A Dark and Deadly Journey

ALSO BY JULIA KELLY

EVELYNE REDFERN MYSTERIES

Betrayal at Blackthorn Park

A Traitor in Whitehall

STANDALONES

The Dressmakers of London

The Lost English Girl

The Last Dance of the Debutante

The Last Garden in England

The Whispers of War

The Light Over London

A Dark and Deadly Journey

An Evelyne Redfern Mystery

Julia Kelly

MINOTAUR BOOKS
NEW YORK

This is a work of fiction. All of the characters, organizations, and events portrayed in this novel are either products of the author's imagination or are used fictitiously.

First published in the United States by Minotaur Books, an imprint of St. Martin's Publishing Group

EU Representative: Macmillan Publishers Ireland Ltd, 1st Floor, The Liffey Trust Centre, 117–126 Sheriff Street Upper, Dublin 1, DO1 YC43

www.minotaurbooks.com

Designed by Gabriel Guma

Library of Congress Cataloging-in-Publication Data

Names: Kelly, Julia, 1986– author
Title: A dark and deadly journey / Julia Kelly.
Description: First edition. | New York : Minotaur Books, 2025. | Series: Evelyne Redfern mystery ; 3
Identifiers: LCCN 2025017922 | ISBN 9781250865540 (hardcover) | ISBN 9781250865564 (ebook)
Subjects: LCGFT: Fiction | Detective and mystery fiction | Novels
Classification: LCC PS3611.E449245 D37 2025 | DDC 813/.6—dc23/eng/20250523
LC record available at https://lccn.loc.gov/2025017922

First Edition: 2025

10 9 8 7 6 5 4 3 2 1

For Diana

ONE

November 20, 1940

I am not an easy woman to shock.

That is not arrogance, but rather mere statement of fact. After all, given that I spent my childhood raised in the bosom of sometimes bohemian, always decadent Parisian society and then, at the age of twenty-two, became a field agent for a government department investigating intelligence breaches during the war, there aren't many things I haven't encountered along the way. However, I can unequivocally and unashamedly say that when I found myself in possession of a safe deposit key and the address for its corresponding box written in invisible ink, I was stunned. The fact that it had been sent from Portugal—if the stamps on the envelope were to be believed—by my estranged father weeks earlier only added to my confusion.

I sparked my silver lighter and held the flame near enough to the seemingly blank paper to reveal Sir Reginald's clandestine message.

London Safe Deposit Company
Lower Regent Street
Box 5297

I supposed that it was possible that my father had a safe deposit box in London. However, why, after nearly five years of silence, would he write to me about it—and in invisible ink no less? After all, as far as I knew, my formidable Aunt Amelia conducted all matters of business on her brother's behalf. If he should send a key to anyone, surely it should be her.

I flicked the lid of the lighter closed and then opened my hand to look at the key I'd held since it slid out of the envelope into my palm. It glinted in the overhead light of the boardinghouse bedroom I shared with my best friend, Moira.

Well, I might be flummoxed as to *why* my father had sent me both the key and the address, but one thing was clear: I had every intention of going to the London Safe Deposit Company to find out what was inside box 5297.

I stuffed the key and the note back into their envelope and then dropped them into my handbag along with my lighter. Then I put on my hat, and out the door I went.

As I descended the stairs, I held my breath, hoping I wouldn't come across one of my fellow boarders, who would inevitably fuss over the "cycling accident" I'd told them I'd been in when I'd returned to our Bina Gardens boardinghouse with a limp. Even three weeks on, I could still feel a faint tug where a doctor had recently removed the stitches from the gunshot wound I'd sustained while apprehending a killer who had dispatched two prominent men at Blackthorn Park, a secret government weapons facility. The fact that the traitor had managed to graze me at all had left me more than a little grumpy.

I hadn't minded lying to most about how I'd ended up bandaged and with a temporary limp, but it had hurt to tell the tale to Moira—even more so when her usually serene expression pinched, lips tightened, and she stared at me a long moment before saying, "If you say so, Evie."

My partner, David Poole, had warned me that life in the Special Investigations Unit could be a difficult one because the secretive nature of the job meant I wouldn't be able to be truthful with the people I loved the most. I'd thought I understood the gravity of becoming an SIU field agent when I'd eagerly joined up two months ago, but I was beginning to learn how isolated an existence it could be.

At the bottom of the boardinghouse stairs, I paused to retrieve my coat from the hooks in the entryway when a key rattled in the lock and Moira opened the front door.

"Evie, fancy meeting you here," she said in a cheerful tone.

"How did your audition go?" I asked.

She grinned, tossing her shoulder-length wheat-blond hair back. "I think the part is mine."

"Moira!" I cried, throwing my arms around her.

"Don't pop the champagne just yet," she said with a laugh as she returned my embrace. "If I've learned anything in this business, it's that nothing is a sure thing until the curtain rises."

Moira had turned her back on the luxurious life of a society debutante in favor of her true love: acting. I knew her real ambition was Hollywood, and she was working hard for her big break, taking roles in every Ministry of Information film and West End play she could while supplementing her half of our rent with a healthy modeling career.

It was a misfortune that her last role, playing a debutante in a comedy of manners called *Whoever Could Say?*, had fallen through when the producer failed to pay his debts and his theater was foreclosed upon.

"I'm certain we'll be seeing your name in lights soon enough," I said. "Well, maybe not lights because of the blackout, but you know what I mean."

"I do. Where are you off to?" she asked with a nod at my coat.

I hesitated. Moira more than anyone else would know how I felt about my father writing to me. After all, she'd been the first friend I made after he ripped me, still mourning my mother's death, out of my life in Paris and dumped me in a British boarding school. However, the mysterious nature of his note held me back.

"I'm just going to make a telephone call." I knew from years of living in boardinghouses—first in Edinburgh, where I'd gone to university, and then under Mrs. Jenkins's roof—that they are not places where you can rely on privacy when you need it most.

My friend raised a brow. "Don't tell me you've gone off the hall telephone because you've acquired a handsome officer you're keeping from all of us."

I snorted. "Hardly. I must telephone Aunt Amelia. She wants to know when I'm coming down to Shaldeen Grange to visit." It was at least a partial truth. I *was* going to ring my aunt, and she always asked when I intended to visit her next.

"Ah, so there's to be a negotiation," said Moira. "Godspeed."

I smiled as I pulled on my coat. "Thank you. I'll see you for supper."

I let myself out of the boardinghouse's front door and made straight for the red box around the corner on Old Brompton Road.

A few moments after giving the switchboard operator the correct exchange, the voice of my aunt's butler filled the line with a somber "Shaldeen Grange."

"Good evening, Henderson. Is my aunt at home?" I asked.

"If you will wait one moment, please, Miss Redfern."

I drummed my fingers against the little shelf in the telephone booth as I waited and watched people hurry by, bundled up in their coats and gloves. With the winter nearly upon us, darkness had fallen some time ago, but mercifully the air raid siren hadn't yet sounded. No doubt all the men and women passing would be wondering what sort of a night the Germans would give us and what would be standing the next morning if bombs did fall on London.

"Evelyne, is that you?" Aunt Amelia's voice pulled me back to the telephone booth.

"Yes, Aunt Amelia."

"Is that charming man of yours with you?"

"Charming man? Do you mean David Poole?" I asked, wondering just what my partner would think if he heard my aunt refer to him as such.

"Yes, Mr. Poole. You really must bring him around again sometime. He can play the piano for me."

"Aunt Amelia, he is neither *my* charming man nor a performing monkey," I admonished. Clearly the decision to take David to my aunt's home as part of our last case had been as unfortunate as it had been necessary.

"That is the sort of attitude that will make you decidedly Down in my books," Aunt Amelia scolded.

I pinched the bridge of my nose hard and prayed to whichever god protected put-upon nieces for strength. I had neither the time nor the desire to examine my place in my aunt's elaborate—and frankly incomprehensible—system of social ranking that declared people Up or Down based solely on her whim.

"I'm certain you're busy, so I won't take up too much of your time," I began. "Has Sir Reginald ever mentioned holding a safe deposit box with the London Safe Deposit Company on Lower Regent Street?"

"Your father has always banked at C. Hoare & Co., just like our father and our grandfather."

"Are you certain that he didn't take a safe deposit box before going on his travels? Perhaps after *Maman* died," I suggested.

Aunt Amelia hesitated. "After Geneviève died, there was nothing that merited being put in a safe deposit box. Your father sold everything. Did you never wonder where all your mother's lovely things had gone?"

"Of course he did," I said, rubbing at the sharp pang in my chest. I suppose I had known that, but I'd been young enough that no one had ever really laid out the truth so explicitly.

"I argued with Reginald that at least the jewels and the furs should be set aside for when you came of age. I had thought that you might like to wear some of your mother's things during your debutante Season, if I could secure an invitation for you to be presented at court, but your father would hear nothing of it. All I managed to salvage was Geneviève's watch and her pearl earrings."

I felt for the bracelet of *Maman*'s watch through my coat sleeve.

"I should have realized," I said.

"If I know my brother, he probably spent the lot of it on women, fast cars, and idiotic schemes that would land a less lucky man in an early grave. I'm very sorry, darling," Aunt Amelia said, her tone softening, "but I suspect that if there ever was a safe deposit box, whatever was in it is long gone by now."

Everything she said made sense. My father was nothing if not profligate and I could easily imagine money—or anything of value, really—slipping through his fingers years ago. But then why send me the key and the vault's address now? And from Portugal for that matter.

"Why do you suddenly have all of these questions about a safe deposit box?" asked Aunt Amelia.

"Moira," I lied automatically. "Or rather Moira's mother. Apparently, Mrs. Mangan is trying to give Moira a few pieces of jewelry because she worries about the safe deposit vault being bombed."

Aunt Amelia sniffed. "Well, if your friend does accept them, you can tell her that she can keep them in the safe here at Shaldeen Grange. That way they'll be out of London."

"That's very kind of you, Aunt Amelia."

"Does Miss Mangan still wish to be an actress?"

I smiled, genuinely touched that Aunt Amelia had remembered what I'd told her about Moira's ambitions. "Yes. In fact, she had an audition today. She said it went well."

"Then I hope Miss Mangan doesn't accept her mother's jewelry. Charity is a slippery slope for a girl trying to cling to her independence."

"I shall remind her of that."

"Do. I'm glad you rang, Evelyne. It's good to hear your voice," said my aunt.

My eyebrows jumped so high they probably brushed my fringe. "Really?"

"Of course!" she barked at me. "You are, as you are often quick to point out, my only niece."

"Then I will ring more often," I promised, finding I didn't abhor the idea.

"Come to visit more often too," she ordered, "and bring that Mr. Poole with you. Goodbye."

The call cut off abruptly, leaving me staring at the receiver in my hand. I shook my head with a laugh and then reached into my handbag for more shillings.

This time, when the switchboard picked up, I asked for the

London Safe Deposit Company. However, the line rang and rang until the operator came back on and asked if I wanted to continue trying.

"No, thank you," I said, "I suspect they're closed for the evening."

I hung up the receiver and then pushed out of the telephone booth to make my way back to Bina Gardens. The vault might be closed for the day, but the following morning I would be there as soon as the doors opened.

TWO

At ten o'clock on the dot the following morning, I walked up to the solid edifice that was home to the London Safe Deposit Company and pushed through the heavy front door.

At the front counter, a balding clerk wearing a gray suit with a faint pinstripe and a pair of steel-rimmed glasses looked up from the ledger he was writing in. "Good morning, Miss. How may I help you?"

"I'd like to request a box, please," I said.

"Very good, Miss . . ."

"Redfern."

"May I please have the box number, Miss Redfern?"

"Five-two-nine-seven," I recited.

As he jotted this down, he asked, "Do you have the key?"

I opened my handbag and took out the envelope, shaking it until the key fell out into my hand.

"Excellent," he said, his smile growing a fraction of an inch wider. "If you would care to follow me, Miss Redfern. We have a private lounge where you may wait for the box to be retrieved."

I slipped my handbag back over my wrist and followed him through a set of doors and down a corridor. He opened a door for me and led me into a well-appointed room done in oak with dark brown leather and hunter-green velvet furniture. It resembled a small drawing room save for a square table placed against the right wall.

"Someone will be with you in just one moment," he said.

"Thank you," I said before settling myself on the sofa and pulling out a copy of *The Postman Always Rings Twice*. The James M. Cain novel was not my normal reading material, and I likely would have passed over it in a bookshop for being too hard-boiled. However, I'd become curious after seeing it in David's car while investigating at Blackthorn Park. I'd asked Moira to slip a copy into a suitcase she'd packed me with additional clothes for an extended stay in the village while investigating the case, and it was only upon returning to London that I'd found my father's letter slipped between the book's pages.

When I'd finally begun reading the book after speaking to Aunt Amelia the previous evening, I'd been fascinated to discover that *The Postman Always Rings Twice* was not a detective novel as such but instead a thriller. It followed the story of a man who falls in love with the wife of a diner owner in California. They'd just concocted a plot to murder her husband, but I had a sneaking suspicion that everything was about to go horribly wrong, as it often does in books.

Despite my preference for the likes of Christie, Sayers, Marsh, and Berkeley, I found Mr. Cain's book tense and tautly written, and I wanted very much to know what happened next.

Not that I would ever tell David that.

I managed to read several pages by the time the door of the safe deposit company's lounge opened again and the same clerk who'd greeted me entered, followed by a strapping man carrying a metal box.

"Here you are, Miss Redfern," said the clerk as his helper deposited the box on the square table with a thunk.

"Thank you," I said.

"We also received a letter from Sir Reginald asking that this envelope be kept with the box," said the clerk, placing a buff envelope on top of the box. "We could not open the box and add it to the contents, but I can assure you that it has been kept safe."

Then the clerk gestured to a small bell set into the wall that I hadn't noticed before. "If you have any questions, you need simply ring. No one will disturb you otherwise."

"Thank you," I said.

When I was alone again, I replaced the ribbon I was using to mark my place in the book and then rose. I reached for the letter first, sliding my finger under the flap to tear it open.

Evelyne,

Inside this box, there is a small tea chest. Take it to a shop on Hatton Garden called H. M. Barlow and ask for a Mr. Morrison.

<u>Do not open the chest.</u>

It is vitally important that you do as you are told and follow my instructions to the letter.

Sincerely,
R.

I scoffed. "As though I was ever going to listen to an order from you."

I fished the key from my handbag and slipped it into the lock of the safe deposit box. I'm not entirely certain that I believed it would fit until that very moment, but it turned without resistance.

I opened the lid and discovered that, sure enough, there was a small tea chest inside. I lifted it out, surprised at how heavy it was, and set it on the table. It was unremarkable except for a small iron lock latching the lid to the front panel of the chest.

I rummaged around in my handbag until I found my lock-picking kit. A few months ago, I never would have dreamed I would be walking around London with such tools on me, but since I'd joined the SIU and been trained with some of the best Special Operations Executive agents in the war, I'd found myself relying on my tension wrench and hook more and more.

The lock was simple, and it took very little work to coax the mechanism to spring open. With a satisfied smile, I lifted the chest's lid and gasped.

It was stuffed full of jewelry. Necklaces of geographic art deco designs wrapped around dangling diamond earrings I knew had once glinted under chandeliers. Rings sparkled in the lounge's yellow artificial light—aquamarines and emeralds and amethysts all set in gold. A golden peacock with sapphires and emeralds studding its tail feathers and a brilliant ruby for an eye nestled next to a stack of diamond-encrusted bangles.

However, it wasn't the value of the exquisitely crafted pieces that took my breath away. It was whom they had once belonged to.

Maman.

This tea chest was full of my mother's most beautiful, precious things.

I lifted out a phoenix brooch peppered with small scarlet rubies and fiery citrines and ran my thumb over one of its wings. I could remember the last time she wore it. She'd had on a dress of black silk topped by a fine net layer embroidered all over with jet beads. I'd watched her sit at the vanity in my parents' Parisian apartment as her maid pinned the brooch to her deep brown hair. Catching my eye in the mirror, *Maman* had dismissed her maid and then called me over to help her slip in some of the hairpins that would hold it in place.

When I was done, she'd announced, "*Parfait, ma cherie*," and deposited a kiss on my cheek that left behind the perfect vermilion imprint of her lips.

I began to pull out item after item, memories flooding back to me until all that was left was the long rope of creamy pearls that *Maman* used to wear in a knot that fell to her waist. I ran the pearls through my fingers.

I had never thought I'd see any of these things again, but they were all there. Every last one.

Anger boiled up in me hot and fast. How *dare* my father let Aunt Amelia and me think he'd sold these things off years ago. How *dare* he.

I began to pack the jewels away, determined to lock everything up again before returning the box to the vault. Then I would pay this Mr. Morrison at H. M. Barlow a visit.

THREE

I reached H. M. Barlow around half past eleven and found myself standing in front of a tiny shop front. This being a Thursday morning in London's traditional jewelry district, I expected that it would be open for business. However, the lights were off, and a *Closed* sign hung in the window of the door.

With a frown, I poked my head into the shop next door. A man wearing a jeweler's loupe looked up as a bell jangled to announce my entrance.

"Good morning, Miss. How can I help you?" he asked.

"Good morning. I'm looking for Mr. Morrison next door. You wouldn't happen to know if he's been in today, would you?"

"I haven't seen Morrison today." Then he frowned. "It's strange. Usually he's like clockwork."

"Is that right?"

"Is there something I can help you with?"

I shook my head. "Thank you. I think I'll slip a note through the door and let Mr. Morrison know I've come to see him."

The jeweler shrugged. "Suit yourself."

Back out on the pavement, I studied Morrison's door once again. Then I freed my notebook and pencil from my handbag. I dipped my head as though I were scribbling something, but instead I was sizing up the shop's locks through my lashes.

The door was fitted with a standard lock, which would present me with no problems, but the rather formidable dead bolt above it would be more of a challenge.

There was a jangle behind me, and I peeked over my shoulder to see a woman with a terrier on a worn leather lead walk by. My lips twisted. Yes, the dead bolt would take time, and I had serious doubts I'd be able to pop it in broad daylight without raising the suspicions of all the people milling about.

I straightened and folded up my supposed note. I was about to push it through the door to complete my charade when a thought struck me. I reached out and twisted the knob. Without a sound, the door swung open.

I gave a little huff of disbelief even as the hairs stood up on the back of my neck. Why would any jeweler worth his salt close his shop but not lock and bolt the door behind him?

With another glance over my shoulder to make sure no one was looking, I slipped into H. M. Barlow. The door closed with a click behind me, and I waited for a moment as my eyes adjusted to the dim light inside. The glass counters in front of me gleamed without a streak to mar them but they were empty of the trays of jewelry I assumed Morrison lined up each morning.

I rounded the counters, acutely aware of the strange silence that hung about the place, and let myself through the door leading off the back of the shop floor. I found myself in a narrow corridor leading to what I guessed would be the back room. Worn wooden boards creaked under my feet, and I was cognisant of the echo of my low heels as I went. When I reached the back door, I twisted the doorknob and held my breath.

The back room was empty of people but filled with utter chaos.

Papers covered in pencil sketches of pieces of jewelry were strewn all over the floor, and a tin can had fallen, sending pencils scattering everywhere. A dark brown stain had half dried on the floor amid the smashed china of a teapot, cup, and saucer, and a stool that I could imagine normally sat pulled up to a wooden workbench had been tossed halfway across the room, where it now rested upturned.

However, it was the door of the huge wall safe hanging drunkenly open that drew my attention.

Moving carefully so that I didn't disturb what I could only assume was a crime scene, I approached the safe. I angled myself to peer inside, half expecting to see it cleaned out. Instead, I was greeted by stacks of black trays and boxes set on one another until they almost touched the top of each of the safe's shelves.

Using a handkerchief to avoid leaving any more fingerprints behind than I already had, I picked up one of the trays and found a row of gold necklaces neatly laid out and waiting for the display case. Another held rings of every gemstone, sparkling in the light spilling into the vault.

I replaced the trays and reached for one of the boxes. Inside lay a pile of what looked very much like oversized rock salt.

Immediately, I put the box back and backed away from the safe.

Up until that moment, I'd assumed that Morrison had been the victim of a robbery. However, considering the tens of thousands of pounds of finished pieces and uncut diamonds I'd just placed back in their safe, I doubted very much that was what had happened here.

Someone had come to H. M. Barlow and torn it apart for another reason.

What did they want?

Where was Morrison?

And what on earth had my father gotten himself into now?

Most people, as soon as they found Morrison's shop ransacked and the jeweler missing, might have rung the police. However, most people are not SIU field agents. Instead, the same instinct that had made me walk into a darkened jewelry shop with an unlocked door and snoop around was the one that had me calmly retracing my steps, wiping doorknobs clean as I went. I had little fear that my housekeeping would wipe away the fingerprints of whoever had turned H. M. Barlow into a tip. This was no common thief taking advantage of an empty shop during an air raid to grab whatever gems they could. The person who had done this had gone to the shop for entirely different reasons, and I suspected they would have taken pains to cover their tracks.

Satisfied that I had eliminated any physical evidence that I'd been inside the shop, I let myself out, closing the front door with a quiet click. Then I walked at a steady, but unremarkable pace down a few roads to a telephone box.

After a few rings, the voice of my department head's secretary, Miss Summers, filled the line. "Good morning, Mr. Fletcher's office."

"Miss Summers, it's Evelyne."

"Miss Redfern, are you well? Mr. Fletcher has been asking after you this morning."

"Does he have something for me?" I asked, my hopes rising. My gunshot wound had landed me desk duty at the SIU's headquarters, translating reports from agents operating in German-occupied France. However, as my leg had grown stronger, so too had my desire to be back out in the field. It might have been easier if David had also been stuck behind a desk, but my partner had disappeared shortly after we'd debriefed Mr. Fletcher and our handler, Mrs. White, upon returning from the murder investigation at Blackthorn Park.

"I rang your boardinghouse this morning, but I must have missed you," she said, deftly avoiding my question.

"There was something I had to attend to. Is Mr. Fletcher in now?"

"One moment," she said, and a few seconds later Mr. Fletcher came on the line.

"Miss Redfern," he said in his usual avuncular tone. One would never guess that he headed up a semisecret department tasked with investigating all manner of crimes in the government's wartime intelligence branches.

"Something strange has happened." I proceeded to explain finding the letter from my father, the safe deposit box, the directive to take the jewels to Morrison at H. M. Barlow, and the state in which I'd found the shop.

"Have you rung the police yet?" he asked.

"No. My previous experience with the police hasn't inspired a great deal of confidence in their abilities." My first encounter with law enforcement had come when, as a child of thirteen, I'd found *Maman* dead in the hotel suite she'd moved into after separating from my father. The detective had taken one look at my mother's body, the little bottle of laudanum that sat next to her water glass on the marble bathroom vanity, the half-empty champagne glass discarded on the sitting room table, and the rows and rows of evening gowns in her bedroom cabinet and decided that her death had been a simple case of a silly socialite who'd been careless with measuring out her nightly dose of sleeping draught. Granted, that had been in Paris and not London, but I'd never forgotten the detective's lack of interest in asking more than the very basic questions about the circumstances of her death when I knew without a doubt that *Maman* would never have abandoned me like that.

"Right," said Mr. Fletcher. "You'd better come to headquarters, Miss Redfern. In the meantime, I'll see what I can find out."

FOUR

A half hour after discovering the scene at H. M. Barlow, I was sitting across from Mr. Fletcher with a steaming cup of tea balanced on my knee. The scene might have been positively domestic—the head of the SIU, after all, had recruited me because he'd been friends with my parents in Paris before their marriage had fallen apart—except that I'd learned that any conversation that happened in this office was bound to be full of surprises.

"There are a few matters I wish to speak to you about, Miss Redfern, but perhaps we should start with the most pressing first," said Mr. Fletcher before taking a sip of tea. "After you rang, I made some inquiries. It transpires that, in addition to his legitimate business, Christian Morrison of H. M. Barlow is a known fence for people wishing to sell jewels on the black market.

"The authorities have been aware of his secondary business for some time due to a bit of trouble he ran into back in thirty-five after the robbery of a socialite named"—he glanced down at a pad of paper balanced on the arm of his chair—"Mrs. Carl Mullins. The thieves managed to steal a diamond-and-sapphire tiara, a sapphire necklace, and an emerald and diamond necklace, bracelet, and earring set from the Mullins family's safe after Mrs. Mullins had the jewels retrieved from the family's bank vault ahead of her daughter's coming out ball."

"I take it that the thieves used Morrison to dispose of the jewels?" I asked.

"Detectives were fairly confident of this, but apparently by the time they managed to piece the case together, the jewels had already been broken down and sold off. Morrison moves quickly."

Mr. Fletcher paused for a sip of tea before continuing. "Apparently he is also a creature of habit."

"Yes. I spoke to the owner of the neighboring shop, and it sounded as though Morrison is usually prompt with his opening time."

"This morning, Morrison's neighbor telephoned the police to report him as a missing person," said Mr. Fletcher. "She is a widow, and he calls in on her every evening after returning home from work. When she did not see him yesterday night, she became alarmed. Normally the police wouldn't consider opening a missing person's case until a greater time had passed, but this neighbor was insistent enough that they made an exception.

"I've asked Miss Summers to continue to monitor the police investigation. If they discover anything, I expect we'll find out soon," he finished.

"Thank you, Mr. Fletcher."

"Perhaps this is as good a time as any for you to walk me through exactly what happened yesterday from when you opened Sir Reginald's letter."

"Right." I took a moment to order my thoughts before recounting everything that had happened since I'd come to realize I possessed the note and key. I told Mr. Fletcher about the vault and the instructions and the jewels I'd thought were long gone.

"Where is the chest now?" he asked.

"Back in its safe deposit box along with the additional instructions Sir Reginald sent me."

"And you're certain there was nothing else in the box other than the letter and chest?" he asked.

"Nothing."

"You said that your aunt is the person who normally handles Sir Reginald's business matters," he said.

"Yes. She wasn't even aware that he had a safe deposit box."

Mr. Fletcher sat back and considered this for a moment. "Why do you think your father wrote to you?"

"I don't know. Truly I don't," I said. "All of this palaver with invisible ink and a second letter to be placed with the safe deposit box, it feels . . . almost paranoid."

It was one of many things that had been niggling at me since I'd opened the box. My father had never been a cautious, meticulous man. He lived his life in huge, often reckless gestures. This level of careful secrecy was an odd fit for him.

"When was the last time you saw Sir Reginald?" asked Mr. Fletcher.

"I haven't seen or spoken to him since I was seventeen. He didn't even have my address."

"Then how did he send you a letter?" he asked.

"He sent my aunt a telegram from Morocco asking for it," I said, recalling my surprise when I'd visited Aunt Amelia a few weeks before and learned of Sir Reginald's request.

"Well, that is interesting," Mr. Fletcher murmured.

"Do you think he's up to something?"

"I won't pretend that this cloak-and-dagger routine paints your father in the best light, but we cannot forget that Morrison does have a legitimate business of buying and selling jewels. And there is also nothing illegal about a father asking his daughter to carry out a bit of business for him while he's abroad."

I scrunched up my nose. "But that's just it. Why is he instructing me from Portugal? If he cared so much about selling the jewelry, why not come back to London and do it himself?"

Mr. Fletcher steepled his fingers and leaned his chin against them. "How much do you know about your father's life abroad?"

"Virtually nothing. I gather he writes to Aunt Amelia from time to time when he is in need of a fresh injection of income. She acts as his representative with his banker, so she's more aware of where he is at any given time than I am."

Mr. Fletcher reached behind him to pluck a file off his desk. He opened it, shuffled through a few sheets, and then said, "Ah yes, here it is. At the beginning of this month, Sir Reginald was in French Morocco before traveling by aeroplane to Lisbon. Earlier this year, he was sighted in Mexico, and last year it was Argentina and El Salvador. We also have reason to believe that he spent several months in Chile before the coup in 1938."

I stared at the file. "Why do you have a list of Sir Reginald's whereabouts to hand?"

The look he gave me felt like a mix of pity and apology. "I know that you will understand that in this line of work, it isn't always possible to be as up-front in all manners as one might like."

Immediately I thought of Moira and how many times I'd had to lie to my closest friend since Mr. Fletcher offered me a job working as a typist in Mr. Churchill's secret cabinet war rooms that had led me to become a field agent.

"Since about a year before the war started, British intelligence has been actively monitoring Sir Reginald's movements. Having known him in a past life, I've taken a personal interest," said Mr. Fletcher.

"Why would British intelligence want anything to do with my father?"

Mr. Fletcher closed the file and set it aside. "What exactly do you think of your father, Miss Redfern?"

"I think of him as little as possible, if you must know. Sir Reginald is a selfish, careless man who has proven time and time again that he is more interested in the renown his next adventure will bring him than in the people around him. At best, he is profligate and careless. At worst, he is a bounder and a cad.

"I understand that some people would say that I'm being disloyal or an ungrateful daughter," I continued. "However, nothing my father has ever done has shown me that he deserves my loyalty. He was unfaithful to my mother, and when she decided to leave him, he set about making her life a misery by dragging her through a painful divorce and a very public custody battle. To this day, I doubt that he ever actually cared about retaining custody of me except for the fact that it was the most effective way to hurt her."

Mr. Fletcher began to say something, but I held up my hand to stop him. "Before you contradict me to try to save my feelings, remember that this is the man who, after *Maman* died, sent my aunt to collect me from Paris rather than coming himself. He then instructed her to dump me in a strange boarding school, in a country I hardly knew, and then proceeded to visit me a total of two times during all my years there. I owe him *nothing*."

"Well, that does rather put a neat button on things," said Mr. Fletcher. "Miss Redfern, in every country your father visits, he is photographed extensively."

"I've never understood the press's fascination with his movements. The allure of explorers and daredevils rather loses its appeal when you realize that gallivanting around the globe serves as an excellent excuse to neglect one's responsibilities."

"Quite," Mr. Fletcher resumed. "However, it has proven incredibly useful in documenting who Sir Reginald has been spending his time with. In El Salvador, he dined with several of those close to Maximiliano Hernández Martínez, who has been an open admirer of Hitler and Mussolini and himself is a fascist. In Argentina, Sir Reginald played polo with several businessmen who have vested interests in Argentina breaking neutrality to supply food to the Germans. And in Mexico, he attended a dinner at which a known arms dealer sympathetic to the Nazi cause was present."

The list only became worse and worse.

"Is there any evidence that Sir Reginald himself has Nazi sympathies?" I asked, dreading what the answer might be.

"That is where things become more interesting," said Mr. Fletcher. "For all of his associations with Nazi sympathizers, your father has also associated with those who support the Allied cause or, in some cases, at least are invested in their countries remaining neutral."

"I suppose that is something."

"It is possible Sir Reginald is indiscriminate about the company he keeps because he truly does not understand the implications of being seen with Nazi sympathizers no matter their nationality. However, any Briton associating with such company is closely monitored until we can more fully assess where their own proclivities lie."

I swallowed around the lump in my throat. "I had no idea."

Mr. Fletcher offered me a smile. "I have no doubt about that, which is why I personally vouched for you when you joined the SIU."

"I imagine Mrs. White had objections," I said before I could stop myself. It was plain as day that my handler didn't particularly like me, but that didn't mean I was supposed to say that out loud.

Fortunately, Mr. Fletcher gave a small laugh. "Never fear. Mrs. White will come to trust your suitability as an agent in time. No, there are forces at work here that are far more formidable than Mrs. White."

"I thought the SIU had a degree of independence from other intelligence departments because we investigate them."

"Yes, but never forget that even the SIU must be accountable to someone," he said.

"Those reports on my father's movements you mentioned were from South America. But what about French Morocco or Portugal? What has he been doing there?" I asked.

"The latest reports seem to indicate that Sir Reginald's primary interests remain polo, automobile racing, flying, and drinking."

"There's no change in form there then."

I leaned back against the sofa, turning things over in my mind.

"Why would Sir Reginald contact me now about jewels he's been holding for nearly a decade?" I asked.

"An excellent question," said Mr. Fletcher.

"It is entirely possible that my father is living well beyond his means," I reasoned. "Aunt Amelia told me a couple of months ago that the sales of his recent books have been weak."

While they might like looking at photographs of him in the papers, the public hasn't been flocking to Sir Reginald's stories of derring-do as they once did. If he was feeling a certain amount of pressure to maintain his lifestyle, it would make sense that he might sell any valuables he had in safekeeping.

"I suspect you may be right," said Mr. Fletcher. "The last time Sir Reginald's name came across my desk, it was in a report filed by a man named Archibald Carter in Lisbon. Apparently Sir Reginald was spending time gambling at Estoril Casino."

"But why Lisbon?" I asked. "I wonder . . ."

Mr. Fletcher leaned forward. "No theory is too outrageous, Miss Redfern. You are probably the person who knows him best."

That, I thought, was a vast overstatement of my relationship with the paterfamilias.

"El Salvador, Argentina, and Mexico are all neutral countries," I started.

"For now," said Mr. Fletcher with a nod.

"And Portugal is neutral. If he is spending his time among influential people on both sides of the war, is there any chance that Sir Reginald could be recruited as an agent to help convince those countries to maintain their neutrality?" I asked.

"I'm glad to see your training already has you thinking in that direction. We have been putting more intelligence resources into our Iberian operation precisely because Portuguese neutrality is so vital to the war effort."

"But what about the Anglo-Portuguese Alliance?" I asked.

"There are some who believe—and I cannot say that I blame them—that relying on a 550-year-old alliance that was drafted before Copernicus conceived of his heliocentric theory is optimistic at best. If Portugal's dictator António Salazar cannot be convinced to join Britain and her allies, maintaining Portuguese neutrality is vital to keeping Franco's Spain in check.

"There was some talk that perhaps Sir Reginald might be recruited to persuade his friends to turn away from their Nazi leanings. Even if he himself has acquired some of their beliefs, he might prove useful by unwittingly rooting out the proverbial bad apples," he finished.

I immediately straightened. "I would like to request permission to travel to Lisbon to sound out whether or not Sir Reginald might be a suitable asset." And ask the man what he had been thinking keeping my mother's jewels a secret for all these years.

"I think, Miss Redfern—"

However, before he could finish his thought the door swung open and Mrs. White strode in, ubiquitous file in hand and annoyance in her eyes.

FIVE

Mrs. White might have dressed like a village librarian in her knit skirt and matching cardigan, but she was a formidable presence charged with the great responsibility of running all field agents in the SIU. As the department's newest addition, I still wasn't confident that she thought any more highly of me than she had on the first day we'd met, when she'd made it abundantly clear she didn't approve of me as Mr. Fletcher's pick to go undercover and investigate a mole in Mr. Churchill's secret underground cabinet bunker under Whitehall.

"Ah, Mrs. White," said Mr. Fletcher as my handler arranged herself in the armchair next to him. "I was just commending Miss Redfern on the excellent job she did catching our Blackthorn Park killer."

I stole a look at Mr. Fletcher and saw him press a hand down through the air as though warning against mentioning the real subject of our conversation.

"And being shot in the process," muttered Mrs. White.

"My leg is healing very nicely, thank you," I said.

Mr. Fletcher did his best to cover a laugh with a cough, earning him a narrowed-eyed glare from Mrs. White.

"We are all very grateful your injury was not too severe and that you are ready to return to the field," said Mr. Fletcher, managing to restore his composure.

I straightened. "Return to the field?"

Mrs. White sighed. "Miss Redfern, against my better judgment, you are needed."

"Now, Mrs. White," Mr. Fletcher gently scolded at the same time I asked, "I am?" with unchecked delight.

Mrs. White opened her file and balanced it on her knee. "One week ago, the head of one of our intelligence branches in Lisbon named Peter Phillips reported that one of his informants requested an urgent meeting and then did not appear. This wouldn't normally be cause for concern—it isn't unheard of for informants to go dark from time to time—but this particular informant is one of the most reliable we have working on the Iberian Peninsula. More than a week's radio silence has caused serious concern among the SIS."

Mrs. White removed a sheet of paper from her file and handed it to me. It was a memo with TOP SECRET typed across the top of it.

"The informant is James Winn, code name Dogwood. This is the last report Phillips filed based on Winn's information," said Mrs. White. "Before his disappearance, Winn contacted Phillips and hinted that he had information that could shift the balance of Portugal's neutrality and drive it toward an alliance with Germany. Not only would such a change leave Spain free to join the Axis powers if Franco wished, but it would give Germany free access to Portugal's mineral deposits."

"Deposits of what?" I asked.

"Wolfram, among other things, is vital to manufacturing armaments," said Mr. Fletcher. "Whoever controls the wolfram mines controls a great deal of the supply chain in this war."

"No one knows if Winn has been killed, kidnapped, or turned—or perhaps he has simply disappeared of his own volition—but he must be found along with the information he holds," said Mrs. White.

"With the increasing amount of German activity in Lisbon, the powers that be have made the decision that the SIU should investigate the matter so as not to pull resources away from existing intelligence efforts on the ground," said Mr. Fletcher. "Due to the urgency of finding Winn, we have decided that we need two of our best on the case."

"Mr. Poole is already in Bristol waiting for his flight to Lisbon," Mrs. White finished.

My pulse quickened at hearing my partner's name. "And I'm to go with him?"

"Yes," said Mrs. White. "Although I have my reservations about sending you on an assignment abroad where you will have less communication with me as your handler at this early stage in your career, my opinion has been overruled."

"Come now, Mrs. White," said Mr. Fletcher cheerfully. "Mr. Poole and Miss Redfern have made an excellent team before. I'm certain that they will again."

"Thank you, sir," I said.

Mrs. White pursed her lips but extracted another page from her file. "You will be traveling with Mr. Poole under the guise of his secretary, Evelyne Moore."

"What is his cover?" I asked as I examined the briefing sheet she handed me.

"David Slater. He is a wine buyer from Berry Brothers and Rudd. He is going on a scouting trip to Portugal in an attempt to contend with the Ministry of Food's quota system that designates how much stock merchants can buy and to ensure that there is a good flow of supply to the company's cellars when the war eventually ends," said Mrs. White.

"With much of France occupied and cut off from us, Portugal may well be the next frontier for wine beyond port," said Mr. Fletcher.

"Shouldn't Mr. Poole and I have been briefed together?" I asked.

"He is not in London as he has been resting after completing another mission," said Mrs. White.

I was surprised how much it stung to learn that David had been sent off on his own without me. It was true, he'd been an agent since before the war and I had only started on my first assignment in September, but we'd worked together well enough that I assumed we'd always be paired up. Apparently I'd been wrong.

"You will have to work quickly to study your briefing sheet, Miss Redfern," said Mr. Fletcher. "We were not certain until this morning that Miss Summers would be able to secure you a seat on the flight to Lisbon as there is intense competition on that route. However, Miss Summers is a wonder and already has all the documents and travel necessities ready for your cover."

"You and Mr. Poole are booked on the nighttime service out of Whitchurch Airport to Sintra Airfield just outside of Lisbon," said Mrs. White. "He is already familiar with all the procedures for keeping me abreast of your progress in Lisbon, so he will be the reporting agent on this assignment. When you land, Peter Phillips will make contact. As Winn was his informant, he will be able to brief you more fully."

"I understand," I said.

"Find out what happened to Winn and do try not to stumble across any trouble this time," said Mrs. White.

I opened my mouth to protest, but then I remembered that my last two missions had ended in murder and I quickly shut it again.

"Mrs. White, perhaps you could let Miss Summers know that Miss Redfern is nearly ready?" prompted Mr. Fletcher.

Mrs. White gave a stiff nod and rose.

As soon as she was out of the room, I said, "Mrs. White doesn't want me on this assignment."

"I did have to fight to send you to Lisbon, yes," Mr. Fletcher admitted.

"Does Mrs. White know about the jewelry shop?"

"No."

"And my father?"

"I didn't think necessary to make her aware of his . . . activities either," said Mr. Fletcher.

"Why?"

"Do you know, Miss Redfern, being a mere civil servant who spends his days behind a desk, I cannot imagine what the life of a field agent is like," he said, changing the subject. "For instance, I imagine there will be stretches of time when you will be at loose ends waiting for an element of your investigation into the disappearance of James Winn to come to fruition, but I couldn't be certain."

"Are you suggesting that I use that time to contact Sir Reginald?" I asked.

"Oh, I would never suggest something like that because I could never authorize an agent to investigate her family member. However, I also cannot account for what an agent does of her own volition."

"If I were to run into my father by chance, what would you suggest I say to him?" I asked.

"I might sound out his leanings. See where his loyalties truly lie. If you believe him to be amenable to becoming an intelligence asset, you should try to convince him to speak to Archibald Carter. He is the chap who has been monitoring Sir Reginald's movements in Lisbon. Carter can take things from there."

"How do I find Sir Reginald?"

"I really couldn't say, but if I were you, I might start with Carter. It's clear from his reports that he thinks we are not doing enough with Sir Reginald and other potential assets in Lisbon. However, I suspect there are things he's leaving out. Things he can't substantiate yet. Find out what he didn't tell us about Sir Reginald's time in Lisbon."

"Yes, sir," I said, rising.

"Before you go, I should warn you to be careful. If word were to get back to Mrs. White that you are working on a personal mission while on assignment, I'm not certain I would be able to prevent you from being removed from the SIU."

"But you're the head of the department. Surely if the assignment came from you—"

"There is no assignment," he said firmly. "There will never be a file detailing this conversation. There will be no record of any of it."

The message was clear: I could look for my father, but it would not be in an official capacity.

"Why?" I asked.

"Because even the head of a department is replaceable if he defies too many orders from on high. I won't sacrifice my position. Not when there is so much of this war left to fight."

"Is Sir Reginald really worth the risk to you or me?" I asked. "There is every possibility that he turns out to be a selfish fool and nothing more."

"Even a fool can be useful, Miss Redfern. I believe that this war will be won not only on the battlefield but also through the acquisition of information and the spread of misinformation. If your father could help us achieve either of those goals, that is an avenue worth exploring."

"I will keep that in mind," I said.

"Do," said Mr. Fletcher before standing up and retreating behind his desk. However, when I was halfway to the door of his office, he called out to stop me.

"Miss Redfern, you may tell your partner about the safe deposit box if it becomes necessary. I leave that up to your judgment. However, you cannot let Mr. Poole become aware of your personal reasons for being in Lisbon."

"Why not?" I asked.

He fixed me with a serious stare. "Because Mr. Poole and Mrs. White are cut from the same cloth. When push comes to shove, they will always choose adherence to the rules over anything else. I suggest that you not put Mr. Poole in the position where he will find it necessary to shove."

SIX

I stepped out of Mr. Fletcher's office, his warnings about David and Mrs. White ringing in my ears, and walked straight into a whirlwind. In rapid time, Miss Summers produced a change of clothes more appropriate for my cover as a humble secretary than the navy trousers I wore. She also gave me a packed suitcase and handbag selected from the SIU's wardrobe for field agents.

"I'll hold on to these things for you while you're away," said Miss Summers, gently removing my own handbag from my wrist and placing it on her desk.

I almost asked to pull out the envelope and key from my father when she added, "We generally find that it is best to leave these things behind. We wouldn't want to send you into the field with something that might give away your cover."

"Of course," I said, taking the packet of documents she handed me. I opened the passport on the top of the pile and glanced at the name *Evelyne Moore*. "At least I'm still Evelyne."

She smiled. "Generally agents keep their Christian names while under cover. It helps reduce the risk that they will not respond when spoken to. Now, you don't want to miss your train. Good luck."

A few hours later, I found myself, standing case in hand, in front of a huge redbrick hotel with all the hallmarks of the previous century's fussiness, having just alighted from the train at Bristol Temple Meads station. In the dark tempered only by the waning moonlight, I could just make out a short man in a bowler hat standing outside the front door. I watched him juggle an attaché case as he tried to spark his lighter and light a cigarette in the quickening wind.

I almost stopped to offer to hold the case for him, but he shot me a suspicious look and gave me his back, so instead I pushed through the hotel's front door.

With the exception of the blackout curtains covering all of the windows, the hotel lobby would have been at home in the previous century. It was done up in dark wood paneling topped with burgundy and gold floral wallpaper and claret carpets that were beginning to go threadbare down the middle. Against the left wall sat a huge empty wooden reception desk with a ledger, pen holder, and bell waiting on top of it. A large vase of sun-bleached silk flowers on a circular table in the center of the lobby hinted at an attempt at luxury, but nothing could hide the old-fashioned feeling about the place. The hotel was like an aging relative who insists on wearing clothing four decades out of date.

I followed the murmur of voices coming from the open door at the end of the lobby and found myself standing at the entrance of a lounge full of men sitting in club chairs. Most of them had a cigarette or pipe in hand, and I could hear several snippets of conversation about Hungary's decision to join the Axis powers. It took me a moment to spot my partner alone in the far corner of the room, reading a newspaper.

Ignoring the looks of curiosity I received from several of the hotel's patrons, I crossed the room and dropped my suitcase at David's feet. He folded down the edge of his newspaper, glanced at the case and then up at me.

"Miss Moore," he said, setting aside the broadsheet. It was strange hearing him address me under another name and with a level of formality we hadn't used since we first met.

"Mr. Slater." I lowered myself into the chair across from him and placed my hands on my knees with a smile. "You didn't think you could leave without me, did you?"

"Go on a trip without my trusty secretary by my side? I would never have dreamed of it. How was your journey down from London?" he asked.

"As smooth as it was unexpected." There was something different about him—perhaps he was a little leaner in the face, or his hair was a bit shorter than the last time I'd seen him driving back from Sussex at the end of our most recent case. "I apologize for not arriving sooner. I was only just informed that I would be needed on this trip."

"Yes, the situation at the office can change rather quickly, can't it?" He shifted and winced.

"What's the matter?" I asked.

"Nothing." He let out a ragged breath before rolling his shoulder carefully. "Nothing at all."

Don't be daft, obviously something's wrong, I wanted to scold, but in case someone was listening, I instead settled for the far more professional, if asinine, "You're hurt."

"Not badly. I dislocated it, but fortunately it popped back in again without too much pain. Serves me right for thinking I could play rugby at my age."

I frowned. Not only had I never once heard of David playing rugby, but I also knew that in our line of work it was far more likely he'd sustained an injury in the field. However, given that we were out in the open of the smoky hotel lounge, I couldn't risk pressing him further about how he'd really hurt his shoulder.

"How have you been since we last spoke?" he asked. "I think you mentioned some trouble with your leg."

Are you still healing from your gunshot wound?

"That's kind of you to remember. I hardly notice it now," I said.

It only hurts when I push it too much, but ours isn't really the line of work where one can complain, is it?

"Good," he said. "Have they had you working on any special projects recently?"

Has Mrs. White sent you out into the field again while I've been away?

"Most of the time I was behind a desk, reading messages from our wine merchants in Vichy," I said.

I've been going mad reading reports from our field agents in France.

"Have you ever been to Lisbon before, Miss Moore?" he asked.

I shook my head.

"This will be a first for me as well," he admitted. "I imagine we will find the situation in the city . . . enlightening. I understand there are many different types of people there these days."

We'll have to keep our wits about us because we don't know what we're walking into.

"I should imagine so," I said.

A man appeared at the lounge door and everyone in the room began to gather up their things.

"I think that is our cue," said David with a nod to the door. "We can speak more when we are in the air."

Under the cover of darkness, David and I were bustled onto the coach with our fellow passengers to be transported to the airport.

"It's a security measure," David explained.

"I imagine everyone flying must have passed the necessary security checks," I mused as I slid into a seat toward the back.

David shrugged and sat next to me. "You can never be too careful these days."

We drove some distance through the outskirts of Bristol, darkened houses flying by in a blur. I knew the city had been bombed as the Luftwaffe tried to target its harbor and shipyards, and I crossed my fingers hoping that we would see no air raids that evening.

When finally we arrived at Whitchurch Airport and passed through a gate topped with barbed wire, I could just make out the outline of an aeroplane on the runway.

As our fellow passengers filed off the coach, a crew member

checked our names against a list. Then David and I both handed our suitcases over to be weighed before a crew member asked for David's weight and then, blushing, mine.

"It's so we can balance the weight of the aeroplane, Miss," he explained. "I hope you understand."

"I'm happy to do whatever will ensure that we make it to our destination in one piece," I said and gave him the measurement.

I followed David as we climbed the stairs at the rear of the aircraft and ducked our heads to enter the aeroplane's arched doorway. Inside, there were twenty-one seats done up in orange upholstery laid out with two seats next to one another and a single seat across the aisle.

"It's not the most calming color, is it?" I asked.

"This is an old KLM plane that the British Overseas Airways Corporation took over at the start of the war. It looks as though they simply painted the body and left the interior as it was," said David.

"Have you flown for business before?" I asked as we settled into our seats.

"Once. Before the war. London to Paris. You?"

"Not like this." I suspected this was not the forum in which to admit that the only times I'd previously been in an aeroplane had been when I'd jumped out of one as part of a parachute exercise with the SOE while training at Beaulieu.

The man in the bowler hat I'd seen outside of the hotel hurried down the aisle, clutching his attaché case so close that he nearly hit David.

"Careful," said David, whipping his elbow swiftly out of the way and wincing as he had in the hotel lounge.

The man in the bowler hat looked taken aback that David had spoken to him. I thought the man might apologize, but instead he ducked his head and scurried to a seat in the second row from the front before dropping out of view.

"Some people have no manners," I murmured. "Are you all right?"

"I think so," said David, testing his shoulder.

"I don't suppose I can persuade you to tell me how you were injured?" I asked in a whisper.

"It's a story for another day."

But before I could protest, a raised voice cut through the murmurs of the boarding passengers. "No, I have told you before, and I will tell you again. I will not stow my case."

I planted my hands on the arms of my chair to peek over the top of the seat in front of me. One of the crew was standing over the man with the bowler hat.

"Mr. Jessup, we have discussed this before," said the crew member with a sigh. "The weight must be distributed—"

"Take someone else's case away," snarled Jessup, curling his body away so that the case could not be snatched from him. "You're not having mine."

"I beg your pardon, but some of us are still waiting for our seats!" came a shout from down the aisle.

The crew member sighed and muttered something I suspected was rather rude. However, from the way Jessup sank back down into his seat with his attaché case still in his hands, I assumed that the crew member had resigned himself to losing the argument.

The passengers down the aisle began to shuffle forward again.

David leaned in and gestured to my once-wounded leg. "How are you really?" he asked softly.

"It hardly hurts at all," I reassured him.

"Good. I would hate to think . . ." He cleared his throat. "Miss Moore, do you have the schedule for when we land? Miss Summers was still preparing it when I left."

I unclipped the clasp of the handbag Miss Summers had provided me with. It was larger than my usual one, and on the train I'd found that, along with essentials such as my passport and identity card, she'd packed a notebook, pen, the details of our hotel in Lisbon, a typed agenda including fake meetings with various winemakers, and contact information for those men in case we needed someone to provide us with an alibi. Nestled innocuously in the middle of the first day was a real meeting with Peter Phillips, the British intelligence agent with whom we were to make contact.

"Here," I said, pointing out Phillips's name. "Do you know him?"

"No, we haven't crossed paths before. I was focused on France before the war, but with the occupation there's been new interest in Iberia's offerings," he said as the last passenger, a man in a dark coat and hat, stopped at Jessup's row. Jessup and the man exchanged a few words, and then the man took off his hat. As he did so, he took a surreptitious look around the aeroplane's cabin.

He must be a spy, I decided. We were trained to constantly assess our surroundings, finding every exit and every vulnerability without even thinking of it.

As the man's gaze fell on mine, he seemed to realize I was watching him because he abruptly disappeared behind the tall back of the seat next to Jessup.

Lucky him. I hadn't gone through a single bit of training that would help me put up with an ornery fellow passenger for a seven-hour flight.

"I wonder what sort of reception we will receive when we arrive," I said to David.

"In my previous experience, the representatives in our foreign offices can be a very mixed bag. Some are delighted to see a friendly face, while others can become territorial. Then there's the worst kind."

"Who are they?"

He grimaced. "Bureaucrats who bog everything down insisting that every 'i' is dotted and 't' crossed before they will make a move. Trying to . . . buy wine with one of them breathing down your neck is nearly impossible."

"Well, let's hope Mr. Phillips doesn't prove to be one of those," I said, pulling out the copy of *Murder in Piccadilly* by Charles Kingston that Miss Summers had also packed for me, no doubt knowing that I would appreciate having some reading material for the long flight ahead. "Until then, I suppose all we have to do is get there."

SEVEN

Hours later, I jolted awake with a start to the hum of propellers. I blinked and then realized from the pain in my neck that I had fallen asleep on David's shoulder.

"Good morning," he said, looking down at me with a small smile.

"Oh, I beg your pardon." I immediately sat up and stretched my neck as I rubbed the sore muscles.

"We seem to keep finding ourselves in this situation," he said in a low voice.

I glanced at him out of the corner of my eye, remembering the time in September when we'd had to duck into a public shelter during an air raid and I'd fallen asleep against him as we read a novel together to pass the time and steady our nerves while bombs fell over London above us.

A jolt of turbulence sent a shock through the plane, and I gripped the arms of my seat as I swayed.

"I hope it isn't like this for our entire descent," I said.

The aeroplane shuddered again.

"It looks as though we might not be so lucky." He glanced at his watch. "We made good time, all things considered. I imagine we'll be there just after six o'clock in the morning."

"Just in time for an early breakfast," I said, my embarrassment at using David as a cushion giving way to hunger because the last thing I'd eaten had been a sandwich purchased at Paddington Station hours ago.

"Before too long you'll be sipping coffee and eating pastries at a café on Rossio Square."

Out of the window I could see the sky beginning to brighten as the aeroplane flew lower, and about twenty minutes later, we made a very bumpy landing in what amounted to little more than a grass field.

"What I wouldn't give for a smooth bit of pavement," I muttered, my hands clutching the armrests of my chair until my knuckles went white.

"At least the worst of it is over," said David, looking a little green himself.

The aeroplane taxied to a stop and our fellow passengers began to stand to collect their things. I reached for my handbag and shifted to button my navy wool coat and reset my matching felt hat from where it had been pushed off the crown of my head. I suspected I looked a state, but there would be time to freshen up once we arrived at our hotel.

I followed David out of our seats and down the aisle to the metal steps leading to the grass airstrip. Beside the aeroplane, we collected our luggage, David gallantly offering to carry mine, and turned to the airfield's little building that marked the exit.

We were halfway across the field when I said, "I believe Miss Summers arranged for a car to collect us. Let me just check . . ."

I opened my handbag, intent on pulling out the typed schedule, when I looked up sharply.

"What's the matter?" asked David.

"My book isn't here."

"Do you remember putting it back in your handbag?"

"I'm not certain." I'd had it before I nodded off and then . . . "I don't think I did."

He glanced back to the thin stream of passengers behind us. All of the luggage was gone and the crew was chatting, cigarettes between their lips, a few feet away from the aeroplane.

"It probably slipped between the seats. You'd better go back and look." He reached for my suitcase. "I'll wait for you inside the building."

I hurried off, hand clamped firmly on my hat to keep the wind whipping across the airfield from stealing it off my head. None of the crew looked up as I approached. I would just slip up the stairs, nip in, retrieve my book, and be on my way, no protracted explanation required.

I tiptoed up the steps, but as soon as I was through the open door, I realized that I wasn't alone in the cabin. Indeed, I could see the top of a man's head leaning against a window asleep.

"What I wouldn't give to be able to sleep like that through turbulence," I muttered before calling out, "Sir, we've landed."

I went to my seat and crouched down. My book was jammed between the wall of the plane and the seat's leg.

I retrieved it, pushing a bent corner of the cover back into place. When I stood, I tucked the book into my handbag.

The sleeping man still hadn't moved.

"Sir," I called out again, taking a few steps down the aisle toward my fellow passenger, "it's time to wake up. We've arrived in Sintra."

I reached the man's seat in the second row from the front and realized he was the one who had almost bumped into David and been so rude about it. Jessup, was it? Whatever his name, his case was on his lap, his bowler hat on top of it, and he was fast asleep.

I reached out to shake his shoulder, and when I did, he slumped forward. His hat slid off the attaché case, and his head lolled forward at an unnatural angle, coming to rest against the seat in front of him.

I jumped back, pressing a hand to my chest.

Someone had broken the man's neck.

There was a time when, despite my love of detective novels, my first reaction might have been to back away and find help. However, the last few months had dramatically altered my relationship to death.

Instead, I swallowed back my instinct to flee and unsnapped my handbag, my eyes never leaving the man's body as I freed my handkerchief.

I guessed that it would only be a matter of moments before the crew finished their cigarettes and someone joined me in the cabin. Moving quickly but precisely, I peeled back the man's jacket lapel and reached into his left inside pocket to retrieve his passport. His passport photograph was serious and unsmiling, and the name *Michael Jessup* was listed next to it. The description stated a few other basic details including his profession—banking—and his county and date of birth—Surrey, England; 23 March 1905.

I slipped the passport back into Jessup's pocket and checked the one on his right side. Inside, I found a slim black leather diary. I flipped the cover open and found a handwritten receipt for a Hotel Metrópol tucked between the endpapers. Replacing the slip of paper, I skipped to the previous day's date, where the flight time was penciled in. I flicked through a few pages, most of which were filled with times and abbreviations I didn't immediately recognize, but when I paged back one more day, something made me stop. It was an entry in pencil from a few weeks ago that read *Winn?* underlined twice.

Why, I wanted to know, did a dead man have our missing informant's name written in his diary?

I began to reach for Jessup's attaché case when I heard the clang of leather-soled shoes on the stairs leading up to the cabin.

I groaned, muttering, "Mrs. White is going to have my head for this," as I swiftly hiked up my skirt and tucked the diary into the top of my stocking. Then, as my hem fell back into place, I let out the unholy scream of a woman who's just stumbled upon a dead body.

EIGHT

Several hours later, a stern-faced man slid into a chair across a wooden table from me, studied me a moment, the furrows of his brow deepening, and then pulled a notebook out of his jacket pocket.

"Menina Moore, I am Capitão Camargo of the Polícia de Vigilância e Defesa do Estado," he said in English. "I understand that you found the body of Senhor Jessup."

"Is that his name?" I asked, making my eyes wide.

As soon as I'd let loose my scream on the aeroplane, the flight's first mate had raced into the cabin, kicking off a rapid series of events. I'd been taught in training that when placed in a situation where it is necessary to lie, it is best to base that lie on a foundation of truth, so I stammered out a story of forgetting my book and returning to my seat to retrieve it. I claimed I'd noticed the sleeping man and tried to shake him awake. All of that was true, I simply omitted the part about sneaking a look at Jessup's passport and taking the diary and tucking it into my stocking, where it had remained hidden ever since.

The first mate planted me in a seat a few rows down from the body and stuck his head out to shout to his fellow crew. I tried to say that I was traveling with my boss, David Slater, who was waiting for me.

To my frustration, the first mate seemed less worried about retrieving David and more concerned with making sure I didn't faint. I imagine that, upon learning about the body on his aeroplane, the captain must have immediately telephoned the Portuguese police, because not long after that, several men trooped on board before one took me by the elbow and bundled me into the back of an unmarked car. I was driven to a squat building that I took to be a police station, where my handbag was confiscated and I was stashed in this room to wait.

And wait.

And wait.

I could only hope that David had figured out where I was and would be at the station when I was finally released. Until then, I would have to play the damsel in distress a little while longer.

"I understand that you and Senhor Jessup were both passengers on the 6:03 flight from Whitchurch in England to Sintra." Camargo glanced up at me, his dark eyebrows furrowing. "Is that correct?"

"Yes," I said, doing my best to make my voice meek.

"Did you speak to Senhor Jessup at any point either in England or on the flight?" he asked.

"No."

He looked up at me. "But you recognized him?"

"Yes. I first saw him in Bristol at the hotel where we were meant to gather before being taken to the airport. Mr. Jessup was wearing a bowler hat. You don't see as many of them outside of the city as you once did, so I noticed him."

"Then you have never met Senhor Jessup before?" asked Camargo.

"No."

"And why did you return to the aeroplane after having previously disembarked?" he asked.

"I forgot my book."

He stared at me. "Your book?"

"Yes. It must have slipped off my lap while I was sleeping," I said.

"Why did you not see it on the floor when you rose from your seat?"

The way in which he phrased the question set me on edge.

"It had become wedged between the seat and the cabin wall. In my hurry to disembark, I overlooked it and didn't realize until I was on the airstrip," I explained.

"And you didn't ask the crew for permission to reenter the cabin and look for your book?"

I hunched my shoulders a little, trying to make myself look smaller and more deferential than was my nature.

"I didn't want to be a bother," I said. "They were otherwise occupied and the stairs were right there. I thought it would be nothing to slip in, find my book, and slip out again without causing anyone any trouble."

"And that is when you claim you found the body of Senhor Jessup?" he asked.

"But, Capitão Camargo, I'm not claiming anything. That is what happened."

He sat back in his chair, watching me for a moment. Then he reached into his jacket once again and pulled out a passport. He flipped it open.

I spotted my photograph. "That's my passport. It was in my handbag. You really shouldn't go through a lady's handbag."

"'Miss Evelyne Moore,'" he intoned, ignoring me. "'Secretary, born in London, England, on the second of May 1918.'" He read out my false details. "Why are you visiting Portugal?"

"I am accompanying my employer, Mr. Slater, on a trip. For business."

"And you just happened to stumble across a dead body?"

"Yes." Although I was beginning to wonder if Mrs. White was right that there was something about me that meant these things simply happened.

"How do I know that you are not the one who murdered Senhor Jessup?"

"Murdered?" I gasped out. "You can't possibly think—"

"His neck was broken. He was murdered. You said yourself that you were alone on the aeroplane with the man."

"It couldn't have been more than two minutes, and he was already dead when I found him," I protested.

Camargo shrugged. "It would not have taken long to kill him, even for a woman."

Years ago, in our boarding school days, when Moira and I had first shared a room, she taught me a trick for conjuring up tears on demand. It had been incredibly useful when extracting myself from scrapes and trying to avoid being gated. Now, as I pulled on that skill, I could feel my eyes beginning to swim even as I tried to think quickly.

"Capitão Camargo, you can't possibly think that I—I can't believe—I didn't do—"

"Menina," he cut me off, "you must understand the position I'm in. I have nothing but your word as to what happened. What is there to say that you didn't return to the aeroplane with the intention of killing Senhor Jessup?"

"But I could never kill anyone!" I wailed. "How could you ever think that?'

He shrugged. "You are English. Those of us in the PVDE have learned that the English cannot be trusted."

"I'm just a secretary," I whimpered.

"And yet . . ."

I was beginning to grow concerned that this was not a normal interrogation of a witness in a murder investigation and that if I stayed in this room for too much longer, I might very well find myself charged with murder and thrown into a Portuguese prison.

"I would like to speak to Mr. Slater, please," I said, making my voice shaky for effect.

"I'm afraid that is impossible. Senhor Slater is being questioned as well," Camargo said.

Bloody hell. If David also found himself locked up, I was fairly certain Mrs. White would leave us to rot in Portugal out of spite.

"But Mr. Slater didn't do anything. *I* didn't do anything," I insisted.

Camargo rose from the table, his chair squeaking against the tiled floor.

"I will return," he said.

"Where are you going?" I asked quickly. "You can't leave me here."

"I have an investigation to conduct. Until that investigation is concluded, I think I shall have to keep you—"

A knock on the door cut him off.

With a grunt he called out, "*O que foi?*"

A young man wearing an apologetic expression opened the door and said something quickly in Portuguese that made Camargo's eyes narrow. Then, out from behind the junior officer stepped a man in a blue suit that bore all the hallmarks of Savile Row's precise tailoring.

"Capitão Camargo," the man said in crisp English, "have you concluded your interview with Miss Moore?"

"For now," Camargo replied.

"Then I am certain you will have no objections to kindly allowing Miss Moore to go," said the man.

"She is a suspect in a murder investigation," said Camargo.

"Are you planning to arrest her and charge her with that murder?" challenged the Englishman.

Camargo looked for a moment as though he was very seriously considering it.

"I would suggest you release Miss Moore now, unless you wish for the British embassy to make this a matter of international concern. I am certain Dr. Salazar will not be pleased to have that conversation with your superiors," warned the Englishman, invoking the name of the Portuguese leader.

Again, Camargo didn't look entirely threatened by that idea. However, after a moment, he turned to address me.

"Menina, I would suggest that you be very careful during your stay in Lisbon. I cannot imagine that a young lady such as yourself would wish to find yourself detained awaiting deportation. Or worse."

I did not want to find out what Camargo considered "worse." My gaze flicked to the man in the blue suit. His expression was grim, but he gave me a slight nod.

"I will be," I said.

"You may go," said Camargo, waving a hand to dismiss me.

I stood and asked in a tiny voice, "May I have my handbag, please?"

"*Devolva a bolsa à menina,*" Camargo ordered the younger man who hovered near my savior's shoulder before switching back to English to say, "It will be returned to you."

"*Obrigada,*" I said quietly, earning another narrow-eyed glare from Camargo, who seemed completely unwilling to believe I was the scared secretary I was pretending to be.

Still, I gamely hunched my shoulders as I passed the captain and walked through the door, praying that Jessup's diary didn't choose that moment to shimmy out of my garter and onto the floor.

As soon as we were out of the room, the Englishman took me by the elbow. "Keep your head down. Don't look at anyone."

"Who are you?" I whispered out of the corner of my mouth.

"My car is parked just out front. We'll speak once we're inside."

Ahead of us, the captain's junior scrambled to grab my handbag from where it rested on a wooden desk. The young man handed it to me with a little bow, and I gave him a wobbly smile.

When we reached the door of the police station, the Englishman opened it for me. Sitting in the passenger seat of a huge black car parked a few feet away was David, who, when he spotted me, hopped out to open the back door for me.

"Miss Moore, are you quite all right?" my partner asked quickly as I approached.

I lifted my chin as though determined to soldier on despite the shock I'd endured. "Yes, Mr. Slater."

"Are you—?"

"I suspect we have a great many things to speak about," said the Englishman as he rounded the car to the driver's side, "but it would be best if we're on our way."

NINE

I sank heavily into the back seat of the car, happy to find that my suitcase was stacked neatly on top of David's next to me. The Englishman and my partner climbed in and, with a roar of the engine, we were off.

As soon as we were out of sight of the police station, I leaned forward through the gap in the front seats and asked, "Who are you?"

"Peter Phillips at your service, Miss Moore," the Englishman answered as he guided the car through morning traffic.

"As soon as I saw the police cars approach the airstrip, I knew something was wrong," David explained. "I assumed that you hadn't made your way back—"

"Because I had landed myself in some sort of trouble," I finished for him.

"I didn't expect it to be murder," David admitted.

"Neither did I," I said.

"Slater says this was all over a Charles Kingston novel," said Phillips, using David's cover name.

"*Murder in Piccadilly.* In my defense, it is a very good book," I said.

Phillips sniffed at that, giving me the distinct impression he was not a fan of detective fiction. Such was his loss.

"It took me some time to convince the Polícia de Vigilância e Defesa do Estado to release you," said Phillips. "The PVDE is not known for its generosity when it comes to anyone, but especially foreigners."

"Why is that?" I asked.

"Portugal has become something of a hotbed of espionage, with Lisbon at the heart of it. This is one of the last routes out of Europe for many people attempting to flee Germany's advances, so the city has been flooded with refugees trying to reach Britain and the United States. It makes it rather easy for the German military intelligence organization, the Abwehr, to operate."

"And us, I imagine," I said.

"Quite," said Phillips.

"Thank you for collecting me. I'm not confident Capitão Camargo had any intention of letting me go otherwise," I said.

"And you really are all right?" asked David, twisting to look back at me.

I smiled. "Other than being a little bored after being cooped up for hours without a book, I'm fine. Did they question you?"

"Not for very long. I was able to ring Phillips as soon as I was released."

"Lucky you," I muttered. "Mr. Phillips, have you ever heard of an Englishman named Michael Jessup?"

"No, I don't think so," he said as he negotiated a turn.

"Apparently he is our dead man." I intentionally glossed over the fact that I'd learned that long before Camargo had questioned me, recalling David's warning that those working on intelligence desks abroad could sometimes be territorial or difficult.

"He'll be in our records somewhere," said Phillips.

"If you wouldn't mind looking him up, that would be helpful. And I would appreciate it if you could secure a manifest for the flight as well," I said.

"You're not thinking of investigating, are you?" asked Phillips with surprise.

"I was almost blamed for a man's murder, Mr. Phillips. It seems reasonable to me that I should want to know at least a little about the victim and the list of suspects," I said.

"Suspects?" Phillips asked.

"Given that Jessup was alive when the cabin door closed at Whitchurch and the aeroplane had only just landed in Sintra when I discovered his body, it seems logical that Jessup was most likely killed by one of our fellow passengers," I said.

"There was only one way onto the aeroplane, and the crew had us disembark as soon as we landed. No one could have boarded or left without being in full view of their fellow passengers," said David in agreement.

"Are you certain that this is a wise course of action, Miss Moore?" asked Phillips. "Capitão Camargo could very well make good on his threat to deport you."

"Rest assured, Mr. Phillips, I am always careful," I said.

"I find that rather difficult to believe given the recklessness with which you behaved this morning," said Phillips.

"Recklessness?" It wasn't as though I had intended to stumble across a body.

"I should drive straight to the office and ring London to report—"

"That will not be necessary, Mr. Phillips," said David sharply. "Evelyne is one of the most instinctive field agents in the SIU. If you want Winn found, you want her on the investigation."

"Besides, the time it would take to replace me could be invaluable for finding Winn," I said.

I could see Phillips's jaw tense. "If you become distracted by looking into this man Jessup's death—"

"I assure you, that will not be a problem. Finding James Winn will be our first priority," said David definitively before glancing back at me as though to ask, *Right?*

"Without a doubt," I said.

Phillips let out a long, labored breath. "What do you know about Winn?"

“Other than the fact that his code name is Dogwood and he appears to have been a prolific source, virtually nothing,” I said.

“I’m glad to see that, after insisting upon sending agents from outside of British intelligence to investigate against my advice, London has neglected to brief you properly,” Phillips grumbled.

“Would you rather we were not here, Mr. Phillips?” I asked.

He glanced at me over his shoulder. “Don’t take it personally, Miss Moore, but you cannot possibly understand the complexity of Lisbon having just arrived. You need to have lived it and seen the changes that it is going through to begin to understand. If you were to ask the Portuguese, even that would not be enough.

“So no, I don’t particularly want you and Mr. Slater poking your noses into places they are not welcome and possibly disrupting the networks of informants that intelligence agents such as myself have taken such care to build over the last eighteen months. It is bad enough that the SOE insisted upon sending their own agents into Portugal. However, it appears that what I want doesn’t matter.”

I could understand Phillips’s frustration to a degree. He had essentially been told from on high that because he had lost contact with an informant he’d cultivated, someone else would have to come in and clean up his mess. It must have stung.

“We will endeavor to do our best not to disturb your work,” I said.

He sighed. “I suppose that will have to suffice. I’ll start at the beginning. As you know, Dogwood is the code name for James Winn. He’s British but has been living in Portugal off and on since 1933. About six months ago, he established contact with me. He said he was in the unique position of having access to sensitive information about Germans’ movements in Lisbon, specifically the Abwehr, their intelligence branch.”

“How did Winn manage that?” asked David.

“I’m not entirely certain,” Phillips admitted. “Winn was a skittish sort—rather paranoid, actually. I know little about him.”

“And knowing that little about him, you trust him?” I asked.

“He was spying for us, not coming around for tea, Miss Moore. Besides, Winn’s information was always spot on,” said Phillips.

"How can you be certain?" I asked.

"I looked into everything he gave me, especially in those early days. At first it was just bits and pieces. Then, about a month in, he came to me with a rather valuable piece of intelligence. It turns out that the Germans were using one of the— Well, that is to say that it had ladies of ill repute who worked . . . well—"

"You can say 'brothel,' Mr. Phillips," I said as David choked out a laugh. "The SIU doesn't generally go in for agents who are inclined to clutch their pearls, regardless of their sex."

I saw Phillips flash a look at David, who shrugged and said, "Evelyne can be plainspoken when she wants to be. You become used to it after a time. For the most part."

Phillips cleared his throat. "Winn reported that the Germans had set up a brothel by the waterfront and were paying the women working there to mine British sailors for information. We interviewed several of the girls before one cracked and admitted it to be true. We issued a warning to all British sailors coming to Lisbon, and we also reported the activity to the PVDE. The establishment was shut down within the week.

"Then there were other, smaller things, like who was planning on passing through Lisbon. Winn knew that the Duke and Duchess of Windsor would be staying at the home of Ricardo Espírito Santo in Cascais in July before we did. Those little scraps can add up to valuable information when put together with the other tips our informants give us."

"And now Winn is gone?" asked David.

"Yes," said Phillips. "The last I heard from him was ten days ago. Normally, that wouldn't concern me. Information and the informants who trade in it can be elusive sometimes. However, Winn left me an urgent message at a café near my flat saying he had information that the Abwehr had a new plot intended to force Portugal out of neutrality and onto the side of the Axis powers. He asked to meet at Estoril Casino that evening."

"Was that out of the ordinary?" David asked.

"Yes and no," said Phillips. "We had met at the casino before, but normally Winn's notes only listed a time and a date, never the actual information he possessed. He was worried about the risk of committing those things to writing, and I agreed."

"Why do you think he made the change?" I asked.

"I worry it was because something had rattled him so badly he'd neglected to follow his own rules," said Phillips. "I went to the casino that evening as instructed, but he didn't appear."

"Why would he arrange to meet you at a casino?" I asked.

"Anyone in Lisbon with the means goes to the casino," said Phillips. "It was a convenient meeting spot because if we were ever overseen talking there, it wouldn't strike anyone as odd. It's a very mixed crowd. There are gardens there too that allow for more privacy than a café or a bar."

"And there's been no word from Winn since?" I asked.

"None," said Phillips.

"Do you have any idea of what the German plot might have been?" I asked.

Phillips hesitated. "I can't be certain . . ."

"Certainty is for official reports," said David. "Any theories you might have will help us understand where to begin looking."

Without taking his eyes off the road, Phillips gave a nod. "An Austrian engineer, Johann Bauer, recently arrived in Lisbon."

"What sort of engineer is he?" I asked.

"One who specializes in refining mining practices. Particularly the extraction of wolfram," said Phillips. "One of my agents, Carter, picked up news of Bauer's arrival in Lisbon a fortnight or so ago."

I recognized Carter as the agent Mr. Fletcher had told me had filed reports on the movements of my father in Lisbon.

"Did Carter make contact with Bauer?" asked David.

"No, but he has been putting together a report on Bauer's movements, who he is meeting with, that sort of thing," said Phillips.

"Then how does Winn tie in to all of this?" I asked.

Phillips hesitated for a moment. "This is pure speculation . . ."

"It still might merit looking at," I said.

"Right," said Phillips. "I think Winn may have come across information about a German scheme to try to use this engineer to tempt the Portuguese into a deal that would increase wolfram production while tying up the export rights exclusively for Germany."

"Which would cut off our supply of wolfram to make armaments and put our munitions production in jeopardy," I said, remembering Mr. Fletcher's briefing on the value of the mineral.

"Precisely," said Phillips.

"We'll need to speak to Bauer," said David.

"I already spoke to him right after Winn disappeared," said Phillips.

"What did he say?" I asked.

"The man proved to be infuriatingly stubborn. He refused to answer any of my questions," he said.

"Perhaps he will be more amenable to ours," said David. "If you will provide us with his name and address."

"With all due respect, I have a great deal of experience recruiting potentially hostile contacts to our side. I cannot see why you would have any more success in speaking to this man than I would," said Phillips.

"And yet we must insist, Mr. Phillips, because while your expertise might lie in recruiting contacts, ours lies in questioning witnesses and suspects," I said.

After a long pause, Phillips said, "Fine. I'll need to consult Carter for Bauer's most recent address."

"Thank you," I said.

"Do you think there's any chance that the PVDE found out about Winn informing for us and deported him?" asked David.

"I would have heard about it from the embassy. They take these matters very seriously," said Phillips.

"Is there any chance that Winn could have been killed?" I asked.

Phillips blew out a breath. "I hope not."

"Could the Germans have turned him?" I asked.

"If that is what happened, Miss Moore, we should all be afraid," said Phillips.

"Do you know where we can find a photograph of Winn?" I asked.

"There might be one in his flat," said Phillips.

"Do you have that address?" I asked.

"I do, actually. He was cagey about things and never would have told me, but I managed to follow him from the casino one night," said Phillips. "He was at number 30 Calçadinha da Figueira in Alfama."

I scribbled that down in the notebook Miss Summers had put in my handbag.

"What about a description?" asked David.

"Medium height, medium build. Light brown hair. Brown eyes. He usually wore a gray suit and gray hat when I saw him," said Phillips.

"That could describe you or me," said David.

"Or virtually any brown-haired Englishman," I added.

"I'm afraid Winn was rather unremarkable, really," said Phillips apologetically. "I suppose it helped him when gathering information. Few people suspect someone they hardly notice.

"I would go with you to his flat, but I'm afraid that I've already pushed back a number of meetings trying to sort out your release, Miss Moore. I can drop you at Rua Limoiero, and then it is a short walk up the steps to Calçadinha da Figueira. When I return to the office, I will see to it that your luggage is delivered to your hotel. I believe we managed to book you into the Hotel Tivoli."

"Thank you," I said and settled back into my seat. I waited a moment until Phillips was distracted asking David something about the county cricket back in England. Then I popped open my handbag and slipped Jessup's diary inside. I would, I resolved, show it to David as soon as we were alone.

TEN

Phillips pulled his car up along the side of a road that slanted steeply upward and pointed to a set of steps sandwiched between a white building and a little patch of green park.

"I'm afraid you'll have to walk the rest of the way. It's about halfway up the hill," he said. "Be careful on the cobbles. It's a little wet underfoot, and they can be slick."

"Thank you, Mr. Phillips," I said.

"You'll locate the Austrian engineer for us?" asked David.

"And the flight's manifest?" I added.

Phillips sighed. "Is there anything else?"

"Not at the moment," I said, tempted to add, *but I'm certain there will be.*

With a grumble, the intelligence agent waved us off and drove away.

"Should you really be antagonizing our contact one hour into making his acquaintance?" asked David in a low voice.

"Should he really be so reluctant about an investigation that has been ordered by London?" I shot back.

"A fair point," said David as we began to climb the stairs.

By the time we reached the door of number 30 on Calçadinha da

Figueira, I was glad it was a cool morning. The exertion of walking up the many steps that made up the road paired with the challenge of making sure I didn't slip on the slicker parts of the cobblestones made for the best exercise I'd had since I'd been shot. I'm not ashamed to say that I was panting slightly when David knocked on the door of Winn's building.

While we waited for an answer, I peered up at the pale yellow facade topped with a red tiled roof. On each of the three floors that rose above us, there was a pair of white French doors that opened onto a black iron Juliet balcony. Flower boxes that must have been filled with cascading blooms in the spring and summer completed the picture.

The black front door swung open, and a woman dressed in a similar somber hue with an apron over her clothes filled the doorway.

"*Como posso ajudá-lo?*" she asked.

"*Bom dia senhora. Fala inglês?*" asked David tentatively.

She crossed her hands over her stomach and gave us a hard stare. "I speak a little English."

"We're looking for a man who lived here," said David.

"A Senhor Winn," I added with a smile.

The woman's expression darkened. "Senhor Winn? What do you want to know about him?"

"Does he live here?" asked David.

"Yes," she said. "I am Senhora Vidal, his landlady. Why?"

"We are looking for him," I explained.

"He is not here," she said, and made to close the door.

"Please," I said quickly. "When was the last time you saw him?"

Her eyes narrowed. "Senhor Winn is a strange man."

"What do you mean?" I asked.

"In six months, he has never spoken to me. He pays the rent by putting it through this door at night." Senhora Vidal shrugged as though this should explain everything. "Strange."

"He's never spoken to you?" I asked.

"His apartment is down there," she said, pointing to her left where there was a window covered in iron bars. "The entrance is around the corner. He is never there when I clean."

"But surely you must have met him when he let the flat," I said.

"My daughter let him the flat when I was in Coimbra visiting my sister." She scowled. "I would never have given the flat to an Englishman. They bring nothing but trouble."

"Does Senhor Winn pay his rent weekly?" I asked.

She folded her hands in front of her. "Yes."

"Then he didn't pay last Friday?" I asked.

"A *woman* came to pay it. She said she is a friend of Senhor Winn's," said Senhora Vidal, clearly unimpressed.

"Was it his girlfriend?" I asked.

The landlady's lips tightened. "I do not know."

"What did she look like?" I asked.

"Like a woman. I don't know. Why are you asking me these questions?"

"Please, Senhora," I implored. "Anything you can tell us would be helpful."

Senhora Vidal studied me for a moment and then sniffed. "She had dark hair. She was a little *anafada*."

"What does that mean?" I asked.

She thought for a moment and then said, "Round. Her shoes were good."

It wasn't the most helpful description I'd ever come across, but it was a start.

"Was she English?" I asked.

She made a noise of disgust. "Portuguese."

"Senhora, would it be possible for us to see Senhor Winn's flat?" asked David.

I thought for a moment that she might turn us away, but then she shrugged and dropped her shoulder to edge between the two of us.

"Senhor Winn has not paid this week's rent yet, so you can see it. If no one pays today, I will let it to someone else," she said as she walked down the steps to the street and led us to a small black door marked 30A a few steps up from her own entryway. Out of her pocket came a set of keys. She unlocked the door to the flat and held it open.

"You have ten minutes," she said before shutting the door behind us.

Not enough time to show David the diary burning a hole in my handbag, but enough time to have a snoop around Winn's life.

I looked around the small sitting room. It was stuffy and held the air of a place that hadn't been entered in some time. However, it was clean and tidy, with no stray books on the small wooden table next to the orange sofa arm or papers on the square dining table around which two chairs were tucked.

I crossed the room, the sound of my heels dampened by a large rug spread out over the floor, and opened a cabinet set into a wall. However, rather than coats hanging neatly from a rod, I saw that it had been converted into a little kitchen of sorts. There was a gas ring and a tin kettle waiting empty next to it. Around the three walls of the cabinet, someone had put up a pine shelf that now held a collection of canisters. I turned one so that I could read the label and found it was a tin of Twinings tea. The other canisters contained coffee granules, sugar, and some powdered milk. A half-drunk bottle of red wine with the cork jammed back into the neck sat next to two unopened bottles. On the far side of the shelf there was a set of cutlery, a plate, a wineglass, and a water glass all neatly lined up.

"It doesn't appear that Winn invited many people here," I said over my shoulder to David.

"What makes you say that?" he asked as he came up behind me, a newspaper in hand.

I nodded to the shelf of utensils. "There's only one fork. What do you have there?"

"This is from eleven days ago," said David, showing me the front page of a newspaper with *11 de novembro de 1940* printed at the top.

"Didn't Phillips say that the last time he'd heard from Winn was ten days ago?" I asked.

David nodded.

"Today is the twenty-second. That means Winn bought this the day before he left a note for Phillips at his café, arranging a meeting," I said.

"Only Winn never materializes at the casino and two days later, on the Thursday, Phillips finally informs London that his contact has gone missing after sending an urgent message," said David.

"But a woman comes by to pay Winn's rent last Friday, the fifteenth."

"We need to find her."

"I agree." I planted my hands on my hips, looking about me. "I'd like to see the bedroom."

"I'll check to see if there's anything useful in the desk," said David.

The bedroom was just big enough for an iron bed with a mattress that sagged slightly in the middle, but it was made up with crisp white sheets. A single bedside table with a small brass lamp on it was the only other piece of furniture in the room.

Reasoning that Winn must have kept his clothing somewhere, I approached one of two doors on the wall opposite the room's two windows. The first proved to be a bath with a small basin and toilet. A straight razor with a worn wooden handle sat next to a shaving brush on the side of the basin, and there was a wood-backed hairbrush and a tin of Brylcreem on the shelf below the mirror. I picked up the brush, turned it over. There were a few strands of brown hair caught in the bristles.

The other door turned out to be a cupboard in which one gray suit, one blue suit, and a dinner jacket hung neatly with three pairs of shoes—two for day and one for night—lined up under them. On the rod there were also several white shirts, and I discovered that a tiny chest of drawers held socks and underthings.

It felt odd rifling through a stranger's intimate garments—although I suspect it would have been all the more unsettling if I'd known Winn personally. Not finding anything tucked among his things, I straightened and began to go through the pockets of his suits but found there wasn't even so much as a spare escudo.

I flicked through the shirts looking for what I wasn't entirely certain when, three shirts in, I stopped. On the collar of one of Winn's white shirts was the unmistakable orangey-red smudge of lipstick.

I unhooked the shirt from the rod but the tail of it caught on something and, unbuttoned as it was, the shirt slipped off the metal hanger and fell to the floor. I stooped to pick it up and, just as I was about to straighten, something caught my eye: a flash of white peeking out from under the chest of drawers. I teased it out with my fingernail and picked it up. It was a burgundy matchbook with "Café Real" printed in black script on the cover.

"Evelyne?" David called.

"In the cupboard."

A moment later, David appeared in the bedroom doorway. "It's a bit spartan, isn't it?"

"Very," I said, holding up the lipstick-stained collar for him to see. "Senhora Vidal will be horrified to know that it appears Winn might have had a girlfriend after all."

"You think the same woman who paid the rent left that lipstick mark?" he asked.

"Quite possibly. And then there's this." I handed him the matchbook.

"Café Real," he read out.

"The café where Winn would sometimes leave Phillips messages," I said.

David flipped the book over and then opened the flap. "Nothing written inside."

"A telephone exchange leading us straight to Winn would have been too easy, I suppose."

"It looks as though we'll have to work a bit harder than that," said David.

"What did you find in the desk?" I asked.

"Nothing much. There was no passport or identity papers. He could have run."

"Or he could carry them on him as a matter of habit, and that would account for why they aren't here. Were there any letters?"

He shook his head. "If Winn had much in the way of correspondence, he didn't keep it in his flat. All I could find were a few pieces of writing paper, several envelopes, and a pencil. I even tried your trick of rubbing a pencil over the top sheet of paper to see if anything appeared."

I had done that during the course of our last case, revealing a list of names that were one of the final pieces of the puzzle to solve a ghastly double murder.

"Did you have any luck?" I asked.

"All I managed to do was turn the paper a uniform shade of gray," said David.

"In that case," I said, pocketing the matchbook, "I want to ask Senhora Vidal on our way out whether Winn had his post delivered here. And then I think it's time to find a decent lunch since we've missed breakfast, don't you?"

That teased a smile out of David. "I think that's a very wise idea, indeed."

ELEVEN

Winn's landlady was sweeping the bit of road outside of number 30 when we left the flat to ask her about the post.

"No letters ever came for him. Nothing," Senhora Vidal snapped, mashing the ground with her broom.

Sensing that our welcome had well and truly run out, I handed her back the key and David and I thanked her before hurrying off.

We retraced our steps down to Rue Limoeiro, winding our way through Alfama in the direction of our hotel thanks to directions from a shopkeeper David managed to speak to in a combination of Spanish, French, and English. Finally, after about twenty minutes of walking, my partner took pity on me and suggested we stop at a café on Avenida da Liberdade, where we had a simple lunch of grilled sardines, boiled potato, and salad. I finished it all with *pudim de ovos*, a crème caramel–like dessert. After months of strict rationing in London, having that much sugar in one sitting felt like the height of decadence.

"I thought you might eat the plate. Shall I order you another?" David asked, watching with amusement as I relished licking every last bit from the spoon. It wasn't very ladylike, but where had being ladylike ever gotten me before?

"No, thank you. I think that is enough for now," I said, reaching for the last sip of my glass of Alvarinho.

"It certainly is a mix of people here," David remarked, looking at the other tables around us.

"A mix" didn't do it justice. There was a cacophony of languages in the café. I could hear not only Portuguese but English, French, Spanish, Italian, German, Polish, and Hungarian. The patrons ranged from well-dressed, with women wrapped in fur coats with beautiful hats perched on their heads and the men in bespoke suits, to those who pulled thin coats around them to ward off a chill even inside. However, one thing was universal: each and every one of them held their shoulders taut as though waiting for the other shoe to drop.

"I have tried, Marie," I heard a middle-aged man reassure his pretty wife, who wore a beautiful necklace of robin's egg–sized pearls, in French at the table next to us.

"Try harder, Henri." The woman whimpered and then dabbed her eyes with a handkerchief. "I thought you said that you knew someone in New York who would sponsor us."

"I do, but he has taken ill, and I cannot reach him. If you would allow me to sell your necklace . . ."

The woman grasped at the pearls. "You *gave* these to me."

The man sighed.

David cleared his throat. "Shall we check in to our hotel?"

"I suppose we should," I said, tearing my attention from the couple.

Our hotel was a short walk away along the beautiful boulevard, and when we stepped inside, the lobby was positively bustling with people.

"*Bom dia*," a man in a smart black suit greeted us at the front desk.

"Hello, I believe you have two rooms for us," said David.

The man glanced between us as though trying to figure out what our relationship might be that we would require two rooms at his hotel.

"The booking should be under Slater," said David. "You might also have my secretary Miss Moore's name."

Understanding lit up the man's eyes, and he quickly lifted the hotel ledger onto the counter and offered David a pen. "Certainly, Senhor Slater. Your luggage has already arrived. I took the liberty of having it brought to your rooms."

"Thank you," said David.

The man busied himself fetching our keys and then handed one to David marked 36 and another to me that was for room 42.

"We are not on the same floor?" asked David with a frown.

"I am very sorry, Senhor, but the hotel is very full," apologized the man.

"Yes, I noticed. Why is that?" I asked.

"Everyone wishes to be in Lisbon," said the man with a tight smile. "Please enjoy your stay."

"Thank you," David and I said at the same time.

A few steps away from the front desk, David said, "I should like to review our itinerary. Shall we meet in ten minutes after you have had a chance to unpack your things?"

Come to my room in ten minutes and we'll discuss the case.

"Yes, Mr. Slater. There's a great deal to review," I said.

You don't know this yet, but I need to tell you about a certain diary I might have lifted from a crime scene.

We boarded the lift together, and he disembarked first with a polite goodbye. When the lift reached my floor, I stepped off and quickly found room 42. Once inside, I sagged against the door. Outside of Camargo's interrogation, my cover hadn't been tested at all. However, it was still exhausting pretending to be someone I was not. Everything was new to me and everyone around me seemed to move through the city with a sense of unease. To top it all off, I'd found a dead man mere hours before.

Pushing off the door, I unbuttoned my coat and slung it over the edge of the bed. I ignored my suitcase waiting on a stand against a wall and instead extracted a comb from my handbag and set about fixing my hair. After a drink of water and a swipe of lipstick, I gathered up my handbag and made my way to David's room.

I knocked sharply on the door of room 36 and, almost immediately, David opened it.

"Come in, Miss Moore," he said.

He'd shed his overcoat and his jacket and had rolled up the sleeves of his shirt, exposing his forearms. I did my very best not to look but didn't quite succeed.

As soon as he shut the door, he sighed. "I've been thinking about it, and I can't see any way around telling Mrs. White about what happened this morning. We're now on the PVDE's list of suspicious people. It could hinder our investigation."

I cringed. "Mrs. White will *not* approve."

"No," he said. "She won't. I'll see if I can head things off in my report this afternoon and reassure her that Jessup will not be our primary focus."

"About that . . ." I began. "I wouldn't say that Jessup is *entirely* out of our purview." I slid my handbag off my wrist and unclasped the top. "Do you have gloves to hand?"

His eyes narrowed. "Why?"

I shot him a look and he turned to his overcoat, muttering, "All right, all right."

"When I discovered Jessup's body, I took the liberty of looking through his pockets," I said as I tugged on my own gloves.

"Before you screamed?"

"Yes," I said.

"You shouldn't have done that."

"Screamed?" I asked.

"Looked through a dead man's things."

I raised a brow. "Why not?"

"Because the PVDE—"

"Jessup was an Englishman killed on a flight from Britain. Are you really telling me that if the roles were reversed and *you'd* found him, you wouldn't have done exactly the same?"

David took a moment seemingly to compose his next sentence, which—I was rather pleasantly surprised to find—was not *You were needlessly reckless, Evelyne*, but instead was, "What did you find?"

I pulled the slim black leather diary out from my handbag.

David blanched. "Don't tell me that's what I think it is."

"Fine. It isn't." I knew it was a petulant response, but the man was being unnecessarily dramatic.

"Evelyne, you took a piece of evidence from a crime scene in another country. If you had been caught—"

"Don't you want to know *why* I took it?"

He pinched the bridge of his nose. "Why did you take Jessup's diary?"

"Because of this." I showed him the page for the thirty-first of October and the notation reading *Winn?*

David swore under his breath.

"I don't know if Jessup's murder has anything to do with Winn's disappearance, but it seemed wise to take a diary linking our missing informant with a man whose neck had just been snapped in what amounts to broad daylight," I said.

"The PVDE took your handbag. How did you manage to sneak the diary off the aeroplane and keep it out of sight?"

"I tucked it into the top of my stocking."

"Bloody Hell, Evelyne." He began to laugh. "No one can say you aren't inventive."

I dipped into a mock curtsey. "Thank you. I haven't actually had a chance to give it a proper look yet because I didn't think Phillips would approve—"

"A good instinct."

"And we haven't been alone and out of the public eye long enough to look. Shall we now?"

David exhaled. "I suppose we should. Why don't we start with that entry for Winn?"

Flicking through the pages of the diary, I found the instance of *Winn?* once again.

"All that's written is his name with a question mark," I said.

"Has anything been erased?" David asked.

I held the page up to the light to see if there was any evidence of ghosting or wear around the entry.

"Nothing." An idea popped into my head. "Can you hand me my lighter?"

Instead of going through my handbag, David gave me his own.

I sparked the lighter and once again performed the trick that I'd used in my boardinghouse room to reveal my father's message. Not a trace.

"Invisible ink?" asked David.

"It was a long shot and apparently an unsuccessful one," I said.

"Let's go through it from the beginning and see if 'Winn' appears earlier," he suggested.

I settled on the edge of the bed and flipped to the first of January while David pulled up a chair, and together we began to read.

Jessup seemed to have regular but modest demands on his time in his early entries. Every Wednesday at half past three there was a notation for a meeting with *E* that I suspected was related to his work at the bank, along with notes about weekend appointments with *Mother*, a *Mrs. S.—Cleaning* every fortnight, and an entry that just read *Dr* in February.

We continued through this survey of the dead man's life until late March when I saw an entry that made me pause.

"Look at this," I said, pointing to the pencil marks.

"'Whit.-Sin., 8,'" read David. "That sounds very much like Whitchurch to Sintra at eight o'clock."

"It does."

I paged back to check that I hadn't missed any earlier entries, but as I suspected nothing earlier made reference to the Whitchurch-to-Sintra route. However, a week later I found a corresponding return.

"Sintra to Whitchurch, ten o'clock," I said. "The way that the flight crew had spoken to Jessup about his case made me certain he was a regular passenger. This could have been the date of his first trip to Lisbon."

David took the diary from me and began flipping through the months.

"Here," he said. "There's a similar pair of entries bracketing the last week of April." He flipped more. "Then another at the end of May."

"What about June?" I asked.

He frowned as he looked. "That's interesting. Jessup took a trip to Lisbon just a fortnight later."

David passed me the book and sure enough, in June, the pattern changed. Instead of notations every four weeks, I started to see *W.-S.* and *S.-W.* every fortnight.

I sat back, thinking. "Air travel is rare enough as it is, but during a war?"

"Tickets are as precious as gold. Half of the aeroplanes are taken up by diplomats and spies. He would have had to have been on very important business for his bank to merit him traveling so often."

We continued on with the diary, finding that Jessup's entries were becoming even shorter and more frequent. Sometime in the summer, he seemed to have acquired the frustrating habit of using only abbreviations or, on occasion, just a set of numbers or a time.

Finally, we were once again on the page with *Winn?* written on it. After a quick check of November and December, we confirmed that there were no other notes related to Winn.

"Where did Jessup stay when he was in Lisbon?" David asked.

"Ah," I said, teasing the receipt I'd seen on the aeroplane out from behind the front cover. "The Hotel Metrópol, if this is to be believed."

"This says he stayed there between the twenty-sixth of October and the sixth of November," he said, reading off the dates from the receipt. "Does that correspond with the dates of Jessup's flights in the diary?"

"It does," I confirmed. "It also means that Jessup was in Britain when Winn last made contact with Phillips."

"Right. We need to put the Hotel Metrópol on our list, but first there are a few messages I must send to HQ after the events of this morning," he said, rising from his chair.

"You aren't telling Mrs. White about me finding Jessup's body, are you?" I asked.

"I'm afraid I must."

"Is that entirely necessary?"

"I promise, I'll make sure she knows how sorry you are that you managed to walk straight into a crime scene," he said with a grin.

I was very tempted to throw a pillow at him.

"Phillips said I could use the secure line in his office. It shouldn't take me long. What will you do?" he asked.

"I should ring around to those appointments Miss Summers arranged for us and let them know we've arrived in case we need someone to vouch for us. I'm not confident that my friend Capitão Camargo was entirely convinced by my innocent secretary act this morning in the interrogation room," I admitted.

"I'll ring your room when I return."

I packed up Jessup's diary and stripped off my gloves before saying my goodbyes and retreating to my room.

I had every intention of ringing those contacts, but I also wanted a moment to breathe and unpack. I was curious to see what Miss Summers thought a wine buyer's secretary would travel with. There was also the promise of a scalding bath with all of that lovely hotel hot water.

When I reached my room, I made straight for my suitcase. I popped open the case's clasps to retrieve Evelyne Moore's toiletries, hoping they resembled the things I would normally use. However, when I lifted the lid, I found a note addressed to *E.R.* lying on top of my clothes that read:

It is vital I speak to you about a familial matter. Please meet me at the Café Nicola on Rossio Square at four o'clock. I will be wearing a red rose.

—A.C.

I glanced at *Maman*'s watch and, sure enough, it was quarter to four.

I let out a groan, frustrated that just this once the spies couldn't stop spying for long enough that I could have a soak and solitary think.

Then I donned my coat and my hat once again and made for the lift.

TWELVE

Five minutes past four, I walked under the elaborate art deco entrance of Café Nicola and stopped to cast my gaze around the restaurant. It was, fortunately for me, not particularly busy and I almost immediately spotted a young man in a gray suit, white shirt, and blue tie with a red rose tucked into his buttonhole. I narrowed my eyes and marched up to his table in a nearly abandoned corner and planted my feet in front of him.

"A red rose? Really?" I asked.

The man looked up and his face brightened. "Miss Moore, how do you do? Please do sit down and join me for a coffee and a *pastel de nata* or two. Some might say it is a little late in the day for them, but that should never stand in the way of enjoyment, I think."

The man's accent was English and, with his light blond hair, ruddy cheeks, and slightly barrel chest, he looked as though he'd only come off the rugby pitch at school a few years ago.

I took the chair across from him while he gestured to a waiter dressed in black and white with a long white apron tied around his waist. I waited until my companion ordered and then asked, "Who are you?" even though I had a fairly good idea given the initials he'd left.

He smiled. "I apologize for the cloak-and-dagger routine, but I couldn't be certain that I would be able to find a quiet moment to introduce myself if you came into the office." He stretched his hand across the gap between us. "Archibald Carter. I work under Mr. Phillips. I was the one who arranged for your luggage to be delivered to the hotel, so I took the liberty of adding a note to your suitcase."

"How do you do?" I took the intelligence officer's hand, studying the man Mr. Fletcher wanted me to make contact with.

"Your note said that you had a family matter to discuss with me?"

"I do." Carter paused while a waiter placed a small cup of coffee and a plate of two custard tarts next to my hand. "Have you had *pastel de nata* before?"

"No," I said.

"You should really try them. They're unlike anything we have back at home."

I picked one up and bit into it, the flaky pastry crumbling with a satisfying crunch that gave way to the yellow custard in the middle.

"Oh, that is delicious," I said, catching a bit of crumb with my free hand before it fell to the pristine tablecloth.

"You'll have to see if a trip to Pastéis de Belém is in the cards while you are in Lisbon," he said with a twinkle in his eye.

Normally I would warm to a man with such high regard for the importance of food. However, I hadn't forgotten the hot bath Carter's message had denied me.

"Your note?" I prompted.

"Yes. I received a cable from our mutual friend in London who made certain disclosures, including your . . . connection to Sir Reginald. I will, of course, continue to call you Miss Moore," said Carter.

I raised a brow. "That's good since it's my name."

"Quite." In a low tone, he added, "I was told that no one should be made aware of your identity or the reason we are meeting, not even Phillips. I wasn't certain how much your partner knows."

With Mr. Fletcher's warning not to risk involving David practically ringing in my ears, I said, "Mr. Slater knows nothing, including that I'm here now. I would prefer if it were to stay that way."

He nodded. "That is the way we usually operate in Lisbon."

"You and Phillips don't share work?"

"Not unless it is absolutely necessary. I keep him apprised of the general nature of my work, but in terms of the details we find it best if we operate independently. There's simply too much work to go around, and it helps keep things neat if someone is compromised or a network of informants collapses."

"Then you wouldn't be acquainted with an informant named James Winn?" I asked.

"Dogwood? Not outside of Phillips's reports. I did think to offer to help find him, but with the influx of refugees and spies into Lisbon in the recent months it's proving nearly impossible to stay on top of everything. Now with Sir Reginald complicating matters . . ."

I sighed. "Yes, he does seem to have acquired a habit of doing that. What is it this time?"

"One of my responsibilities is monitoring the manifests of the ships and flights out of Portugal and making note of any people of interest. Sir Reginald arrived in Lisbon about a month ago on the twenty-fourth of October on a flight from Casablanca. The next day, he made something of a splash at the roulette tables at Estoril Casino. Over the course of his time here, he established himself as a regular at the casino. Then, without warning, Sir Reginald vanished."

"Vanished?" I asked.

Carter leaned forward. "I haven't been able to identify anyone who has seen him since the thirteenth of November. There is no record of him leaving Lisbon on a flight or a boat."

"What about crossing the border to Spain?"

"That would have required the necessary paperwork to travel, but my sources have found no evidence that he made any such request. It appears that Sir Reginald is in the wind."

First James Winn and then Sir Reginald. There appeared to be a rash of English expats disappearing in Lisbon.

"So you see, Miss Moore, I had hoped that perhaps you might

know where your father is," Carter continued. "When was the last time you spoke?"

"When I was nearly eighteen," I said.

"Oh. And I take it that you are not . . ."

"Currently that age? No. I was in my last year at school. Sir Reginald drove me up to London and took me for a rather awkward lunch at his club. I think both of us realized after that that an arm's-length relationship would be for the best."

"And you haven't heard from him since?" he asked.

"That's just the thing, Mr. Carter. Not only have I not seen Sir Reginald in years, there hasn't been so much as a letter, telegram, or telephone call in all of that time. But then, seemingly out of nowhere last month, he asked my aunt for my address," I said, telling him about the key and the safe deposit vault address. I described how I'd been delayed in opening the envelope until two days ago because of work, and about the jewels I'd found in the safe deposit box. Then I told him about Morrison's ransacked shop.

At the end of my story, Carter blew out a long breath. "Well, that certainly doesn't bode well for Mr. Morrison . . ."

"I fear you may be right," I said.

"You don't think your father . . . ?"

"I have very little regard for Sir Reginald's character, but I find it highly unlikely that he would have ransacked Morrison's shop after instructing me from Lisbon to take the jewels to that very same man. If he were traveling to London, why not keep the safe deposit key and use it himself to retrieve the jewels?"

Carter rubbed the knuckles of his right hand against the palm of his left as he looked off in the distance. "That's true."

"Besides, it isn't the most straightforward thing to slip into the country undetected these days," I said. "If he'd returned to Britain, I'm certain one of our respective employers would know about it."

I chewed on my lower lip for a moment and then asked, "What did Sir Reginald do in Lisbon outside of gamble and go to parties?"

Carter pulled a black leather-bound notebook out of his inner jacket pocket and flipped it open. "He checked into the Hotel Aviz—it is a miracle that he was able to secure a room as it's been booked up for weeks—and proceeded to spend every night he was not invited to a dinner or party at the casino."

"Do you know the company he kept?" I asked.

"The usual wealthy expat crowd that buzzes around the princess."

I laughed. "A princess? Why am I not the least bit surprised?"

"Why do you say that?" asked Carter.

"Let's just say that if I was forced to be generous and name my father's one good quality, it is his charm—or at least his ability to appear charming when he wishes to be to people who he believes are important. He is particularly skillful with convincing women of a certain class he is a delight."

"I did wonder how the man managed to marry three times . . ."

I gave a snort. "It's a wonder it's not more. It would be just like him to ingratiate himself with a member of a royal family."

"She isn't quite that kind of princess. Princess Petrova is more aristocrat by marriage than royal," he explained.

"Russian?"

"British, actually. She was born Miss Camille Lang. Her father was a prominent London barrister, and as far as we can tell she had a fairly conventional upbringing for a girl of her class. She was educated at one of the better girls' schools until she was sent to be finished in Switzerland. There she met Prince Yevgeny Igorevich Petrov's sister, Yelizaveta. She was the one who invited Miss Lang to the family's Parisian home and that is where Miss Lang met Prince Petrov."

"Did they go back to Russia after they married?" I asked.

"It appears that they lived mostly in Paris but would return to St. Petersburg annually until the revolution put an end to that." He consulted his notebook again. "In 1925, Prince Petrov died. The couple's son, Oleksandr, received the bulk of his father's fortune, but a healthy settlement was left behind for the princess with an additional income to provide for her during her lifetime. She lived primarily in Paris, but then, in 1938, she moved to Lisbon, where she has since installed herself as the doyenne of expat society. At first it was just the British, but with all of the people pouring into the city after war was declared, she's expanded to include all manner of nationalities."

"German?" I asked.

Carter closed his notebook and tucked it away again. "I think you'll find, Miss Moore, that there is more blurring of social lines between supporters of the Allies and Axis countries than you might expect here. People are happy to sit at the same baccarat table and take each other's money night after night. The princess holds monthly 'soirees,' as she calls them, that certainly have a few Abwehr spies dotted throughout."

"Doesn't that concern you?" I asked.

"Not so long as we have plenty of our side there too to keep everything in check."

"And you think my father attended one of these soirees?" I asked.

"I know for a fact that he did. Phillips is always invited, and he reported seeing Sir Reginald there."

I made a mental note to ask Phillips whether Winn had ever been invited to the princess's home.

"I wonder . . ." Carter began. "Your father's instructions that you should take a box of jewels to a London jeweler strike me as odd."

"Why is that?" I had my own reasons for finding the instructions strange, but I was curious to hear Carter's perspective.

"Well, one of the things Sir Reginald did early in his time in Lisbon was visit a series of jewelry shops."

"That is curious," I said.

"I have notes on the names of the jewelry shops and the dates back at the office. I'll find them for you."

"That would be very helpful, thank you."

"Sir Reginald also had a habit of rotating around the various hotel bars," Carter added.

"Do any of them stand out?" I asked.

"Not particularly. Many people here have nothing to do but wait while they apply for the necessary visas and other paperwork to travel on to their final destination. In a single day, you might see the same man in three different cafés and two hotel bars, simply biding his time."

Carter glanced down at his watch. "Right, I should be making my way back to the office."

"Thank you for your help," I said, rising. "I haven't had the impression that Mr. Slater and I are entirely welcome."

"Has Phillips not made you feel right at home?" asked Carter with a laugh.

"I wouldn't call his the warmest welcome I've ever had," I said.

"Give him time," said the intelligence agent. "It ruffled a few of his feathers when London insisted on sending you both."

"Didn't we ruffle any of yours?"

"Miss Moore," he said as he dropped a few escudos on the table, "I promise that I could not be more delighted to have your assistance, in whatever form it comes."

THIRTEEN

By the time I returned to the Hotel Tivoli, it was a quarter past five. I stopped at the front desk to ask whether there were any messages for me in case David had returned in my absence. Finding none, I retreated to the quiet of my room.

Tempted as I was by the prospect of a bath without a queue of my fellow boardinghouse women waiting impatiently outside the door, I decided that I couldn't ignore my work any longer, and the first thing I did after I toed off my shoes was pull on my gloves and reach for Miss Summers's agenda.

I was just lifting the telephone receiver to make my first call when there was a knock on my door.

"Who is it?" I called out.

"Mr. Slater."

There was a degree of urgency in David's voice that, while not alarming, still made me hurry to open the door.

When he saw me with no shoes on, he turned bright pink. "Oh, I beg your pardon. I didn't realize you were in a state of undress."

Really, my stockinged toes could not have been *that* much of a sight.

"Is there something I can help you with, Mr. Slater?"

"Yes." He glanced either way down the corridor. "May I come in?"

"I think my reputation can risk it."

With a sigh and a shake of his head, he stepped through and, as soon as the door was shut behind us, asked, "Your reputation? What if someone had been listening?"

"Then they would have assumed that, despite your role as my employer, there was something more intimate between us," I said.

When I turned, I found that my partner's eyes were glued firmly on the ceiling as though he was trying to summon the strength to cope with such a suggestion.

"Come, David. Don't be so prudish. Besides, it's useful, really, for explaining any slip in formality while we're in public," I said. "Now, am I to assume that you have news?"

He shook his head at my admonishment, but nonetheless said, "I do."

I gestured at the wooden chair pulled up to the desk in the corner of the room. "Will you sit?"

David took the chair gratefully and I sat on the edge of the bed as I had earlier while examining the diary in his room.

"How angry is Mrs. White?" I asked, knowing that I might as well rip the plaster off.

"I'd say that she's not quite volcanic, but she did not sound happy."

"You spoke to her?"

"Yes, Phillips had his secretary arrange it. We had some difficulties, but we managed to finally make the trunk calls line up. I can't imagine telephone calls will be a luxury you and I can become accustomed to if she ever allows us back out into the field abroad again, but given the circumstances, it seemed prudent."

He paused and then said slowly, "Mrs. White did have some choice words about your ability to find dead bodies around every corner."

"An ability, I would like to point out, that I did not develop until Mr. Fletcher recruited me for the SIU," I shot back.

"Noted," he said. "The fortunate news is that, as far as Mrs. White is concerned, your stumbling over Jessup's body hasn't altered our mission. We are to focus on finding out what has happened to Winn with no further distractions."

"Did you . . . ?"

"Mention the diary you stole from a crime scene?" He scowled. "No, I didn't see the need to wade into details until we are certain that the two cases are, in fact, connected."

Despite his sour expression, David had protected me from incurring any more of our handler's wrath than necessary. For that, I was grateful.

"How was Phillips?" I asked.

"More gracious than this morning. However, I am concerned that if he learns about the diary—"

"He'll go straight to Mrs. White and demand our removal from the case, which, I think you'll agree, she would be more than happy to fulfill given her rather low opinion of me," I finished for him. "We need to find a way to ask Phillips about Winn and Jessup without letting him know what we've found until we are certain Jessup's death ties in to Winn's disappearance. A scribbled note in a diary is not enough."

"We can sound Phillips out tonight. He suggested we go to the casino this evening to see where he and Winn used to meet," said David.

I stilled. "The casino?"

"Phillips said he would be bringing along one of the agents who works for him who might be able to tell us more about the Austrian engineer, Bauer." David must have seen the worry in my expression because he asked, "Is that a problem? You don't have a moral stance against gambling that I'm not aware of, do you?"

"No, it isn't that."

I rose and threw open the top of my suitcase.

"Evelyne . . . ?"

I began to pull out garments and hold them up before discarding them. "These are not my clothes. In fact, I've never seen this suitcase in my life."

"It's a Miss Summers Special," he said.

"Is that what we call it?" I asked, not bothering to look up from my sorting.

"That's what I call it. I couldn't speak for our compatriots."

"Well, I'd say Miss Summers is rather too good at her job," I said, discarding a white cotton blouse with a Peter Pan collar.

"Why is that?"

"Because she gave me the clothing of a secretary accompanying her boss on a business trip, and what secretary of good reputation expects to go to dinner and a casino with said boss?"

Understanding dawned on his face. "You don't have an evening dress."

"Or shoes, or a bag, or a wrap." I glanced at the little clock on the bedside table. "And where in Lisbon am I going to find them at nearly half past five on a Friday?"

FOURTEEN

I have never wanted to kiss a man out of gratitude the way I wanted to kiss the concierge at the Hotel Tivoli that late Friday afternoon. After I pulled on my shoes and coat, David and I went downstairs and straight to the desk to ask if the concierge could think of a dress shop supplying evening dresses that might be willing to accommodate a desperate Englishwoman in need of something for the casino that very evening.

The man simply smiled and said, "Menina Moore, it would be my pleasure to direct you to the shop of my sister. If you will allow me to make one telephone call."

Twenty minutes later, we were ushered into a discreet shop in the Chiado neighborhood by a tall woman in a beautifully fitted chocolate-brown skirt and jacket who wore her dark hair scraped back into a low bun.

"*Boa noite*, Menina Moore. I am Senhora Ferreira. My brother, Alexio, said you need a gown?" asked the shop owner.

"Yes," I breathed. "I'm afraid there's no time for alterations either. I'm meant to be going to the casino tonight."

"I see. Please come in," said Senhora Ferreira, who gestured for David and me to follow her to an area with two armchairs, a raised platform, and a long mirror. "I have chosen some things based on what Alexio was able to tell me about you. They are just behind that door." Then she turned to David. "If you would care to sit, Senhor."

In the dressing room, I found half a dozen dresses hanging up on gold hooks set into the wall. Alexio must have given Senhora Ferreira a sense of my coloring because they were all the deep greens, blues, and reds that suited me best. I chose to ignore the fact that he also must have guessed at my measurements because, mercifully, they all looked as though they might fit.

"I would suggest you start with the blue, Menina Moore," came the dress shop owner's muffled voice through the closed dressing room door just as I was pondering where to start.

Without a quibble, I brought the navy dress to the front and began to unbutton my coat.

When I stepped out of the dressing room, Senhora Ferreira was ready to assess me from top to toe.

"Good," she announced, "but maybe not the best. Do you have shoes?"

"I have nothing."

She held up a finger as though to tell me not to worry and went to a cabinet from which she produced a pair of black velvet evening sandals with a heel and a little black velvet bag held closed by a gold clasp. She handed me the bag and then helped me ease on the shoes.

"You are tall," she said.

"Not as tall as some," I replied, although it was true that I stood a good few inches above many women I knew.

"But you like it?" she asked.

I nodded.

"Good," said Senhora Ferreira. "A woman should make the most of what she has. Now, go show your husband."

"Oh, he's not my husband," I protested. "Mr. Slater is my employer."

Senhora Ferreira raised a brow. "Even more reason to show him."

As though on cue, David called out, "Miss Moore?" from outside the dressing room.

"Go," urged Senhora Ferreira, giving me a little push of encouragement.

When your best friend happens to be an actress and a model, you become used to every eye following her when you walk into a room. However, without Moira to stride in next to me, I was acutely aware of the moment that I passed through the door and David's attention focused on me. He sat up a little straighter and touched the knot of his tie. Then he smiled.

"Do you like it?" he asked.

I looked down, smoothing my hands over the bias-cut silk. "It's beautiful."

"But not right," Senhora Ferreira announced as she stepped out behind me and touched the fluttering sleeve that covered my arms to the elbow. "You should not wear sleeves in the evening."

"It's really all right," I protested, crossing my arms over my chest and letting my hands slip under the silk of the sleeves as I was acutely aware that both the shop owner and my partner were now examining me with a critical eye.

"Try the green dress," said Senhora Ferreira firmly.

"Do you mind?" I asked David.

He spread his hands in front of him. "Not at all."

"A man never minds waiting for a beautiful woman," said Senhora Ferreira, making me properly blush before she turned me around and marched me back into the dressing room, shutting the door with a snap.

I dutifully peeled off the navy dress and unhooked the gown of deep emerald from its hanger. The cool fabric slid through my fingers as I pulled the dress on. It was bias-cut like the last one, but instead of the slashed boat neck of the navy dress and fluttering sleeves, this one had two long strips of silk that gathered under the bust to form the bodice. The straps then tied at the back of the neck, leaving my shoulders and arms bare and the long tails of the straps dangling down the open back.

I felt far more exposed in this dress, but it was undeniably stunning. Or at least I assumed it would be when I finally managed to wrestle the slippery ties into place at the nape of my neck.

I was just about to call out to Senhora Ferreira for help when the telephone rang somewhere in the shop.

"I must answer that," said the dress shop owner through the door.

"But I—"

I stopped at the soft retreat of the other woman's shoes on the carpet.

I tried again to simultaneously push my hair out of the way and tie the straps, but my waves went everywhere and the bodice sagged forward. Alone in my hotel room, with my hair pinned up and out of the way, I would be able to master this dress, but now?

With a sigh and the straps gathered in one hand, I opened the door of the dressing room and, cheeks flushed, poked my head out into the area where David was sitting.

"Could I bother you for some assistance?" I asked. "This gown ties at the neck and I can't quite manage."

He hesitated a moment and then stood.

When I stepped out fully from behind the door, his brows jumped. "That is quite a dress."

"Yes, well . . ." I trailed off, not knowing quite what to do with the awkwardness that had seemed to descend over the room. This was David Poole, my partner. The man had tended to me as I lay bleeding on the ground, for goodness' sake. What was there to be awkward about around him?

He cleared his throat. "Right. If you'll turn around."

I did as he said, giving him my exposed back, and a moment later he took the ties from me. Keeping the tension on them, he said, "Tell me if this is too tight."

I nodded.

"Could you lift your hair?" he asked.

"Of course," I said. "I'll probably wear it pinned up."

"That's a shame. You have beautiful hair."

I went hot all over. "David . . ."

"Simply a statement of fact."

I chanced a glance at the pair of us in the large mirror to my left. A soft smile played on his lips but then, when he lifted his arm to loop one of the ties, he winced.

"Oh, your shoulder. I should have thought."

"Don't worry about my shoulder, Evelyne."

"But if you injure it again—"

"I am not thinking about my shoulder at the present moment," he said.

That made me purse my lips.

What felt like an agonizing age later, David said, "There," and stepped back, the silk ties falling from his hands and brushing my open back. "You should have a proper look."

I stepped in front of the mirror and rolled my shoulders back. Senhora Ferreira had been right. Emerald was my color. It picked up the mahogany tones of my hair. All I needed was a little red lipstick to top it off.

"I think this is the one," I said, looking back at David in the mirror.

He nodded stiffly, and then took his seat again. I was about to step away from the mirror and retreat to the dressing room to change when David said, "Evelyne, where were you this afternoon?"

I looked up sharply. "This afternoon?"

"I rang you from Phillips's office. The hotel switchboard said you weren't picking up the telephone in your room," he said.

"You didn't leave a message."

"No."

"Why did you call?" I asked.

"Where did you go?"

I stared at him for a long moment, hating not being able to tell him the truth about my search for my father.

"Why have you still not told me what happened to your shoulder?" I asked, hoping to pull his attention away.

"It's a personal matter."

"Well, this is too."

"You have a personal matter in a city you've never visited before?" he asked.

"I know it is difficult to believe, but I did have a life before I met you. I do know other people."

I watched him struggle with that, his lips twisting until they settled into a thin line.

"I worry about you, Evelyne," he finally confessed.

I shifted my weight from foot to foot. "Because you think it's likely I'll wind up landing myself in some sort of mess?"

"Because not so long ago I lost someone I couldn't protect." His voice caught on the last word.

I wanted to ask who she was because I felt certain it was a woman, but indulging in my curiosity was a dangerous game that would expose me to a set of uncomfortable questions all my own.

"I'm more than capable of handling myself," I said.

"You have proven that time and time again. However, there are things—"

"Have you made your choice, Menina?" Senhora Ferreira asked as she glided back into the room. The shopkeeper took one look at the two of us, and her mouth formed an O.

"Yes, Senhora, *obrigada*. I will take this dress," I said.

"Very well," she said. "There is the matter of payment."

"I will see to that," said David.

"And how will you be paying, Senhor Slater?" asked Senhora Ferreira.

"With escudos?" he asked as though wondering how else he might be expected to pay.

Her expression brightened. "Very well."

"What else do people pay with?" I asked out of curiosity.

"The other day a Viennese lady tried to pay me in rubies." Senhora Ferreira made a face. "Every foreigner seems to have rubies, diamonds, and sapphires in Lisbon, but what many of them don't have is real money. Menina Moore, if you will." She gestured to the dressing room door.

"*Obrigada*, Senhora Ferreira," I said, and retreated to the dressing room, where I took off the green silk dress and wondered whom David had lost not so long ago.

FIFTEEN

At seven o'clock on the dot, I walked out of the Hotel Tivoli's lift and spotted David in a dinner jacket, sitting on one of the lobby's blue sofas with Phillips across from him. My partner caught sight of me as I approached and immediately stood, followed swiftly by Phillips.

"Gentlemen," I said, coming to a stop in front of them. It shouldn't have mattered, but I was suddenly pleased I had taken time over my appearance, applying my lipstick with care and weaving a few magnolia blossoms the hotel had been happy to provide me into my hair.

"Miss Moore, you are a vision," said Phillips, taking my hand and planting a kiss on the back of it. As soon as he released it, I pulled the silk and wool evening wrap Senhora Ferreira had insisted that I purchase a little higher up on my shoulders, wondering at why the intelligence agent had transformed from put out about my presence in his adopted city to charming in a matter of hours.

"Thank you, Mr. Phillips. Mr. Slater tells me that you have graciously arranged for us to have supper before the casino?" I asked, ignoring the fact that David seemed to be studiously avoiding my gaze. A tension had hung in the air between the pair of us since we'd left Senhora Ferreira's shop in Chiado and walked back with a big white box and matching paper shopping bag containing my new wardrobe. We'd said goodbye at my door, and I'd done my best to put out of my mind the sensation of his fingers against the back of my neck as he tied my dress.

I shivered and fixed my attention on Phillips, who offered me his arm.

"I have managed to secure a table at a wonderful little restaurant not too far from here," said the intelligence officer as he guided me to the door. "They have an excellent wine list, which I thought might be useful in Mr. Slater's search for new vintages. Then we will make our way to Estoril. It isn't too far, and the drive isn't entirely unpleasant even with the winter approaching."

"That sounds delightful. It is very kind of you to have invited me along as well," I said, glancing over my shoulder. I was very conscious of David trailing behind us, but he seemed to be lost in his own thoughts.

"Not at all, Miss Moore. I imagine after all of the excitement of this morning, you might welcome a little bit of luxury. Not to mention the rationing back in Britain, of course. I cannot imagine what it is like needing to think about how much tea one drinks," he said with a shudder.

"Mr. Phillips, I wonder if you've had the chance to locate the Austrian mining engineer you thought Winn might have wanted to speak to you about," I said in a low voice.

"Bauer?" He patted my hand. "All in good time, Miss Moore."

"And the manifest showing who was on the flight this morning? I would very much like to know the name of the man sitting next to Jessup." That passenger seemed the most likely to be our murderer. Who else would have had the opportunity to quietly break Jessup's neck while we were in flight?

"Miss Moore, your enthusiasm for your job is commendable, but you can't possibly expect a man to think about business on an empty stomach," said Phillips.

"Perhaps we might discuss matters in the car—"

"Here we are," Phillips cut me off as an attendant opened the hotel's door and revealed Phillips's large black car waiting outside.

My mouth twisted in frustration, but then I caught sight of the man who emerged from behind the steering wheel. It was Carter. He'd traded his gray suit and red rose from our meeting that afternoon and now wore the same uniform of black dinner jacket, white shirt, and black bow tie as the other men.

"Miss Moore, Mr. Slater, may I introduce Archibald Carter?" said Phillips.

Before I could say anything, Carter extended his hand and inclined his head just slightly. "How do you do, Miss Moore?"

"How do you do, Mr. Carter?" I asked, playing along with the charade that he hadn't just briefed me about Sir Reginald's Lisbon life over coffee and pastry a few hours before.

"Carter's a rather good sport and offered to drive us tonight," said Phillips, clapping his junior on the shoulder. From Carter's rictus smile, I couldn't tell whether he'd felt press-ganged into driving duties that evening or whether he simply wasn't all that fond of his employer.

It was shaping up, I decided, to be quite the evening.

"I hope you've all enjoyed your supper," said Phillips a few hours later as we piled out of the restaurant and back into the car.

While the food had been wonderful—and far richer than anything I'd had in Britain on the ration for the past year—the atmosphere had been . . . strange. David had brooded and Carter had been almost subdued compared to the confident young man I'd met that afternoon, deferring to Phillips at every turn. That had left it to me to carry the conversation with Phillips. Fortunately, there wasn't much need for me to do more than interject an "I see" or an "Is that right?" from time to time. Freed from the responsibilities of his actual work, Phillips seemed more than happy to speak about himself, his prowess on the cricket pitch, his fellow Old Etonians, and how he'd sailed at Cowes and ridden with the Quorn Hunt. The man was, I realized, socially tiresome, and by the end of supper, I was ready for new company.

However, he was also David's and my contact in Lisbon and therefore a necessity until we located Winn.

Carter started the car and navigated down the road. As soon as we were away from the restaurant, Phillips twisted in the front passenger's seat to face David and me. "I do apologize for all of that blather in there, but I find that cultivating a reputation as something of a bore has been rather useful in my line of work."

"Useful?" I asked.

"It serves my purposes well for the Abwehr to believe that British intelligence is filled with public school boys who haven't a thought in their head for anything except for sport. We know who they are, and they know who we are—there's no escaping that fact—but I want them thinking I believe Lisbon is some sort of holiday from rationing and the Blitz rather than real work," said Phillips.

"And you find that approach effective?" I asked.

"It is indeed. You must remember, Abwehr agents assume that, because we are English, we are naturally inferior to them. It is an Achilles' heel of sorts," said Phillips.

I had to admit, it was a genius approach to spy craft when your fellow spy already knew your identity.

"Was the Abwehr there tonight?" asked David.

"The next table over," said Phillips. "Carter spotted him before I did."

"You come to recognize the signs," said Carter, "but in this case it was more straightforward than usual because we'd already identified the agent. His name is Berndt Köhler."

"Chances are good that you'll see him again this evening," said Phillips.

"Why is that?" I asked.

"Because everyone who is anyone comes to Estoril Casino, Miss Moore," said Phillips with a grin.

"That means you should both be careful this evening," warned Carter without taking his eyes off the road.

"Indeed," said Phillips. "Be mindful of what you say in public spaces. Few people are who they seem in Lisbon, even among the upper crust. It's probably wise if you stay close to me tonight. I'll make some useful introductions."

"To whom?" asked David.

"Princess Petrova for one." Phillips then reiterated much of what Carter had told me that afternoon about the princess's background before ending with a warning. "The princess might seem like a flighty wealthy widow whose chief concerns are for her gowns and her diamonds, but don't underestimate the power of her connections."

"But it is also worth mentioning that her friends are not all drawn from our side," added Carter. "Do not make the mistake of believing that the princess's sympathies lie only with the Allies."

Phillips started shaking his head. "The princess is apolitical as far as we can tell."

"And you think she might know Winn?" I asked.

"I doubt the princess would ever be interested in Winn. He isn't in the echelon of people she surrounds herself with," said Phillips. "However, she is a font of knowledge when it comes to gossip. It is possible she knows someone who has encountered him who could be useful for your investigation."

I nodded, secretly hoping that the princess might also be able to shine some light on Sir Reginald's whereabouts given Carter's assurance that my father had been to one of her parties.

"Mr. Phillips, now that we no longer are at risk of being overheard, did you happen to secure the passenger manifest from the flight David and I came in on?" I asked.

The intelligence agent shot me a regretful smile. "I haven't had the chance, I'm afraid. We had an important report due for London that had to make it into the embassy's diplomatic bag before the next flight took off from Sintra this evening. Given that I had to spend my morning retrieving you from a police station, we were rather behind."

I wasn't certain whether I was supposed to apologize for the inconvenience my finding a murdered man had caused or not.

"I will send word to one of my contacts and let you know as soon as I have it in my hand, Miss Moore," Phillips promised.

"Thank you." I glanced at David, who gave me a small nod. "Do you know whether the victim, Michael Jessup, ever did business with Winn?"

"Not that I'm aware of, but I wasn't Winn's nursemaid," said Phillips. "What makes you ask?"

I shrugged, hoping Phillips would see my curiosity as grasping at straws rather than a pointed question. "When one British expat disappears and another is murdered in a short space of time, it does make one wonder whether it is too much of a coincidence."

"The fact that they were both British doesn't mean that they knew each other," said Phillips.

"We noticed on the aeroplane that Jessup seemed familiar to the flight crew. Is there any possibility he's one of ours?" asked David.

"I'd never heard of the man until this morning, and I am beginning to wish I never had," muttered Phillips. "Carter, do you know anything about this Jessup fellow?"

Carter shook his head. "He's not one of our agents. If he traveled back and forth to Sintra, it's likely he's in our files, but we haven't kept a close eye on him. I can quietly ask around to find out more if you like."

"I don't think that will be necessary, Carter," said Phillips. "His death is a matter for the PVDE to investigate. Not us. What *we* should focus on is finding Winn."

"I still think the fact that Jessup was murdered on a BOAC aeroplane is notable," I pushed.

Phillips twisted in his seat, his expression distinctly annoyed. "If you don't wish to find yourself in a Portuguese jail because that captain at the PVDE decides that he likes the look of you for the man's murder, I would suggest you leave the circumstances of Jessup's death be."

David cleared his throat. "You haven't managed to locate the recently arrived Austrian mining engineer, have you, Carter?"

"It appears that Herr Bauer has moved from the hotel where he had been staying. I'm working on locating him," said Carter.

"You were meant to be across this," said Phillips sharply.

"I have been focusing my attention on other areas," said Carter.

I caught his eye in the rearview mirror, and I knew without having to ask that those other priorities related to my father.

"Refocus them. Mr. Slater and Miss Moore do not have unlimited time," said Phillips.

"Yes, sir," said Carter tightly.

"How did your investigation progress today, Mr. Slater?" asked Phillips. "You can imagine, I'm eager for an update."

I did not miss that Phillips addressed my partner rather than me.

"Evelyne?" David prompted, deferring to me.

"Winn's flat was rather spartan," I said carefully. Phillips might be our contact, but he was not our handler. We had no obligation to provide him with anything more than the basic details to keep our investigation flowing. Still, he was the person who seemed to know Winn best, so I thought it prudent to answer.

"We found a newspaper that was nearly two weeks old and a matchbook from a Café Real, but very little else," I said.

"Café Real was where Winn would leave word for me if he needed to meet. I suppose he picked up a matchbook on one of his visits," said Phillips.

"What was your arrangement there?" I asked.

"There is a table in the corner by the window that has a gap between the tabletop and the metal that finishes the edge. He would hide a scrap of paper there, and I would go every morning for a cup of coffee as cover to check whether he'd left me anything or not," said Phillips.

"Have you been going since he disappeared?" I asked.

"Yes. I had hoped he might reemerge, but so far nothing," said Phillips.

"Well, that sends us nearly back to square one, except for the woman," I said.

"Woman?" asked Phillips.

"Winn's landlady mentioned that a woman had come around to pay his rent in his absence last week. Did he ever mention a girlfriend?" asked David.

Phillips frowned. "No, I don't think so."

"The landlady said this woman was Portuguese. Dark hair like mine, but shorter," I said.

Phillips shook his head. "That doesn't ring any bells."

"Evelyne also found a shirt hanging in the cabinet with a lipstick stain on the collar," said David.

"So now you are looking for the girl?" asked Phillips.

"The girlfriend and the engineer seem to be our best leads so far." Which wasn't saying very much.

"We're here," Carter announced, swinging the car around into the drive of a huge white building. Coming from London, where the blackout had plunged the city into darkness each night for more than a year, it was almost disorienting seeing the brilliant lights of the casino shining out like a beacon. Ahead of us, I could see a diminutive gentleman in evening clothes help a whip-thin woman slide out of the back seat of a car and arrange her long black skirts around her evening shoes. It seemed incredible, witnessing this scene, that elsewhere on the Continent, a war was raging.

Phillips glanced back at us. "Are you ready?"

"Lead on," I said.

Carter parked the car and climbed out to open the door for me. Then he leaned down as though to hand me out of the car as David clambered out of the other side.

"I have some of the information for you," he said in a low voice. "As soon as you can get away without raising Phillips's and Slater's suspicions, meet me at the coat check."

"All right," I said.

He straightened and, in a normal tone, said, "There you are, Miss Moore."

"Thank you, Mr. Carter," I said, looping my wrap around my shoulders as I looked up at the casino's brilliant facade and prepared myself for whatever was inside.

SIXTEEN

If the illuminated brilliance of Estoril Casino's exterior had stunned me with its contrast to darkened London, there was something more familiar inside. At first glance, the men in their somber evening dress and women in brilliant silks and satins in the main gambling hall could not have been further from those huddled in a London air raid shelter, but there was an underlying manic urgency to all of this drinking, gambling, and jocularity that I recognized immediately. It was the desperation of a group of people doing their very best to smother their worry and bury it under a layer of forced fun.

Phillips hugged the edge of the gambling hall's floor, and the clatter of roulette wheels and laughter filled my ears. However, as David, Carter, and I followed him, we didn't stop to observe who was winning and losing. Instead, we walked through an arched doorway to another room, almost as large, that was lined on one side by a long bar facing a sea of full tables.

"Welcome to the casino's bar," said Phillips.

"I can see why you said everyone comes here," I said, looking around at the crowd. My eye was caught by a beautiful icy blond in her mid-fifties who sat at a wide table placed in an alcove on a sort of mezzanine level. She was dressed in scarlet, and even from my position across the room I could see the flash of a wide collar of huge rubies and brilliant white diamonds at her throat. Around her sat a semicircle of men and women all facing her as though she were the sun.

"That," whispered Phillips, nodding in the woman's direction, "is Princess Petrova."

"She certainly looks as though she's holding court," I said.

Phillips graced me with a little laugh. "I suspect she would be delighted to hear you say as much."

"You know her well?" I asked.

He lifted a shoulder. "I'm not certain anyone could claim to know the princess well. Her approach is to cast a wide net of what one would call the right sort of acquaintances rather than to confide deeply in a single person. It suits me to be pleasant to her and find myself invited to her parties because they make for excellent people-watching. Our side goes and their side goes, if you understand my meaning. Carter doesn't entirely approve of the princess, but he's surprisingly old-fashioned about things."

I glanced back to see whether Carter had overheard but found he was no longer standing next to David.

"He excused himself as we were passing through the gambling hall," said David by way of explanation.

"I suspect he has his own business to conduct tonight," said Phillips. "Come along. I'll introduce you to the princess."

As we approached her table, the princess's eyes flicked over from the man with the precisely waxed moustache she was speaking to and then in a flash dropped again. If I hadn't been looking right at her, I wouldn't have noticed the way she seemed to take the three of us in, assessing us in a split second.

"I beg your pardon for the interruption, Princess Petrova," said Phillips with a slight bow of his head.

"Mr. Phillips," she said, as though only just seeing him for the first time. "I am still cross with you. You said you would come to my dinner party last week, and on the very same day you sent your regrets. My entire seating arrangement was off. Do you know how difficult it is to find a spare man these days? Mrs. Farris almost had to see herself in to dinner, but fortunately I had just met a charming opera singer the night before who was able to stand in."

Phillips affected a deeper bow. "I must apologize, Princess. I was called away on urgent business. The war . . ."

"The war." She sniffed, sending her dangling earrings flashing like fire in the light of the chandeliers. "All anyone talks about these days is the war. I expect you wish me to forgive you?"

"If you would be so kind," said Phillips as though he found the entire petulant display rather amusing. "You are, after all, the most generous hostess in Lisbon."

The little bit of flattery seemed to do the trick because the princess cast another eye over him and then flicked open a painted silk fan. "See that it doesn't happen again, or I shall have to seriously reconsider your standing invitation to my little soirees." As she fanned herself, she nodded to David and me. "Who have you brought me?"

"May I present Miss Evelyne Moore and Mr. David Slater," said Phillips, stepping back to bring David and me to the forefront. "They are both new arrivals in Lisbon who are keen to make your acquaintance."

The princess smiled as though it was the most natural thing that we should want to know her and then raised a hand for David and me to shake in turn. "How do you do?" She paused. "Miss Moore, you look remarkably familiar."

"Do I?" I asked.

"Have you ever lived in Paris?"

I could feel David tense next to me at the mention of the city of my birth. However, I simply gave a laugh. "Paris? I should be so lucky. I've always dreamed of going to Paris."

"Perhaps one day," said the princess. "Mr. Phillips, Miss Moore is without a drink, and you know how I disapprove of a lady being too long without liquid courage."

"An oversight that I will soon have corrected," said Phillips with a little bow. "What will you have, Miss Moore?"

"A gimlet, please," I said.

"And I will take a martini, very dry, Mr. Slater," said the princess.

David's lips quirked as though he was trying to smother a laugh at the woman's high-handedness. "As you wish."

As soon as the men were gone, the princess turned to me and said, "I fancy a bit of fresh air. The casino can become so stifling at this time of night. Join me, Miss Moore."

She rose, and I followed her down the steps from the mezzanine to the casino bar's floor.

"What brings you to Lisbon?" asked Princess Petrova as together we wove around tables.

"I am Mr. Slater's secretary. He is in the wine trade," I said.

"Scouting out our Portuguese wines, I imagine. He'll find they have very little to recommend them compared to the French. It is most inconvenient not being able to rely upon supplies from France these days, but I suppose all of us must make sacrifices."

I fought to keep my expression neutral at the suggestion that the princess's wine cellar was a worthy sacrifice in the face of what the French people living under German occupation must be living through.

I didn't have to *like* the princess, but I did recognize the unique opportunity presented to me now that we were alone.

"You must meet a great many people in Lisbon," I said. "I've noticed so many different languages being spoken."

"Yes, everyone seems to rattle through here eventually," she said with the wave of a hand.

"I had thought to look up a friend of my brother's while I was here," I said, concocting a fictional sibling on the spot. "His name is Michael Jessup. I don't suppose you've met."

"English?" she asked, without a flicker of recognition at the name of the murdered man.

"Yes. They were at school together. Harrow," I said, borrowing David's old school for my purposes.

The princess thought for a moment. "I don't recall meeting a Mr. Jessup. You said he has been in Lisbon for some time?"

"I think so. I will admit I haven't seen him in an age."

She shot me a sly smile. "This isn't an *affaire de coeur*, is it?"

I tried my best to look bashful. "I really couldn't say."

"Well, my dear Miss Moore, I shouldn't be too worried. I know every Englishman who is worth knowing in Lisbon, but I don't know this Mr. Jessup, ergo . . ."

I almost laughed at the snobbery of her statement but persisted. "Perhaps you've heard of another of my brother's friends. James Winn?"

"Your brother does have rather a large number of friends from school, doesn't he?" she asked as we reached a set of gilded French doors.

"Oh, Mr. Winn is not a friend from school. My brother did some business with him in London," I said, hoping that wouldn't hedge me in too much.

Rather than responding, the princess opened the door off of the casino bar and stepped out into the inky black night.

"Much better," she said, breathing in deeply. Then she reached into a small beaded evening bag and produced a gold cigarette case and lighter and an ebony holder. I watched her fit the cigarette into the holder and then light it.

"I hope you won't mind if I speak very frankly, Miss Redfern."

I froze at the sound of my real name. "I beg your pardon?"

"Oh, yes, I forgot. You are calling yourself 'Miss Moore' while you are in Lisbon, aren't you?" asked the princess, with a light laugh around a stream of smoke. "What a lark."

"I'm not certain I understand your meaning, Princess. I *am* Miss Moore."

"Come now, there's no need for that. It's all so tiresome, you pretending I don't know your real name, me continuing to press you. Shall we simply agree that I know that you are really Evelyne Redfern, daughter of Sir Reginald and Lady Redfern?"

"Why do you believe my surname is Redfern?" I asked.

"Because, not very long ago, Sir Reginald sat in my sitting room and—whether you like it or not—you bear a striking resemblance to him. You have Geneviève's coloring, I'll grant you that, but if you swapped your brown hair for blond, the resemblance would be undeniable to even the most casual of your parents' acquaintances."

I swallowed. "I'll have to take your word for it."

"There we are," said the princess, seeming all the more pleased for my admission that I was who she said I was. "Now we can speak more freely with one another."

"What is it that you wish to speak to me about in my guise as Miss Redfern that you would not be able to ask Miss Moore?"

"Your father, naturally," she said. "Do you know, I hadn't seen him in nearly twenty years until last month when he strolled up to me in the casino bar as though no time had passed?"

"You don't say."

"I remember the parties your mother used to throw. Wild affairs that would start with dinner and end who knew where. They would go on until the small hours of the next morning, and I recall sometimes watching the sun rise in my taxi home. She spared no expense, Geneviève."

"I remember only the beginnings of those parties," I said.

"Yes, your mother would trot you out during cocktails before we sat down to supper," said the princess with a smile I didn't entirely enjoy. "You were such a dear little thing. Always so well-dressed. Precocious too. I remember you telling Joan Miró that you didn't much like his latest painting your mother had taken you to see. The man went red as a tomato."

I still didn't like the man's work, if truth be told.

"Which leads me to wonder, why the charade of being Miss Moore?" she asked.

"A pseudonym can be useful when one's childhood has been written about in every international newspaper. No one wants a secretary who distracts from proceedings," I said.

"I think you'll find many men do, but that's not your meaning, is it?"

When I didn't respond, she gave a little laugh. "The poor little Parisian orphan, trying to make her own way in the world."

"There's nothing wrong with honest toil," I said, ignoring her invocation of the nickname numerous journalists had bestowed upon me during the coverage of the custody battle that had stemmed from my parents' divorce.

"You certainly didn't learn that sentiment from your father. I don't think Sir Reginald has done an honest day's work in his life," said the princess.

"It wouldn't suit him."

"No, I don't think it would. He's the kind of man made for sitting at the wheel of a shiny new sports car, not behind a desk in a dreary London office."

"What did Sir Reginald want from you when he visited?" I asked.

Her lips twitched in amusement. "Help. Why do you want to know?"

"I am trying to find him," I said honestly. "Lisbon is the last location my aunt Amelia knew him to have been, but she has lost touch with him. When Mr. Slater told me he would be making a trip to Lisbon, I thought I might try my luck."

"Drawn by the pull of daughterly affection, no doubt," said the princess with a raised brow.

"Something like that. What kind of help did Sir Reginald want?"

"Money. What else? That's what everyone in this city ultimately wants. Money can solve so many problems," she said.

"Like what?"

"It can smooth the way for exit visas. It can purchase tickets on ships and aeroplanes. It can make the PVDE look the other way."

"And which of those did Sir Reginald need it for?" I asked.

"I would never be so crude as to ask directly," the princess started, "but I had the impression that he may have found that he was becoming low on funds. It's the story of so many people who come to Lisbon."

I frowned. "But unlike those refugees, he entered the country not from occupied Europe but through French Morocco after arriving from South America."

A slow smile slid across her face. "Now how did you learn that?"

"A friend."

"Peter Phillips?"

"Just a friend," I repeated firmly.

She looked at me as though she was reassessing me. "You have worked quickly if you already have friends in Lisbon."

"Did you agree to help Sir Reginald?"

Princess Petrova took a drag on her cigarette. "I did, actually."

"By lending him money?"

"I am not in the business of lending anyone money. If I did, I would find myself indebted to nearly everyone in that bar. However, since Sir Reginald is an old friend, I offered to make an introduction to someone who might be able to help him."

"Who is that?"

"A man named James Winn," she said. "Now, you told me that your brother had done business with Mr. Winn in London. Given that I know Sir Reginald and Lady Redfern never had a son, I wonder why you would go to such lengths to concoct such a story."

"I am trying to find him too."

"Why should a nice girl like you wish to be mixed up with a man like Mr. Winn?"

"What does 'a man like Mr. Winn' mean?" I asked.

"He is the sort of person who is good to know but is also unscrupulous."

"In what way?" I asked.

"All of this"—she cast her hand in the direction of the wall of windows into the casino bar behind us—"is one side of Lisbon. The tip of an iceberg, if you will. But the rest of the city—the bit below the surface—is far darker than I should ever wish the daughter of an old friend to know about."

I suspected that I knew more about darkness than the lady would ever have guessed.

"Mr. Winn lives in the shadows," she finished.

"What does that mean?"

"He has connections to people who have a flexible relationship with legality. This makes him a good person to know in a city full of people in difficult situations that cannot be solved through conventional means."

"How did you become acquainted?" I asked.

"I had a little trouble with some jewelry that I sent out for repair. The jeweler—a scoundrel of a man—claimed it had become lost through no fault of his. A man at the casino overheard me lamenting the loss of my jewels and said he had a friend who might be able to help if only I would tell him the name of the jeweler." She touched her necklace. "I was skeptical until one day my jewelry was delivered in a cloth bag by a taxi driver. There was a note inside from Mr. Winn telling me it had been a pleasure to help."

"Did he ask for money?"

She shook her head.

"Can I see the note?" I asked.

"I threw it away long ago."

"When was this?"

"Over the summer. June? Maybe July," she said.

"Did you not think it strange that Mr. Winn didn't ask for anything in return?"

"Not in Lisbon. People do any manner of things for reasons other than money," she said.

"How does one contact him?" I asked.

"One doesn't."

"If you offered to introduce my father, you must have had some manner of reaching Mr. Winn," I said.

"Mr. Winn has a way of appearing when one needs him most. I assume he keeps a close ear to the ground to learn which people are in distress and intercedes where he wishes."

"That makes him sound like a folk hero," I said.

She smirked. "I would hardly call him Robin Hood."

"Could you introduce me to the man from the casino who first told you about Mr. Winn?" I asked.

"I've never seen him again in my life. And even if I could, I wouldn't. Despite his usefulness, young ladies should not go about seeking the company of men like Mr. Winn."

"But if my father spoke to Mr. Winn, he might know something about where he is," I pushed.

"As far as I know, Sir Reginald and Mr. Winn never met," said the princess.

"How can you be certain?"

"The day after Sir Reginald asked me to make the introduction, he rang and told me that he no longer required Mr. Winn's services."

"Why?" I asked.

"He wouldn't say. Sir Reginald always has been like that. Gracious when he needs help and then, when he doesn't, he becomes rather sharp and imperious," she said.

"Yes, I remember that," I mused.

"It is growing cold," said the princess, removing her burned-down cigarette from its holder and throwing it aside on the veranda. "Shall we return to our drinks?"

SEVENTEEN

The hum of voices in the casino bar hit me like a wall as I followed the princess back inside. Imperious lady that she was, people seemed to dart out of her way as she glided along. However, we weren't twenty feet from the stairs to the mezzanine when a small man dressed in a tired dinner jacket with lapels that were far too wide for fashion darted into her path. His face was gaunt, and he clenched and unclenched his hands in front of him as he said, "Princess Petrova, a moment of your time please."

The princess stopped abruptly and then sighed. "Mr. Fortescue, are you here again?"

"I *must* speak to you." The man grasped her arm before seeming to remember himself and dropping it hastily. "Please."

"I have told you before, Mr. Fortescue, that I cannot help you," said the princess firmly.

"But it is a matter of great importance," Fortescue protested.

"I am not a charitable organization," the princess insisted.

"But you promised—"

"Ah, Princess Petrova," said Phillips, stepping in between the princess and Fortescue while brandishing a martini. "Your drink."

"Thank you, Mr. Phillips," said the princess, turning away from Fortescue to accept the glass.

"Your gimlet, Miss Moore," said David, handing me my drink.

"Thank you. The princess and I have been having a refreshing conversation outside," I told him before taking a little sip.

He inclined his head, and I gave a tiny nod. We would talk later.

"Mr. Slater, come sit by me," said the princess, sweeping up the stairs and safely out of Fortescue's orbit.

With clear reluctance, the scorned Fortescue slunk away as we arranged ourselves around the princess's table.

"Your charming secretary was just telling me you have an interest in Portuguese wine, Mr. Slater," said the princess.

"It's a necessity these days," said David.

"Who did you say you work for?" asked Princess Petrova, touching the collar of rubies that hung around her neck.

"Berry Brothers and Rudd," he said.

"Yevgeny, my late husband, and I always ordered from Berry Brothers when we stayed in London," she said with a nod of approval.

"We appreciate your custom, madam," said David.

"*Miss Moore* was also asking whether I had made the acquaintance of two of her brother's friends," said Princess Petrova, placing an emphasis on my false name, no doubt to show she would use it. For now.

"Two friends?" asked Phillips with clear interest. "How fortunate it is that Miss Moore should have two friends in Lisbon."

I looked down at my folded hands, hoping that I looked like the model of a bashful secretary. "It was silly, really. Lisbon is such a large city, but Mr. Phillips had told me so many things about the princess's wonderful parties that I wondered whether she had come across them."

"I am glad to hear that Mr. Phillips enjoys my little gatherings," said the princess.

"Oh, but I do," said Phillips.

"And were you able to help Miss Moore, Princess?" asked David.

"I'm afraid not," said Princess Petrova, setting down her glass and rising. "If you will excuse me, gentlemen."

"A brother?" asked David in a low voice as I shifted to take the princess's now-vacant seat.

"I always did want a brother," I whispered.

"You said you used to meet Winn here, is that right?" David raised his voice to ask Phillips.

"Yes," said Phillips, who was smoking a cigarette. "In the gardens. There are a few dark alcoves where it's possible to wait undetected until someone is almost upon you. If we arranged a meeting and he couldn't attend for whatever reason, we had a drop point as well."

"Where was that?" asked David.

"I can show you if you like," said Phillips, unfolding himself from his seat to stand.

"Would you like to come with us?" David asked me.

I shook my head, knowing this would likely be my best opportunity to meet Carter. "I'm still chilled from being outside. Perhaps I'll speak to a few members of staff to see if anyone has seen Mr. Winn or a man matching his description recently."

"I've already spoken to the staff most likely to have encountered Winn," said Phillips.

"I can't imagine everyone in Portugal has the warmest feelings toward members of British intelligence," I said.

"It isn't as though I walk around identifying myself," protested Phillips.

"You said yourself that you and the Abwehr agents know one another, which means that members of staff probably do too. I imagine the same goes for the Spanish and Russian intelligence agents who are no doubt here as well," I pointed out.

He opened his mouth as though to protest, but then seemed to think better of it when David patted him on the shoulder.

"Miss Moore will be fine," he said before turning to me. "Meet us back here when you're done."

I found Carter sitting in a chair just a few feet away from the casino's cloakroom, a lit cigarette dangling from his fingers.

"I'm sorry to keep you waiting," I said, stopping in front of him. "First the princess wanted to speak and then it took me a few minutes to figure out a way to leave our party without raising their suspicions."

"Where are they now?" asked Carter.

"The garden. Phillips is showing Slater where our mutual friend liked to meet."

Carter nodded. "Good. Shall we walk?"

I took the arm Carter offered me and we began to stroll down the casino's corridor like any other couple might. As we passed the entrance to the restaurant, the noise of the gamblers and diners began to die down. To my left, through the windows framed in swags of fabric, I could see the faint outline of the casino's garden stretching out into the night, the paths picked out in white that glowed in the moonlight.

When it became clear that, finally, we were alone, Carter stopped and reached into his jacket pocket. "I went back through my notes on Sir Reginald's movements in Lisbon. I had remembered correctly that he visited three jewelers." He unfolded a scrap of paper. "On Monday the twenty-eighth of October he went to Joalharia Dom Pedro, just across the way from where I met you this afternoon on Rossio Square. Then the following day he went to Ourivesaria Andreia on Rua Aurea in Baixa, followed by a visit to Joalharia Coelho on Travessa do Carmo in Chiado."

I frowned. "I still don't understand why my father went to a set of Lisbon jewelers when he had a safe deposit box full of jewelry in London."

"That I'm afraid I don't know," said Carter, handing me the paper.

I stared at the list. "Do any of those names stand out to you?"

"No. They all have good reputations."

"Nothing to do with the black market?" I asked.

"Not these particular jewelers, no."

"The princess told me something that might be of use," I said, relaying the story of Sir Reginald asking for assistance with money.

"So she offered to put the word out that your father might be interested in Winn's help, but then he rang the next day and told her he no longer needed assistance?" asked Carter.

"Which begs the question: did Sir Reginald stop needing money, or did he find another avenue for securing funds that he thought was better or faster than Winn's help?" I asked.

"Or did he find himself suffering from a case of cold feet?"

"Sir Reginald is a proud man. I doubt he would have stooped to asking for help with money unless he was truly running low on funds," I said. "But if that was the case, why not simply wire my aunt to have his banker release more funds? Or wire his banker himself?"

"Maybe he didn't have sufficient funds in his bank account to cover his needs," Carter suggested.

"It's possible," I said slowly. "But that still doesn't explain why Sir Reginald then turned around the next day and called the entire thing off, or why he wrote to me in London about my mother's jewels."

"Do you think Winn's and Sir Reginald's disappearances are connected?" asked Carter.

I blew out a long breath. "I sincerely hope not."

"If they are . . . ?"

"Then hopefully we find both of them soon. Thank you for the names of the shops," I said, folding the paper and tucking it into my clutch.

"It's my pleasure," said Carter. "It might be best if we return to the table at different times."

I nodded. "You go. I'll hang back."

I watched Carter make his way back down the corridor toward the casino bar. I needed to question some of the casino staff to give credence to the story I'd given Phillips. However, I wanted a few moments to think. There must be a loo on this side of the building, away from the noise and hubbub of the main gaming room, bar, and restaurant. I would take refuge and check my lipstick.

I set off in the opposite direction Carter had gone, my heels sinking into the plush carpet, and took a left following the corridor. To my left was a bank of windows, and on my right, the wall was hung with a series of large landscape paintings. Every dozen feet or so, there were groupings of armchairs where patrons could have a quiet word, although no one seemed interested in taking advantage of them that evening.

I frowned. There must be a loo somewhere . . .

I was about to round a corner when, from out of my sight, I heard Princess Petrova say in her haughty tone, "You have displayed a shocking lack of good manners tonight, Mr. Fortescue."

I slowly edged behind one of the corridor's elaborate curtains. I was fairly certain that, unless someone was looking directly into the window I now stood by, I was shielded from the view of most passersby, yet I could still hear when Fortescue replied, "You do not understand the difficulty I find myself in, Princess."

"Clearly I do not," she said.

"I am asking for your help," he pleaded.

"I really don't see how I can help you—or why I should, for that matter, after the way you have behaved."

"But I was told that you were the one to come to in order to discuss matters relating to—"

"You were incorrectly informed, Mr. Fortescue," she said.

"I'm certain I'm not," he said, menace edging his voice now. "He took something from me—something very valuable—and I want it back."

"Whatever agreement there was between you is no concern of mine," she said.

"But they say you are the one who can contact him," he insisted.

"You have been incorrectly informed. Now, if you'll excuse me, there are people expecting me," said Princess Petrova.

I heard the rustle of fabric but then it stopped abruptly and the princess snapped, "This is the second time you have placed your hand on me this evening. Remove it at once!"

"If you won't help me, I will find him myself," said Fortescue, his voice low.

"You do that, and see how much he likes it," she hissed.

Fortescue must have let go of her because a moment later she came storming around the corner, and I caught a glimpse of red silk through the gap in the curtain.

I waited for a few moments for Fortescue, but he never appeared, so I assumed he went in the other direction.

Cautiously, I stepped out from behind the curtain. The coast was clear.

It sounded very much like Fortescue was desperate to find Winn because he believed Winn had stolen from him, which earned Fortescue a spot right at the top of my list of suspects.

I had to find David. However, as I turned on my heel to make my way back to the gambling hall, I noticed a stream of smoke dancing above one of the scattered club chairs dotting the corridor. Slowly, a tall man in a dinner jacket who wore his bright blond hair cropped close to his skull rose from the chair and turned to face me.

"Miss Moore, I have not had the pleasure of making your acquaintance," said the man with an easy smile that some women might have found appealing but—accompanied by the jarring experience of hearing a German accent after months of being at war—made me decidedly uncomfortable.

I crossed my arms over my chest, feeling suddenly exposed in my evening dress. "We have not."

"That is a great oversight as we have a mutual friend of sorts," he said, rounding the chair. Everything about him was precise, from the cut of his jacket to the pristine white of his shirt, yet somehow he looked . . . off. It took me a moment to realize that it was because he wore his evening clothes like a military uniform.

"Who might that be?" I asked.

"Your Mr. Phillips."

I tensed but lifted my chin nonetheless.

"Ah, I see I have shocked you. I should explain, it is a little joke between us professionals," said the German man, coming to a stop in front of me. He placed a hand to his chest and made a bow. "I am Berndt Köhler, at your service."

The German Abwehr agent Phillips had spotted at dinner and warned David and me about.

"I make it a point to learn about anyone interesting who arrives in Lisbon," he continued.

"I can't imagine what could possibly interest you about me," I said.

"Other than the fact that you are British and a very pretty girl? You are a secretary in the employ of a Mr. David Slater of Berry Brothers and Rudd, which I am told is a distinguished wine merchant," he said. "You arrived in Lisbon this morning via a flight into Sintra, yet you did not go to the Hotel Tivoli until this afternoon, which leads me to wonder what you were doing during that time."

"Mr. Slater had a meeting. I attended to take notes and keep his diary," I lied smoothly. "Afterward we had lunch in a café. I'm surprised you don't know that."

"You attended a meeting right after alighting from your flight?" he asked.

"Shortly after, yes. We did have to drive into Lisbon first."

He reached into his jacket pocket and produced a silver cigarette case with an unmistakable swastika etched into the front of it. He flicked it open and removed a cigarette. He was about to replace it when he stopped himself with a laugh. "Please excuse my poor manners. Would you care for a cigarette?"

"No, thank you."

He shrugged and lit the cigarette. "As you wish."

"Now, was there something in particular you wished to speak to me about, Herr Köhler, or did you simply want to prove that you know when I landed in the country and which hotel I am staying at?"

He laughed. "Miss Moore, you make my motives sound so sinister. I only wished to make the acquaintance of the woman who found a body on a British Overseas Airways Corporation aeroplane at Sintra's airfield this morning."

It should not have surprised me that the man knew about Jessup's body. Any intelligence officer worth his salt lived and died by his network of contacts, no matter which side he was on.

"It was a horrible thing to discover a dead man like that," I said.

Köhler blew a stream of smoke toward the ceiling. "Not just a dead man, but a murdered one. I would have imagined a simple *secretary* such as yourself might be more . . . upset by such a discovery, and yet you are here, enjoying the delights of Estoril."

"You forget, Herr Köhler, that I have been living in London during the Blitz. This was not the first dead body I've ever seen."

He smirked and tilted his head as though to concede that this was understandable.

"If there is nothing else, I should return to my party," I said.

I made to round him when he stopped me with an arm on my elbow.

"You are lying to me." His fingers tightened around my arm. "I do not like when pretty girls lie to me, Miss Moore."

"And I don't particularly like when brutish men manhandle me," I said, my voice low with warning as I glowered up at him.

"Miss Moore!"

Köhler's head snapped up, and I took the opportunity to wrench free from the man's grasp.

"Miss Moore, I have been looking for you," said David as he hurried up, looking between the German agent and myself.

"I apologize, Mr. Slater," I said.

"Mr. Slater, I too must apologize for detaining your secretary," said Köhler. "I was only expressing my concern at the distress she must have felt at this morning's events."

"This morning's events?" David asked.

"Yes," I said, stepping forward. "The unfortunate incident at the airfield. Herr Köhler knows all about it."

David glanced at me, and I could tell he understood my warning that Köhler knew more than he should.

"Thank you for your concern, sir, but Miss Moore is made of stern stuff," said David.

Then, gentleman that he was, he offered me the crook of his elbow, and together we walked briskly away as the cigarette burned down to Berndt Köhler's fingers.

EIGHTEEN

I expected David to guide me back into the gambling hall, but instead we made straight for the entrance of the casino, where Phillips waited with my wrap.

"There you are," said Phillips with not a little bit of annoyance in his tone as soon as he laid eyes on us. "We're going."

"Going? Already?" I glanced up at David.

His lips formed a thin line, but he took the wrap from Phillips and draped it over my shoulders while Phillips marched ahead to the car, where Carter waited behind the wheel. David opened the back door and then slid in next to me.

As soon as Carter set the car into gear, Phillips twisted around in his seat. "What were you thinking speaking to an Abwehr agent?"

"We saw you through the windows of the corridor when we were on our way back from his meeting spot with Winn," said David by way of explanation.

"I can assure you that it wasn't my choice," I said. "Herr Köhler approached me—or rather accosted me—and insisted on introducing himself."

"What did he say?" asked Phillips.

"He wanted to make it very clear that he has been observing

David and me since we arrived at Sintra. He knows that we are staying at the Hotel Tivoli, but there is some time he cannot account for between the airfield and the hotel. I lied and told him that we attended a meeting. I also suspect that he does not believe for one moment that David and I are employed by Berry Brothers and Rudd," I said.

"Bloody Köhler," Phillips swore before clearing his throat. "Pardon me, Miss Moore."

"No need," I said.

"The Abwehr are well-informed—often frustratingly so—however, given your association with me, I suppose that it was only a matter of time that he guessed you might be working with or for British intelligence," said Phillips. "Did he ask you about Winn?"

I shook my head. "His name didn't come up. However, he did know that I was the one who found Jessup's body."

"Do you think the PVDE would have informed the Abwehr?" asked David.

"I doubt it. The PVDE takes a rather dim view of the espionage activity of any country other than their own. It's more likely that someone associated with the airfield told him," said Phillips.

"Did Herr Köhler threaten you?" asked David.

I flexed the arm Köhler had tried to crush when he told me he didn't like "pretty girls" lying to him. Well, I didn't particularly like being reduced to merely a pretty girl.

"He didn't threaten so much as make it clear that he has taken an interest in me and what I am doing in Lisbon," I said.

"Which will no doubt make your job here more difficult," said Phillips.

"What did you find in the garden?" I asked.

"Nothing of note," said David. "The drop point is a fountain at one of the farther corners of the grounds. It was empty, and there was no evidence that it's been used since Winn disappeared."

"If Winn couldn't make an appointed time or for whatever reason felt that he might be compromised if he waited for me, he would put a message in a tin, wrap it with oil cloth, and then bury it under a rock at the back of the fountain," Phillips explained.

"And I take it there was nothing there this evening either?" I asked.

David shook his head. "No fresh footprints, and no conveniently dropped train tickets with a destination printed prominently on the front to tell us where Winn has gone. What did you find when you questioned the casino staff?"

"Very little," I lied, meeting Carter's eyes in the rearview mirror.

"Which is as much as I said you would learn," said Phillips.

I was tempted to fire back the very helpful fact that I had overheard Princess Petrova and Fortescue arguing, but I wanted the chance to speak to David without Phillips's interference first. Besides, the last thing I wanted was for Phillips to accuse me of wandering off on my own and leaving myself vulnerable to Köhler or some such rot.

However, I did allow myself one question. "Who is Mr. Fortescue?"

"A nuisance, that's who he is," muttered Phillips before saying, "I believe this falls under your area of expertise, Carter."

"Walter Fortescue. Forty-four years old, born in Staffordshire, if my memory serves," said Carter. "Fortescue once worked in shipping, but he ran into some trouble in Egypt earlier this year. There were some suspicions of smuggling and bribery, I believe, but nothing stuck.

"From Alexandria, he traveled to French Morocco, where he managed to negotiate his way across the Mediterranean. However, he's been stuck in Lisbon ever since. I gather there is some trouble with his passport, and he has been denied both entry into Britain and an exit visa from Portugal. I imagine he is currently living in a state of perpetual fear that he will eventually be deported somewhere but will have few options when it comes to places to go."

"If he was denied entry to England, where could he go?" I asked.

"The last I heard, I believe he had designs on the United States or Canada," said Carter. "However, his attempts to secure a visa to enter either country have been futile to date." From the angle I was sitting at, I could see Carter smile. "I have a counterpart in America who contacted me with a few questions about Fortescue. I doubt that, by the end of our conversation, my American friend was terribly impressed with Fortescue's character."

"The princess did not seem particularly warm toward him either," I said.

"The princess is always eager to pick up waifs and strays, but she doesn't keep all of them around. I believe she cut Fortescue loose after less than a week of his acquaintance," said Phillips.

"Why was that?" I asked.

Phillips shook his head. "I'm afraid to find that out, you'll have to ask the princess."

I settled back into my seat, knowing that the next time I saw the princess I had every intention of doing just that.

NINETEEN

David and I waved our goodbyes to Phillips and Carter from the curb in front of the Hotel Tivoli, and then we retreated inside out of the cold.

"I know it's late," I said, slipping into my secretary cover in case anyone was listening, "but could I have a few moments of your time, Mr. Slater? There are several matters I wish to address before our meetings tomorrow morning."

"As you wish, Miss Moore," he said.

"I have the schedule in my room."

We walked to the lifts together and rode up to the fourth floor in silence. Once we were in my hotel room and out of the hearing of anyone, I let out a heavy sigh.

"It's exhausting keeping a cover going, isn't it?" asked David, scrubbing a hand over his face.

"More so than I realized it would be," I said.

"Are you really all right after your run-in with the Abwehr?"

I gave him a small smile. "It will take more than an arrogant German spy to frighten me off."

"I have no doubt, but nevertheless—"

I placed a hand on his elbow. "I'm fine. I promise. Besides, there is a more pressing matter at hand. Princess Petrova knows who I am."

He glanced down at my hand and frowned. “What do you mean she knows who you are?”

I let my hand fall away. “She recognized me because apparently I bear a striking resemblance to my father—something I am not particularly pleased to learn. She was friends with my parents in Paris.”

“Does this compromise you?”

“I don’t know. It might have made her more forthcoming with me than she would otherwise have been. She told me that Winn helped her with a problem securing some jewels that disappeared after she sent them off for repair.”

“Then she knows how to contact Winn,” he said.

“Yes and no.” I explained the princess’s description of discreetly putting out the word that Winn’s services were needed. However, I left out the fact that I knew all of this because Sir Reginald had asked Princess Petrova to contact Winn on his behalf.

After working two cases together, I had grown used to confiding in David, and an instinct tugged at me to voice the questions rattling through my mind about what my father was up to. However, I couldn’t shake Mr. Fletcher’s warning not to trust David with my secondary assignment in Lisbon because I feared that if my partner learned about my father and the company he’d been keeping, David might well feel obligated to report back to Mrs. White. After finding Jessup’s body, the last thing I wanted was to give our handler another reason to order me on the next flight back to Britain.

When I finished, David sighed. “Then the princess doesn’t actually know where Winn might be.”

“She does not, but there might be someone who does. Do you remember Fortescue, the man who stopped the princess at the stairs? Just before Köhler approached me, I overheard Fortescue and the princess having a disagreement in a quiet part of the corridor away from the gambling hall.”

David raised a brow. “Were you following them?”

“Believe it not, I wasn’t. I overheard them just as I was about to round a corner, so I stopped and listened.”

"From behind a sofa?" he asked.

"I was hiding behind a curtain, if you must know."

"A classic move of spy craft," he said with a laugh. "What if someone had seen the toes of your shoes?"

"No one saw my shoes."

"I'll have to take your word for it. What did Fortescue say?"

"He seemed rather desperate," I said.

"Desperate for money? Desperate to leave Portugal?"

"Desperate for something to be returned to him. Something that he believes Winn stole."

"What did the princess think of that?" he asked.

"She maintained she couldn't help him."

"It sounds as though tomorrow we need to find Fortescue and pay him a visit," he said. "Hopefully by then Carter will also have dug up the new address of Bauer, the Austrian mining engineer, for us. Until then, I think it's best if we get some sleep."

We said good night, and as soon as my partner was gone, I shed my dress and heels and fell onto the bed with an exhausted sigh.

The next morning, I finally had the chance to avail myself of the luxury that was the Hotel Tivoli's seemingly unlimited hot water. After a good soak in the deep bath, I dried off and dressed. I chose the most sober combination of a navy suit, a white shirt, and black shoes that Miss Summers had provided me with in my suitcase. A slick of lipstick as the final touch made me feel secretly a little bit more like Evelyne Redfern and a little less like Evelyne Moore. With my gloves on, my hat securely in place, and my handbag on my arm, I was ready for breakfast.

I found David already at a table laid for two in a corner of the hotel's dining room.

"Good morning, Mr. Slater," I said as a waiter drew back my chair.

"Miss Moore, did you sleep well?" he asked, playing the role of benevolent employer rather well, I thought.

"Not particularly. I found myself expecting the air raid siren, even if Lisbon hasn't seen any bombing."

"It is a hard habit to shake," David agreed. "I suspect there is also always an element of anticipation that keeps one on the edge when traveling for work."

No doubt that element of anticipation was one of the things that also kept us out of danger.

We ordered our breakfast and the waiter brought a second silver pot of strong, hot coffee to match David's. I took my first sip, grateful for the hot drink even if I would have preferred my usual cup of tea in the morning. However, when in Lisbon . . .

I was halfway through my cup when a boy dressed in the jacket of a hotel page approached the table.

"Menina Moore?" he asked.

"Yes?"

"*Chegou um telegrama para si*," he said, holding out a silver tray with a folded paper on it.

"*Obrigada*," I said, taking the telegram and placing a coin on the platter for him.

He bowed and hurried off.

"Is everything all right?" asked David as I opened the telegram and scanned it with a frown.

I turned it to show him the scramble of letters that was undoubtedly a code.

"I suspect the telegram is from Miss Summers with a bit of information on a matter I was looking into before I was told I would be needed in Lisbon," I said.

"Is there anything I should know?"

I hesitated. "Not at this time. I should probably figure out how to read this."

"Did she leave you with a key?"

I popped a piece of bread into my mouth and chewed thoughtfully. "Do you know, I think she might have. What will you do while I'm working this out?"

"I took the liberty of ringing Carter," said David. "He said he was still tracking Bauer down, but he should have something for us later this morning. He also thought he could furnish us with Fortescue's address if we give him some time.

"Until then, I am going to be going through the manifest of every ship and aeroplane that's left Lisbon since the day Winn disappeared. Apparently Carter has access to those records, and he said that he would have everything ready for us in the office this morning. Well, ready for me."

I scrunched up my nose. "I can't say I'm jealous. I think I've had enough of paperwork and desk duty over the last three weeks to last me a lifetime."

"How is your leg?" asked David.

"A bit tight in the mornings, but better and better every day. How is your shoulder?" I asked.

"Much the same."

I waited for him to elaborate. When he didn't, I simply shrugged. "Where shall I meet you when I'm finished with this business in Miss Summers's telegram?"

David glanced at his watch and set his napkin aside. "Why don't I ring when I have those addresses?"

"All right," I said.

We finished our breakfasts and then David left for Phillips's office while I retreated upstairs to my room.

I pulled the telegram from my handbag and smoothed it flat. Miss Summers never would have sent me a coded message if she wasn't confident that I would have access to the key needed to read it. Fortunately, I had an inkling of an idea where she might have hidden a code in plain sight.

I picked the copy of *Murder in Piccadilly* up off of my bedside table and began flipping through it, stopping when I found page sixty-seven's number circled in light pencil.

I smiled. "Very clever, Miss Summers."

A book code had been what had helped me crack my very first case, and no doubt Mr. Fletcher's secretary had enjoyed the little joke of using a book code once again.

Taking my notebook, telegram, and book to the hotel room's desk, I wrote out the alphabet and then went down the page writing each letter as it appeared so that A became M and so on. Then, with my book code in place, I began translating the message.

C. Morrison found shot in air raid shelter in Clerkenwell. Murder investigation underway.

I exhaled. I hadn't exactly expected that Morrison would be alive, but knowing that my fears had been realized . . .

Sir Reginald had sent me, with a tea chest full of my mother's jewelry, to a jeweler and known fence who, from the looks of it, had been abducted, shot, and killed.

I had to find my father.

TWENTY

I was just about to pick up the telephone to tell Carter about Morrison's murder when it rang.

"Hello?"

"I have a telephone call for Miss Evelyne Moore," said the switchboard operator.

"Thank you. I'm Miss Moore," I said.

I waited for a moment while the operator connected the line, and then David's voice filled my ear. "Good, you're still in your room."

I glanced at my watch. "Where are you?"

"Phillips's office. I only just arrived, but Carter was waiting for me. He's tracked down Fortescue's hotel, and he's found Bauer. Can you meet me at Café Branca, Rua da Graça 94?"

I scribbled the address down in my notebook. "What is special about Café Branca?"

"It's across the road from where Bauer is staying." I could hear the muffled sound of someone off the line speaking before David said, "Apparently it will take me ten minutes to walk there, but you'll be longer."

"I'll ask the concierge how to get there."

"Once we speak to Bauer, we can try to find Fortescue at his hotel."

"Excellent. Is Carter there?" I asked, picking up the translation of Miss Summers's telegram again.

"Would you like to speak to him?" David asked with some surprise.

"Please."

There was the sound of a telephone being passed from hand to hand and then Carter came on. "Miss Moore?"

"I received a telegram this morning from London. The jeweler is dead. He was found shot in Clerkenwell."

"Well, that changes things," he said.

"It does." Even if I had very strong doubts my father was responsible for Morrison's death, it was too much of a coincidence that he'd sent me to the man's shop just before Morrison had been killed.

"Tell David I'll see him as soon as I can make my way to Café Branca," I said.

As soon as I rang off, I pulled on my things and made my way down to the hotel lobby, where I asked the concierge for directions to the café.

It turned out that the café was in the Graça neighborhood, nestled in the hills of the city. The attendant insisted that I take the tram, so, armed with my directions for the stop on Rua da Conceiçao, I ventured out and caught one of the little yellow vehicles I'd seen trundling along the tracks sunk into the city's roads. With the help of a kind older gentleman with a cane, I managed to find the right line and pay my fare. Since he was going the same way as me, he took the seat next to me.

We rattled along for about a quarter of an hour until the gentleman pointed out where I should alight. When the tram came to a stop, I thanked him and stepped down onto the pavement.

I could see the red and green painted sign of Café Branca ahead of me, and in the window, with a newspaper and a cup of coffee, sat my partner.

I entered the café and slid into the seat across from David. "Hello. I didn't realize you read Portuguese."

"I don't, but with my French I can make some of it out," he said as he set the paper down.

"Any stories of note?"

"Apparently we're still at war."

I gave a short laugh. "Yes, I gathered that. I hope you weren't waiting too long."

"Not long at all," he said. "Were you successful in cracking the code?"

On the tram ride over, I had contemplated how I would answer this question.

"I was," I said carefully. "It's an ongoing case that I thought would remain quiet while I was away. Apparently I was wrong."

"If there's anything I could do to help . . ."

I shot him a tight smile. "I will let you know. Until then, we should focus on our elusive engineer."

"Right. That," he said, pointing to a building across the way, "is the flat where Johann Bauer is staying at the moment. Carter seems to think we have a good chance of finding Bauer at home because, outside of applying for visas, he seems to do little else."

"And we still think Bauer might be the key to learning what Winn wanted to tell Phillips before he disappeared," I said.

"Outside of Princess Petrova, Bauer seems to be our most likely lead."

"Well"—I rose to my feet—"I suppose then that there's no time like the present."

I do not want to speak to anyone," came the voice through a heavy wooden door a few moments later. "I am a very busy man."

David glanced at me as I leaned against the wall just outside of Johann Bauer's flat door. When he'd knocked, the engineer had opened the door a crack wide enough to peer out, but Bauer did not seem at all inclined to lift the chain and invite us in.

"Herr Bauer," David tried again.

"Why should I speak to you? Two weeks ago it was the Portuguese and the British. Last week it was the Spanish. Three days ago it was the Germans. I want to be left alone," said Bauer, shutting the door firmly in my partner's face.

David stepped back, his hands spread wide as though to say, *What else can I do?*

"May I try?" I asked.

"Please do," he said.

I switched spots with him, cleared my throat, and rapped gently on the door.

"Go away!" came the muffled cry from the other side of the door.

"Herr Bauer, I understand that you're frightened," I called out.

Immediately the door wrenched open. "I am *not* frightened," said the man fiercely.

"Are you certain?" I asked, my arms crossed as I studied the engineer with a shock of white hair standing in all directions and an unbuttoned waistcoat. "Because you seem rather scared to me."

"Madam—"

"Miss," I corrected. "It's all right to be afraid. I might be, in your shoes."

Bauer pulled himself up. "Nothing frightens me."

"Then it will be nothing to speak to us for a few moments," I said with a smile. "Herr Bauer, be reasonable. We are British. You are Austrian. We are on Portuguese soil—*neutral* ground. There really is nothing we can do to you."

He held my gaze for a long moment. "*You* might not, but there are some who don't have the same scruples."

"You said the Germans visited you?" I asked.

"And visited me and visited me. I had to move from my hotel into this"—he gestured behind him—"this *Hölle*."

"Perhaps we can help you," I offered.

"How?" he asked.

I had a good idea, but precisely no authorization to make any promises. I shot David a quizzical look over my shoulder. He shrugged.

"I think those sorts of things are best discussed indoors where there is less chance of being overheard. May we come in? Please?" I asked.

Bauer's expression remained reluctant, but after a moment the engineer removed the chain and allowed us to enter the flat.

It was not the most luxurious space I'd ever been in. The entire flat was the size of the room I shared with Moira at Mrs. Jenkins's boardinghouse, with an unmade bed crammed in one corner. An open suitcase covered a tiny table framed by two battered wooden chairs. Next to the door was what amounted to a kitchen if a couple of shelves and a gas ring could be called a kitchen.

Bauer must have caught me looking around because he said, "I have not had time to unpack, and what would I unpack into?"

"It is a little short on space," I agreed.

"I spend most of my time writing letters or waiting at the British embassy to see anyone who will speak to me," said Bauer. "When I think I've finished all the paperwork, there are passport stamps to collect. When I've done that, I'm told I cannot travel to London without making additional arrangements. I've written to everyone I know from Oxford to Newcastle, but still I'm told I must wait."

"Why did you leave Austria?" I asked.

He shot me a look that told me he thought I must be an idiot. "Not all of us welcomed the Anschluss. Our chancellor told us that the referendum meant the people could decide whether Austria joined Germany or remained a sovereign state, but how can one trust a vote that is not done in secret?

"After Austria was annexed, I thought that if I focused on my work and did not say anything to anyone, they might leave me alone." Bauer made a disgusted noise. "I should have known that was foolish."

"What happened?" I asked.

"I heard that some of my colleagues who had spoken to me so openly about their distrust of the Nazis suddenly were working for them. Those who refused began to disappear. And so I left," he said.

"How?" I asked, genuinely shocked that an expert in mining—something so vital to any country's war effort—had been allowed to flee.

His expression grew grim. "I received permission to travel to Paris to visit my sister, who is in ill health. From there, I managed to make my way through France and cross the Pyrenees into Spain on foot. From there I was helped into Portugal.

"I thought that I would be safe here, but not a week after I arrived an Englishman approached me at a café. He knew who I was without me introducing myself. He said that he wished to speak with me."

Phillips had said Carter hadn't made contact with Bauer but instead contented himself with compiling a dossier on the man. It was possible that the SOE could have found the engineer, but when I saw the way my partner was looking at Bauer, I knew that we were both thinking in a different direction.

Winn.

"Do you recall what he looked like?" asked David.

Bauer glanced at my partner. "He was not as tall as you with . . . I think it was brown hair. He wore a gray hat like yours and he kept it on the entire time we spoke, so I can't be certain."

"Did he give you his name?" I asked.

Bauer shook his head. "He said he was someone who had powerful friends who could help me, but in exchange he wanted information. That if I helped him, he could speak to someone who would expedite my petition for a visa with the British embassy."

"What did he mean by information?" I asked.

That earned me a shrug. "I don't know. The man said I would see him again, but I never did."

That certainly sounded like Winn, and the timeline would match up. Had Winn planned to bargain with Bauer? Information about the German plans for Portugal's mining efforts in exchange for Phillips's help approving Bauer's request for a visa?

"You said the Germans approached you a few days ago?" David prompted.

"They sent a woman," said Bauer, his disdain clear in his voice. "She tried to tell me that the Abwehr were watching me and if I wasn't careful, they would have the PVDE deport me back to Austria. I told her that if they wanted to do that, they would have done so by now."

"You didn't think the threat was real?" I asked.

"I believe it was real. I think they would send me back this very moment if they could, but if they do, there will be outrage," said Bauer, puffing his chest out a bit. "If the Portuguese were to allow me to be kidnapped and taken back to Germany, it could be seen as an act of complicity that could threaten the balance of neutrality."

"Are you not afraid that the Germans might do it anyway?" I asked.

"Of course I am," said Bauer. "That is why I left my hotel for this place where no one knows I am."

The fact that we had found him didn't seem to enter his thinking.

"Now," Bauer glanced at his watch, "I will have to ask you to leave. I must return to the British embassy and see if there is any news."

"Of course, Herr Bauer," I said. "But before you go, perhaps you could give us a description of the German woman who approached you."

"German?" He snorted. "She was Portuguese."

I frowned. "But you said—"

"She was working for the Germans. I am certain of it. Or if she isn't, she is being tricked into giving them information. She asked all manner of questions about my work under the guise of trying to seduce me," he said.

"Are you certain—"

"I am," he said, firmly cutting me off. Then he stood up. "Now I must insist you leave. I am a very busy man."

After Bauer saw us out, David and I wound our way down his building's staircase and out into the road. Standing on the pavement looking up at the building with its faded blue and white tiles and yellow plaster, I asked, "Do you think Winn was the British man who approached Bauer?"

"It certainly sounds like him, but if it was Winn, something about the entire thing doesn't add up," said David. "Winn told Phillips that he had information that could be vital to maintaining Portuguese neutrality, but Bauer himself seemed to be well aware that if anything happened to him in Lisbon, it could spark a diplomatic event."

"And Bauer wasn't exactly hiding himself away at first. He said himself that the Portuguese had been to see him, and both the Germans and the Spanish have approached him," I said.

"What was it then that Winn claimed would upset the balance here so badly it could threaten the war?" David asked.

"A plot to kidnap Bauer? Perhaps Bauer's confidence in his position is unfounded and he really is under threat from the Abwehr," I said.

"We should ring Phillips," said David. "There was a telephone booth in the café."

We nipped across the road and back into Café Branca. David raised a hand to a waiter and then pointed to the telephone booth. The waiter nodded his head and went on with his business.

David slid into the small booth and left the door open so that I could hear what he was saying from where I lingered outside. He gave an exchange I assumed was for Phillips's office and after a moment said, "Hello, Miss Larkin. It's David Slater. Is Mr. Phillips in?"

After a pause, David covered the receiver and said to me, "He's not in, but Carter is."

He dipped his head again and said, "Carter, Slater here. Miss Moore and I have just spoken to Bauer. Yes. Yes, that's right, he thought moving would make it easier for him to stay anonymous, but your instructions led us right to him. If you could find him in less than twenty-four hours, I think Bauer is more vulnerable than he realizes."

I listened to David quickly brief Carter on our conversation with Bauer and his report of being approached by a Portuguese woman he was convinced was working with the Germans—knowingly or not.

He fell silent for a moment, listening to Carter, no doubt, and then he said, "I think that's for the best. Very good. Goodbye."

David replaced the receiver. "Carter is going to see about making arrangements for Bauer's safe removal from Lisbon to London.

He's ringing the embassy now to see if anyone can expedite Bauer's visa application, and he's suggested that Bauer be moved to a more secure location in the meantime. It sounds as though we have some bolt-holes we can stash him in on a temporary basis."

"If Bauer will agree to it," I said.

"I suspect he will when Carter dangles his visa in front of him," said David. "Apparently there will be two men, Winslow and Harriet, watching the building in thirty minutes or so."

"And until then?" I asked.

"One of us sits and enjoys a cup of coffee here, never letting the front door out of our sights," he said.

"And the other?"

"Back door, if there is one."

"Well," I said, "I know which one I'm choosing."

David sighed. "I'll go see if there's an alley I can stand in."

TWENTY-ONE

About three-quarters of an hour later, a man wearing a red carnation in his buttonhole appeared at the café door. After looking about, he spotted me and approached.

"Miss Moore, I presume," he said in a rather cheerful voice, tipping his hat to reveal a mop of sandy hair.

"It depends who is asking," I said.

That earned me a hearty laugh. "Winslow." He stuck out his hand and gave mine a firm shake. Then he dropped into the seat across from me, unbuttoned his suit jacket, crossed his legs at the ankles, and peered out the window at Bauer's building.

"So that's it?" he asked.

"That's it."

"Harriet has gone around back. I don't suppose you could give me a description of the chap in case he decides to go for a walk?" asked Winslow.

I did my best to give him as much detail about Bauer's appearance as possible before Winslow put his hand up to stop me. "Excellent work. Now, I'm going to see about a coffee. I don't suppose you fancy one before you go?"

I was beginning to feel rather jittery what with my cups at breakfast and while watching Bauer's building, so I declined.

“Suit yourself,” said Winslow.

I said goodbye and then hurried across the road and around the corner. Sure enough, there was a narrow road running behind the building and I could see my partner on the cobbles ahead of me speaking to another gray-suited man.

David broke off and strode over, pulling his coat a little closer around his neck.

“It’s about time the reinforcements came. It’s chillier than it looks out here,” he said.

“I’m certain you’ve been in worse in London let alone some of the places our lot are sent,” I said.

“Yes, but I’m not normally standing outside with nothing to do,” he grumbled.

“You can warm up on the tram while we travel to Fortescue’s hotel. Where is it?”

“The Hotel Metrópol.”

I blinked. “That’s the same hotel that Jessup had a receipt for in his diary.”

“The very one.”

“What are the odds?”

“That,” said David, “is precisely what I have spent most of the morning asking myself.”

David and I alighted at the tram stop at Praça da Figueira and walked up a short distance to the Hotel Metrópol on Praça do Rossio. We had decided on the tram that we would see if Fortescue was in and then ask hotel management about Jessup.

We joined the steady stream of people entering the lobby. The place was as busy as our hotel, and to my left, I could just see through a pair of open doors to what looked like the hotel bar, which, at this time of the morning, was filled with people sipping coffee.

At the front desk, we were greeted warmly by a man who

introduced himself as the hotel manager. However, when we asked after Fortescue, his face fell.

"You wish to speak to Senhor Fortescue?" he asked.

"Yes. Would you know whether he is currently in his room?" asked David.

"I will check," said the manager with a weary sigh he only partially managed to stifle as he lifted a white telephone receiver. *"Por favor, ligue-me ao Sr. Fortescue, que está hospedado no quarto 523."*

After a moment, the manager switched to English. "Senhor Fortescue? A gentleman and a lady are here to see you. Their names?"

At the manager's raised eyebrows, David said, "Mr. Slater and Miss Moore. We are friends of Princess Petrova."

The manager, seemingly unaffected by the mention of a Russian aristocrat, relayed the message, nodded, and hung up the telephone. "Senhor Fortescue asks if you will wait for him," he said, gesturing to one of several of the lobby's seating areas arranged for conversation.

"Thank you," said David.

We settled ourselves on opposite ends of a leather sofa that faced an armchair and, sure enough, a few moments later out of the gold lift doors came Fortescue. I watched him scan the lobby, skipping right over us.

David leaned over and whispered, "I thought he might recognize you from the casino."

"I'm clearly not as memorable as either of us think," I said.

David huffed a little at that, and we both rose as he called out, "Mr. Fortescue," capturing the red-faced man's attention.

Even from where I was standing, I could see the slight fraying at Fortescue's collar of what was clearly a well-made shirt, and as he approached, I noticed that one of the buttons on his jacket was loose.

"Are you Slater?" asked Fortescue, stopping in front of David and ignoring me entirely.

"I am, and this is my secretary, Miss Moore," said David, gesturing to me.

Fortescue spared me little more than a glance before turning back to my partner. "Do we know one another?"

"We don't, but we were hoping you might help us," said David.

Fortescue rocked back on his heels. "Look, I don't mean to be rude, but I have rather a busy schedule—"

"We are looking for James Winn," I said, cutting across Fortescue's excuse.

"I don't know anyone of that name," he said.

"I think you do," I said.

"You do, do you?" he asked, his tone positively pugnacious.

"Yesterday, at Estoril Casino, you spoke to Princess Petrova about needing to find Winn," I said.

For the first time since David had hailed him, Fortescue took a good look at me and frowned. "You were there when I spoke to the princess."

"I was there in the casino bar," I said.

"But I didn't mention anything about Winn. I'm certain of it," he said.

"Not then you didn't."

"Shall we sit down?" asked David, pointing to the chair behind our suspect.

Fortescue shot me one more look that seemed a mix of annoyance and wonder before unbuttoning his jacket and taking a seat.

I felt it was neither the time nor the place to point out that it was bad manners for a gentleman to sit before a lady, but I certainly noticed it.

Arranging myself on my end of the sofa, I asked, "Why were you so keen to locate Mr. Winn at the casino yesterday evening?"

"Why are you?" Fortescue fired back.

"Consider us an interested party, just like yourself," I said.

"An interested party with connections that can make things very difficult or very easy for a man in your situation," said my partner.

David delivered this in the mildest of fashions, but Fortescue narrowed his eyes nonetheless. "Who are you two? Intelligence? Foreign Office?"

"We understand you're in something of a limbo here," I said, ignoring his questions.

I could see the man's jaw tense, but he gave a curt nod. "I am having some difficulties reentering Britain, despite the fact I'm English. It's a bloody nuisance, and it means that I've been in Lisbon for far longer than I expected."

"And you think that, somehow, Winn can help you?" I asked.

"I don't think Winn can help. The man has been useless as far as I'm concerned. He never even bothered to speak to me," Fortescue shot back.

"But you told the princess he'd stolen something from you," I said.

Fortescue scoffed. "How could a man I've never met before steal something from me?"

"Then who were you arguing with the princess about yesterday evening?" asked David.

"A bounder of the highest order. Blasted Michael Jessup," said Fortescue.

David and I exchanged a look. Fortescue hadn't been speaking about Winn at all but rather our murdered aeroplane passenger.

"What did he take from you?" I asked.

"It's expensive staying indefinitely in a place like this," said Fortescue, sidestepping my question as he waved a hand at our surrounds. "The hotels have figured out that they can prey on people like me who need accommodation, and they're charging astronomical prices. Not to mention the fact that every meal needs to be eaten out."

"You could always stay somewhere a little less central," David suggested.

"And less grand," I added.

Fortescue scowled. "You don't understand, Mr. Slater. It's the inexpensive hotels that go first. They're all booked up, and the only thing left is places like the Metrópol."

Having just come from Bauer's bolt-hole, I somehow suspected that Fortescue's choice of location had more to do with pride than anything else—a fact he confirmed when he added, "Besides, I'm not going to live in squalor like a refugee."

"And how did you think Jessup could help you change this situation exactly?" I asked.

Fortescue sat back and crossed his arms. "You were right to ask about Winn. I had initially thought to deal with him. Among a certain kind of person, he has something of a reputation."

"A reputation for what?" asked David.

"If a man finds himself short on funds and in a bit of a bind, Winn can sometimes offer assistance," said Fortescue.

"Were you were looking for a loan?" I asked.

"Not as such. I was told that if I had something to sell, Winn could get the business done quickly and discreetly," he said.

"What do you have to sell?" I asked.

Fortescue looked away for a flash and then back again. This time when he spoke, he lowered his voice to a near-whisper. "When I was in Egypt, I acquired some . . . items given to me by a friend. Old ugly things really, but they're made of gold. I've taken them around to some antique dealers here, but none of them will touch them. My friend didn't furnish me with papers of authenticity before I left Egypt, so dealers are reluctant to take them on because they are under an increased level of scrutiny from the Portuguese authorities."

I suspected that the antique dealers also had a good idea that the gold artifacts were stolen and wanted nothing to do with them.

"Someone told me that Winn might be able to help, but to do that I'd have to speak to the princess," said Fortescue. "A snob of the highest order, she refused to vouch for me because of one little incident at one of her awful parties."

"Incident?" I asked.

The man's cheeks reddened. "I had rather more to drink than I expected that evening, and I may have made use of one of her potted plants."

"Made use?" I asked.

"It was not clear where the facilities were and—"

David cleared his throat. "I think we can surmise what happened."

"The princess banned me from her infernal soirees. I never got the chance to ask her about this Winn fellow."

"Then how did you become involved with Jessup?" I asked.

"I was having a drink in the bar here and a man asked to share my table because there was a shortage of seats. I was feeling fairly low, and he must have been able to tell because he began speaking to me—quite unprompted, mind you. I don't know why, but I told him about my dwindling funds, and he asked if I had anything of value to sell. When I mentioned the antiques, he said he might know someone who could help me, but he would need a sample to show them what sort of thing they would be purchasing from me."

"And you just gave him one of your antiques?" I asked.

"I was desperate," said Fortescue. "He told me his name was Jessup and he was a frequent guest at the hotel. I could ask the staff to vouch for him. I agreed to meet him again that evening and, after asking around about him, gave him one of the pieces as instructed. He promised to be back in touch, but I never heard from him."

Fortescue leaned forward, his hands on his knees. "The man stole from me, and I want my gold back."

"Why do you think the princess can help you?" I asked.

"Because when I told this Jessup I'd intended to ask the princess for help, he told me he knew her and thought she was nothing more than a trumped-up wealthy woman trying to stave off boredom by pretending to have a connection to Winn. I happened to agree. The princess talked about Winn like some sort of mythical beast."

"The princess told me she didn't know Jessup," I said.

"She knows him. I'm certain of it," he said with conviction.

"When did Jessup approach you?" David asked.

"It was the first day of the month. I recall because I had to pay my hotel bill," said Fortescue.

"Well," said David, pulling out his notebook and jotting something down before tearing the sheet out and handing it to Fortescue, "if you do think of anything else, we are staying at the Hotel Tivoli."

Fortescue took David's note and stuffed it unceremoniously in his pocket.

"What a charming man," I said, watching Fortescue storm off.

"Charming and with plenty of motive to want Jessup dead if what he says is true," said David.

"Perhaps. Anger and a feeling of injustice can prompt men to do so many things."

"You sound doubtful," said my partner.

"I fear Fortescue had neither the means nor the opportunity to kill Jessup. Carter said Fortescue hasn't been able to return to the UK. How could he then be on the aeroplane with us when Jessup was murdered?"

"He hired someone else to do it," said David.

I considered this but shook my head. "With what money?"

"Do you believe that the princess knew Jessup?"

"She wouldn't be the first suspect to lie to us during the course of an investigation," I said.

"And she won't be the last."

"If she did know Jessup, she could be the linchpin between him and Winn. That and the diary entry."

"We don't even know what the diary entry means." David sighed. "What next?"

I glanced at *Maman*'s watch. "I want to speak to the princess again, but while we're here I think it's best to confirm Jessup's story. I'll see if any of the staff in the hotel bar remember seeing Jessup and Fortescue speaking."

"I'll go see if the manager can tell me anything about Jessup's stays here," said David. "His habits, who he met with, who he telephoned. That sort of thing."

"I'll meet you back here in half an hour," I said before making for the hotel bar, determined to find out what I could about what exactly Jessup had been up to during his stays at the Hotel Metrópol.

TWENTY-TWO

The bar of the Hotel Metrópol was a strange place. It was so densely crowded it was a wonder that the patrons didn't knock elbows every time they lifted a glass to their lips. Given the early hour, most seemed to be partaking in coffee rather than stronger fare, but I did spot a few glasses of wine planted in front of several people. A cacophony of voices filled the space, and I found that I was becoming used to the noise of Lisbon's social life.

A waiter in a crisp white shirt and black jacket approached me and executed a little bow. "Senhora."

"It's 'Menina,' actually," I said with a smile.

He placed a hand to his chest and deepened the bow in apology. "*Peço desculpa.* May I show you to a table?"

"Yes, please," I said, although looking around I wondered where exactly he proposed to put me.

The waiter led me through the crowd, weaving expertly around tables until we reached the far end of the room, closest to the bar. There, tucked away in a corner, was a little table set for two. He drew back one of the chairs for me.

"*Obrigada*," I said, taking a seat and deciding to take a risk. "May I please have a cup of tea?"

He nodded and made to turn, but before he could retreat, I added, "I wonder if you could also help me. My friend, Mr. Jessup, was a guest at this hotel. Did he ever come into the bar?"

The waiter smiled apologetically. "I will ask Angelo. He is the head waiter. He would know."

I thanked him and occupied myself watching the people around me. A few minutes later, another man dressed in a waiter's austere uniform approached my table with a teapot, a cup and saucer, and a little pot of milk.

"*Uma xícara de chá*, Menina," he said as he placed the tea down on the table in front of me. "Martim said that you were asking about Senhor Jessup."

"Yes. We were supposed to have dinner together three days ago, but he never came," I said, rapidly concocting a lie to explain why I was poking around about Jessup. "It wasn't like him at all, and I'm worried."

Angelo's lips pursed into a thin line. "I'm very sorry, Menina. I didn't realize that Senhor Jessup had returned to Lisbon, but sometimes people come and go very quickly."

I could hear the undertone in his voice. Lisbon was a beautiful city, but there was darkness lurking in the corners.

"I was hoping that by retracing Mr. Jessup's steps I might find out what happened to him. He told me he had a drink here from time to time," I said.

"Senhor Jessup did visit the bar in the late afternoon every day he stayed at the Hotel Metrópol."

"To meet someone?"

Angelo shook his head. "He usually read the newspaper and waited for a telephone call. The switchboard knew that if any calls came for him, he would be here."

"Did he receive many calls?" I asked.

"Often," said Angelo. "Not every day, but many times one of the other waiters or I would be asked to fetch him for the telephone."

"Were they local calls?" I asked.

"The hotel switchboard operators would know best, but I do know he always placed a trunk call the night before he checked out of the hotel. He would ask me or one of the other waiters to remind him of the time so that he did not miss it."

"That's very helpful, thank you," I said. "I met one of Mr. Jessup's friends the other day. A Mr. Fortescue? I believe he is a guest at this hotel as well."

The head waiter sucked in a breath that told me that he enjoyed having Fortescue as a guest about as much as the hotel manager did. "I am aware of Senhor Fortescue, yes."

"I don't suppose you remember the two of them ever sitting together."

Angelo shook his head. "I am sorry, Menina, but no. When it is very busy, I will sometimes help behind the bar. Maybe it was one of those days. Normally Senhor Jessup chose to sit alone. Although, I do remember him joining another patron a few weeks ago."

"Another patron?" I asked, trying to keep the excitement out of my voice.

"An Englishman."

Had the meeting between Winn and Jessup actually happened?

"Do you remember the man's name?" I asked.

"Oh yes. He is called Sir Reginald."

That pulled me up short. "Sir Reginald? Are you certain?"

"Yes, Menina. Sir Reginald began coming to the bar about a month ago. He would request the same table every time and sit with a cocktail for an hour. One day, while it was very crowded, Senhor Jessup came in as usual. I was seating guests, but when I tried to find him a free table, he said he was meeting Sir Reginald. I didn't know the two were acquaintances."

That made two of us.

"But surely if Sir Reginald and Mr. Jessup both had the habit of sitting in the bar in the afternoons, they might have met before," I said.

He shook his head. "Maybe they did, but I never saw them speak before that day."

"You didn't happen to hear what they talked about, did you?" I asked.

Angelo puffed out his chest, clearly insulted by the implication that he might have been eavesdropping. "I did not."

"I apologize," I said quickly. "I'm simply trying to learn anything that might help me find Mr. Jessup. I'm very concerned about him."

He seemed to soften a little at that. "I did not hear anything, but I can tell you that the conversation did not seem heated. They spoke for about twenty minutes and then Sir Reginald left."

"Did you see them speak again after that?" I asked.

Angelo shook his head. "I haven't seen Sir Reginald since."

"You don't recall what day this meeting was, do you?" I asked.

"It was the last day of the month, thirty-first of October," he said. "I remember because it was the same day Mr. Jessup placed a trunk call to London."

"His usual one?" I asked, trying to remember the annotations in Jessup's diary as to when his previous trip had ended.

Angelo shook his head. "No, he stayed for some days after that."

I sat back and considered this. My father and Jessup had met at the hotel bar and spoken for twenty minutes, and then Jessup had placed an expensive call to London much earlier than his usual call on his final afternoon in Lisbon. Less than a week later, Jessup *did* make his usual call, according to Angelo, and then left for a fortnight. On his return to Lisbon, he'd been killed.

What about the conversation with my father had prompted Jessup to break his habits and place that extra telephone call?

"Thank you, Angelo," I said. "You've been very helpful. There's just one more thing. Could you tell me where the hotel switchboard is located?"

"In the basement," he said with a smile, and then, no doubt anticipating my next question, added, "I will arrange for Martim to show you the way."

TWENTY-THREE

True to his word, Angelo sent Martim over as soon as I'd finished my tea to show me downstairs. I was still turning over what I'd learned about my father and Jessup's meeting. If I had been skating on thin ice taking Mr. Fletcher's secretive assignment to speak to my father, now I was in truly dangerous territory. Sir Reginald's name had been connected to a murdered banker on a Lisbon, Portugal-bound aeroplane, a murdered jeweler in London, and a missing informant. To make matters worse, no one seemed to know where Sir Reginald could be found.

I needed to tell David what I'd learned, Mr. Fletcher's warning be damned. David was my partner and he had a right to know that the case of a missing informant had just become more complicated than either of us could ever have anticipated.

But first, I wanted to follow the thread of Jessup's trunk calls while I had the chance.

The basement had little of the glamour of the more public spaces like the lobby and the hotel bar, trading soaring ceilings for cramped corridors painted in functional white. These were the sorts of spaces guests were never meant to give a thought to if a hotel was well-run, and I suspected it was only my story about being worried about Jessup's whereabouts that bought me access.

Martim stopped in front of a door with *Mesa telefônica* stenciled on it in blue paint. When he opened the door, I was hit by the sound of a half dozen women's voices speaking in rapid Portuguese, English, French, and German. Just beyond the door, I could see an older woman lift her head and frown as she connected a call and then removed her headphones.

"*Não permitimos convidados aqui*, Martim," the woman said in a sharp tone, her expression pinched.

Martim glanced back at me and, in English, said, "Angelo asked me to bring Menina . . ."

"Moore," I supplied.

"Menina Moore here," finished Martim.

"I'm very sorry to be a bother," I said, doing my best to play the role of the polite English secretary I was supposed to be, "but I'm trying to find a friend who was a guest here at the Hotel Metrópol. It really is urgent that I locate him, and Angelo thought that you might help."

The woman assessed me with a cool eye that told me she was no more impressed with my somber suit and prim blouse than I was. "Why do you think *I* might be able to help?"

"You or one of your switchboard operators. He placed a trunk call to London. I was hoping I might find out who the call was to."

The woman sighed and reached for a book that sat next to her right hand. "What is your friend's name?"

"Michael Jessup. I believe the call would have been on the thirty-first of October at five o'clock in the afternoon," I said.

Her eyes narrowed. "You seem to know a great deal about this call already."

"Angelo was very helpful," I demurred.

She made a low noise in her throat and flipped open her book to page through it. She stopped and took a moment to read through an entry before saying, "Senhor Jessup booked a trunk call to London, exchange SWI 7832, on that date."

SWI 7832? The exchange didn't ring any bells.

"Who arranged the call?" I asked.

"Luiza Barbosa."

"May I speak with her?" I asked.

The head of the switchboard glanced at her watch. "She is supposed to have a break now. If she wants to speak to you, you can speak to her for ten minutes. Menina Barbosa!"

From around the other side of the switchboard, a woman with abundant dark hair, beautifully smooth olive skin, a round face, and a red pout poked her head. The head of the switchboard gave her a series of instructions in Portuguese, and I watched as her gaze flicked to me, hardened, and then turned back to her superior.

"Menina Barbosa will speak to you," said the switchboard's head.

"What does she want?" Menina Barbosa asked sourly in English.

"Menina Moore will ask you herself," said her superior. "Menina Moore, if you will follow her."

"*Obrigada*, Menina Barbosa," I said as I fell into Luiza's wake as she breezed by me, the yellow skirt of her dress swishing about her silk-stocking-clad legs. Even with my long stride, I had to scramble to keep up with her.

"I do not like how the English say 'Barbosa.'" She sniffed, not bothering to look over her shoulder as she addressed me.

"I apologize," I said.

"Call me Luiza."

"Thank you for being willing to speak to me, Luiza—"

She gave a short laugh. "I don't like that either."

"I just had a few questions—"

"I will only answer what I know," she said, pushing out of a side entrance door and into the decidedly less glamorous back of the hotel property. The clang of pots and pans from a nearby doorway told me that this was the service entrance to the kitchen, a fact confirmed by the stacks of boxes filled with produce waiting to be brought in and the empty packing crates haphazardly stacked for when someone would come along and break them down for the rubbish.

Luiza fished out a packet of cigarettes from her handbag, lit a match, and took a deep draw. She blew out the smoke in a steady stream, her free hand planted on the curve of her hip in a way that gave her a weary look.

"What do you want?" asked Luiza.

"I'm looking for a man named Michael Jessup. He was a guest at this hotel," I said.

She flicked the end of her cigarette dismissively. "Senhor Jessup? Yes, I remember him."

"He seems to have disappeared, and it's rather urgent I find him," I said, holding back the fact of his murder for fear it might make her even more reluctant to speak to me.

Her eyes raked over me before she took another draw on her cigarette. "What do you want to know?"

"Angelo in the bar told me that Mr. Jessup often waited in the bar for a telephone call when he was staying at the Hotel Metrópol. Do you know who was calling him?" I asked.

She crossed her arms under her chest. "I only took the telephone calls and directed them to the bar's telephone, where one of the waiters would fetch Senhor Jessup."

"Surely you must hear the caller from time to time, even if it's just as you are making sure the connection is clear."

"Rarely," she said with a smirk.

"Then you couldn't tell me whether he was speaking to a man or a woman?" I asked.

"No," she said shortly, lifting her cigarette to her lips again.

"Angelo said that Mr. Jessup was in the habit of booking a trunk call the night before he left Lisbon on every visit, is that right?" I asked.

"Yes," she said.

"But he also booked a trunk call to London on the thirty-first of October, which wasn't his habit because he stayed on for several days afterward," I said.

"Yes," she repeated.

"Who was the trunk call on the thirty-first of October to?"

She threw her hands up in the air. "I book the calls that I'm told to book. He gave me the same telephone exchange that he always gave me, but with much less notice. It ruined my afternoon trying to make sure his trunk call was arranged."

"He wanted to place a call to SWI 7832?" I asked. "The same place he always rang just before he left?'

"Yes. He called it every time he was staying at the hotel, usually just before he left. That is fine because we know he always wants a call the night before he leaves. But this time he said it was urgent."

"Did he say why?" I asked.

"Guests do not share why anything is urgent. All I can tell you is he wanted two trunk calls during that stay. One on the thirty-first and one on the fifth, the day before he checked out of the hotel." She threw her cigarette down and ground it under the toe of her black leather heel. "I must return to my place."

I watched her march back into the building, leaving me among the rubbish of the alleyway.

TWENTY-FOUR

I gave Luiza a few minutes' head start and then doubled back through the service door to retrace my steps past the switchboard room until I reached the door Martim had originally directed me through. When I caught Angelo's eye across the bar, I raised a hand to the waiter in thanks and headed for the lobby once again.

As promised, David was lingering at the sofas where we'd interviewed Fortescue. As I approached, he folded his hands behind his back and asked, "Where are you coming from?"

"The switchboard room. I went there after the bar because I discovered something," I said, and I related the story of what I'd found—with the parts surrounding my father omitted because I knew I should save those for a more private place. When I reached the news of the telephone exchange, David frowned.

"That's a London exchange," he said.

"Which makes me wonder why Jessup was telephoning a London exchange every time he stayed at the Hotel Metrópol when the next day he would be flying back to London?"

"Telling his wife about his plans to come home?" he asked.

"That would be a very expensive habit. Besides, if he did have a wife, why telephone her when it would have been far less expensive and faster to send a telegram?"

"Telephoning his employer?" David asked.

I shook my head. "Again, why waste the expense of telling your employer you are returning when the dates of your trip are already planned?"

"Well, it sounds as though you had a more successful time of it than I did. The hotel manager was not particularly helpful. He can't remember whether Jessup and Fortescue ever met," said David.

"Angelo in the bar couldn't remember either, but that doesn't rule out the possibility that it happened." I stopped myself. "David, there's something I need to discuss with you."

He glanced at his watch. "Can it wait? I need to report, and I thought I'd wire Miss Summers to see about that telephone exchange."

I shook my head. I'd waited long enough already. "I need to speak to you now. Somewhere private."

"But our hotel—"

"Now," I insisted.

"Right," he said, standing up. "I have an idea."

David led me through the hotel, walking with purpose as though he not only knew the place but belonged. As we left the buzz of the lobby behind, things became quieter. We wound down several hallways until we saw a bank of doors.

"See if any of them are open and free," he said, trying one handle.

I tried the door across from him. It gave, and I found myself looking at a dark room half filled with tables and chairs.

"This one," I said, flicking on the light.

David followed me in and, when the door closed behind us, asked, "What's the matter?"

I looked down at my hands. I could hear Mr. Fletcher's warning to keep my search for Sir Reginald to myself, but that had been before I'd learned that Jessup and Sir Reginald had definitely met. Before I knew that Morrison had been shot and killed.

My father was connected to too many dead men to keep things from David any longer.

I drew in a deep breath and started at the beginning. "Before I left London, I received an envelope in the post. Inside was a key and an address written in invisible ink."

"You can't be serious," he said with a laugh.

"Unfortunately, I am."

"Who would send you a key?" he asked.

"My father."

"But I thought you don't speak," he said.

"We don't," I said with a nod. "The address led me to a safe deposit box and a tea chest of my mother's jewels I'd thought had been sold off a long time ago. There was also a letter with instructions that I was to take the box to a Hatton Garden jeweler named Christian Morrison. When I arrived, I found a ransacked shop and no Morrison. I learned this morning that he was shot and killed. His body was found in an air raid shelter."

"That was the telegram you received at breakfast?" asked David.

I nodded. "Miss Summers let me know."

"Do Mr. Fletcher and Mrs. White know about this?"

"Mr. Fletcher does. Mrs. White does not," I said. "If she did, she would never have agreed to send me on assignment with you."

"Why? You couldn't have known about the connection between your father and a murdered jeweler," he said.

"Sir Reginald is here in Lisbon—or at least he was until he disappeared."

He stilled. "Disappeared?"

"Carter had been keeping an eye on him, but Sir Reginald vanished."

"Why has Carter been monitoring him?"

I looked down at my hands, knowing just how poorly I would take the news that David had withheld anything about an assignment from me if our roles were reversed.

"The intelligence services are assessing Sir Reginald as a potential asset to influence significant figures in neutral countries because of the company he keeps. However, there has been some resistance to the idea. Mr. Fletcher thought I might be able to speak to Sir Reginald and persuade him to become an asset."

"Why don't I know about this?"

I sighed. "Because I was given instructions not to tell you. It wasn't until I met with Carter while you were reporting to Mrs. White yesterday that I learned of Sir Reginald's vanishing act."

David stared at me. "Is there anything else you neglected to tell me?"

I winced. "Do you remember when I told you that Princess Petrova recognized me as Sir Reginald's daughter when she met me at the casino? She also told me that Sir Reginald had approached her for help. She said she believed it had to do with money. She had planned to effect an introduction between Sir Reginald and Winn, however, the day after my father asked for the favor, he rang her and told her it was no longer necessary."

"Your father was in contact with the very man we are looking for and you thought it wise to hold that back from me?" David asked, his voice shaking a little as I suspected he was holding back his anger.

"He never spoke to Winn so I thought it wouldn't matter," I said quickly.

"No, you *hoped* it would not matter. You had no right to make that decision on your own, Evelyne."

"I will have you know that I am fully capable of making my own decisions—"

"We are *partners*," he snapped. "We are meant to be working together. We have to tell Mrs. White."

"No."

"Evelyne, be reasonable. You have gone on an assignment in a foreign country without disclosing a huge conflict of interest to your handler. What happens if we realize that your father really is involved and you must make a difficult decision about what to do? You could jeopardize the entire investigation."

There it was, the crossroads that Mr. Fletcher had warned me about. If David was asked to choose between loyalty to me and loyalty to the job, the department, and the country, he would choose them every time.

"Mr. Fletcher knows," I said stubbornly.

"Mr. Fletcher is not your handler."

"But he is our head of department."

"No one is infallible. Not even a head of department. If Phillips were to find out about this—"

"He would demand that I was removed, just like Mrs. White. But I can't be, David. Not when we have just had our first real break connecting Jessup and Winn," I said.

"I should be picking up the telephone right now and making arrangements for you to be on the first flight back to Whitchurch."

"Please don't do that," I said. "*Please.*"

"You lied to me." The fact that he sounded more hurt than angry cut me to the core.

"I was given an assignment and told expressly that I should not disclose it to you unless absolutely necessary."

"You lied," he repeated.

"The moment I realized the extent of the connection between Winn, Jessup, and Sir Reginald, I resolved to tell you. I just couldn't do it in the middle of the Hotel Metrópol's lobby," I said.

"You said Jessup. How does Jessup factor into this?" he asked.

"At the Hotel Metrópol's bar, I found out that Jessup and Sir Reginald met around the same time Sir Reginald approached the princess. I think that Jessup might have offered my father some sort of deal that made him turn away from Winn."

"Do you think Winn killed Jessup?" asked David.

"No," I said quickly. "If Winn was on that aeroplane, Phillips would have spotted his name."

"Not if Winn was traveling under false papers."

"It still doesn't fit. Why would Winn go missing for days before Jessup's trip only to risk leaving Portugal and returning on a flight from Britain to kill him? Besides, Winn sounds like he liked to keep a low profile. The plane was so crowded that if something went wrong while he was breaking Jessup's neck, we all would have heard it and he would have been trapped on that aeroplane. No, I think Winn was somehow in competition with Jessup, but I don't think he is our killer."

"Could Sir Reginald be our killer?" asked David.

"Why would Sir Reginald kill a man who was supposed to be helping him out of trouble? Besides, if my father had been a passenger, I would have recognized him."

"Are you certain?" he asked. "You said yourself that you haven't seen him in years."

"Mr. Fletcher showed me a series of recent press photographs. Sir Reginald looks much the same as he always did."

I hated the guarded look in my partner's eyes as he studied me, almost as though he didn't know whether he could trust me any longer.

"I am sorry, David," I said. "I promise I only trusted the seriousness of the connection between Winn, Jessup, and Sir Reginald when I spoke to the head waiter at the bar."

"And Princess Petrova's offer to introduce Sir Reginald and Winn?" he asked.

My shoulders sagged. "I had a lapse in judgment. I can understand why you might be skeptical, but I promise you I never would have held back from you the fact that Sir Reginald is in Lisbon if it had been up to me." I leaned over and put my hand on his. "You are my partner."

He stared at our hands for a moment before covering mine with his free one. Then he took a step back.

"Where does that leave us?" asked David.

"I don't know," I said, not entirely certain whether he was referring to the case or to our partnership.

"I can go to Phillips's office and send a wire to Miss Summers asking her to look into the telephone exchange you found," he said stiffly.

"That's a good idea," I conceded.

"In the meantime, why don't you go to the place on the matchbook you found in Winn's flat? The one Winn and Phillips used to use as a drop point?"

"Café Real?" I asked.

"Maybe they remember Winn meeting someone," said David, his tone still formal.

"I suppose it's worth a look," I said. "I might also stop into one of the jewelry shops Carter said Sir Reginald went to when he was new in town."

"Fine," he said. "I'll see you back at the hotel then."

And with that he left me in the half-full storeroom feeling about six inches tall.

TWENTY-FIVE

I could not deny that I was terrified, upon leaving that Hotel Metrópol's storeroom alone, that I had ruined David's trust in me by keeping Mr. Fletcher's assignment from him. However, there was no going back. I couldn't change the decisions I'd made. Instead I would have to show David that I was the partner he deserved once again.

I resolved to tell him everything I learned, and I would begin with my trip to Winn and Phillips's café.

Using directions from the Hotel Metrópol's concierge, I wound my way through the city's streets and, about twenty minutes later, found myself in front of Café Real. It was far more modest than Café Nicole, where I'd met Carter the day before, with no embellishments outside except for a green awning and the establishment's name hand-painted on the glass above the door.

As I walked through the door, a waiter looked up. He stepped forward to greet me and after determining that I had little Portuguese and he had little English but both of us spoke French, showed me to a table in the window that afforded me an excellent view of the road.

"Could I please have a cup of tea and two *pastel de nata*?" I asked in French. "Oh, and do you have any matches?"

"Yes, Menina," he said, and hurried off.

A few moments later, he deposited the teapot, cup, saucer, and milk on my table. Next to these, he set a plate of pastries, and then handed me a fresh matchbook. It was an exact copy of the one I'd seen in Winn's flat.

"Thank you," I said. "I'm very glad my friend recommended this place to me. You might know him. James Winn? He's English like me."

The waiter smiled. "We have several English customers, but I don't remember a Senhor Winn."

"That's a shame. He spoke so highly about your coffee," I said. "I think he might have met his friend Mr. Phillips here."

The waiter brightened. "Senhor Phillips? He comes in for coffee every morning. Sometimes a lady joins him."

"A lady?" Phillips, you dark horse.

"From time to time. Senhor Phillips likes to sit over there." The waiter pointed to a table pushed up against a wall.

"I might move to that table, if you don't mind," I said.

The waiter shrugged his shoulders. "Yes. If you like."

"Thank you," I said with a smile.

The waiter took my things over to Phillips's usual table, and I settled myself in the chair and took a sip of tea and bit into my *pastel de nata*. While I chewed, I surreptitiously ran my hand along the ridge that finished the raw edge of the wood underneath the table, looking for the gap that Phillips had described when he told us about exchanging notes with Winn. My fingers brushed a rise in the metal, and I worked a fingernail between the wood and the ridge. Could that be the spot?

I pulled my notebook out of my handbag and tore a strip of paper out of the back of it, coughing to cover up the noise. I folded up the paper and sat with it cradled in my palm. Then I sat, sipping tea and watching the café's staff mill about and my fellow patrons chat away. As soon as everyone's back was turned, I quickly dropped my head to look under the table. Sure enough, there was a gap between the metal and the wood just as Phillips had said, but it was empty. When I slipped the folded paper into the ridge, it held.

Swiftly, I sat up and dropped the folded paper and my notebook into my handbag before my waiter emerged from the kitchen carrying a fresh cup of coffee for a table in the front. I took another bite of pastry just as the café door opened and the man walking in met my gaze. It was Capitão Camargo.

I suppose I shouldn't have been surprised that the PVDE officer walked straight over to me.

"Menina Moore," he said.

"Capitão Camargo, what a coincidence seeing you again," I said.

The PVDE officer raised a brow. "I spotted you through the window, Menina. What are you doing in Bairro Alto when your hotel is on the Avenida da Liberdade?"

"As Mr. Slater did not have need of me this afternoon, I thought I would take in the sights of your beautiful city. It's not so very far to walk, is it?" I asked with a wide smile.

"But a café like this? It is not where foreigners go."

"I thought it looked charming."

"And the Hotel Metrópol?" he asked. "That is where I followed you from."

"You followed me?" I gasped, playing at being the easily shocked Miss Moore. It was a convenient expression because it covered for the fact that I was furious at myself for not realizing that I had acquired a tail.

"I wondered what the woman who found the body of Senhor Jessup was doing at his hotel," said Camargo.

My hand flew to my mouth. "His hotel? I didn't know."

"Then why were you there?" he asked.

"Mr. Slater had a meeting, but there was some confusion and the vintner who he was meant to see never arrived," I said, hoping that Camargo hadn't seen David speaking to the hotel manager or me while I'd been in the bar or returning from the switchboard. "The man's secretary sent a telegram to our hotel to rearrange the date, but as we were out at another meeting, we didn't receive it until I rang the Hotel Tivoli's desk to check whether we had any messages."

Camargo raised a brow, but instead of pushing any further, he said, "I hope you have been keeping yourself out of trouble, Menina Moore."

"I do try my very best. Have you found out more about what happened to the man who died on the aeroplane?"

"We have some leads," he said.

"I hope you do find whoever killed him. It's a horrible situation," I said, giving a little shiver to punctuate my point.

"I have been meaning to telephone your hotel, Menina Moore, because some more questions have arisen as part of my investigation," he said.

"Questions?"

"Did you notice that Senhor Jessup was carrying an attaché case when he boarded the flight from Whitchurch to Sintra?"

I pretended to think about this. "Yes, I think I did see him with one. In fact, he made something of a fuss over keeping it with him despite the crew wanting to stow it. Something about weight distribution on the aeroplane. In the end, they allowed him to have it."

"And did you notice that case when you discovered his body yesterday morning?"

"I really couldn't say," I said, even though I knew I had because I sincerely regretted not having enough time to search Jessup's case. Still, the diary had proven to be a boon.

"Try," he suggested dryly.

"When I realized he was dead, I— Oh, it was horrible," I said, pulling a handkerchief from my handbag to hold to my lips.

"Menina, please. It is important that you answer the question," he said with less patience than I might have wanted if I'd been a real weeping witness.

"I think there was a case." I hesitated. "Yes, I remember now. It was resting on his lap."

"Did you touch it?" he asked.

"No."

Camargo made a low "hmm" noise in the back of his throat that told me he wasn't entirely convinced that I was telling the truth.

"Why do you ask?" I asked.

"Because when we examined the case more closely, we discovered that it was fitted with a false bottom."

"Why, it's like something out of a spy novel! What was inside?" I asked, letting my natural curiosity at this new tidbit of information show through.

"Nothing," he said.

"Nothing?"

He nodded.

"Then it's not like a spy novel at all," I said. "How disappointing."

"You seem to be very well acquainted with spy novels, Menina Moore. You should know that espionage is not allowed in Portugal," he said sternly.

"Well, I should think not." I blinked as though just catching his meaning and then laughed. "Surely you can't mean me? Oh, Capitão Camargo, I can reassure you that I wouldn't even know where to begin being a spy. I do think it would be rather glamorous, though, don't you?"

"No, I do not."

I smiled up at the captain, who was clearly not enjoying this interaction with me in my guise as Miss Moore.

"What do you think Mr. Jessup was doing with an attaché case with a false bottom?" I asked.

"That is not for you to ask or me to say, Miss Moore. If you remember anything that could be relevant to the case, I will ask you to contact me immediately. And"—he leaned down over the table—"I would remind you that I am never far, Menina."

He clearly meant it as a threat, but I beamed up at him and said, "That is very reassuring, Capitão Camargo. I feel all the safer for it."

His eyes narrowed, but then he straightened and gave me a curt nod goodbye, leaving me to my rapidly cooling tea and my half-eaten pastries.

I waited a good ten minutes after Camargo left to call for my bill. The waiter who had been so accommodating when I first entered Café Real looked positively terrified when he dropped the slip off, and I couldn't blame him. Who wouldn't be frightened after a PVDE officer came into their café and began to question an Englishwoman who had just herself been asking any number of questions?

Outside, I was delighted to find that the sun had come out, so I left my navy coat open and tilted my face up to catch a little bit of its warmth. I retraced my steps through Bairro Alto to Rossio Square and the Hotel Metrópol because I knew that at least that way I could find my way back to my hotel without having to ask for directions.

I also wanted to think.

I can't say that I was entirely surprised my father had found himself mixed up in something unsavory. Ever since Mr. Fletcher had told me about the company Sir Reginald kept in South America, I'd known that my father's morals might be more flexible than most. Could Sir Reginald actually be responsible for Jessup's murder or Winn's disappearance?

I couldn't imagine it. Sir Reginald's first instinct had always been for his own pleasure and his own benefit before anything else. He was selfish, unfaithful, and arrogant, but he was not a murderer.

However, a theory was beginning to form in my mind—one that I couldn't ignore for much longer—and I wanted to test it.

As I entered Rossio Square, I dug into my handbag for my notebook, out of which I drew the list of names Carter had given me the night before. One of the stores was Joalharia Dom Pedro just across the way.

Keeping the statue of Dom Pedro IV on my left, I began to walk anticlockwise around the square, looking at the shop and restaurant names as I went. Sure enough, a few minutes later, I found myself looking up at a beaux arts sign for the Joalharia Dom Pedro. I pushed open the glass plated door of the shop, a small bell announcing my arrival. Behind a counter, an older gentleman looked up and smiled.

"*Bom dia, Menina*," he greeted me as he set aside a gold men's watch he had been examining as I entered.

"*Bom dia*," I said.

Immediately the man's smile widened. "Would you prefer to speak in English?"

I gave a little laugh. "If you don't mind."

"English, French, German, Italian," he rattled off languages. "It is helpful for a shop owner to know a little of all of these. That is a very pretty pair of earrings you are wearing."

I reached up to touch the pearls *Maman* had given me. It probably wasn't wise to have brought them or her gold watch while my cover was a working secretary, but I was loath to leave them behind in London when they were talismans of sorts.

"Thank you," I said. "They were my mother's."

"The pearls are a good size, perfectly matched." He smiled. "Your mother was a woman of discerning taste."

"She would have been delighted to hear you say that."

"My condolences," he said graciously.

"Thank you."

"How may I help you?" he asked.

"I was hoping you might be able to tell me about a customer who came into the shop. I believe it was at the end of last month."

The jeweler's previously sunny expression faltered a little. "You must forgive me, Menina, but so many people come into the shop . . ."

"I understand," I said with a sigh. "It must be impossible to remember all the names and faces. It's just that my father has gone missing—"

"Your father?" he asked.

"Yes. I've come all the way from England to find him. He sent me a message saying that he would be arriving on a ship a month ago, but he never appeared. My sister and I fear the worst might have happened," I said, swiftly concocting another fake sibling to help my story, because if I'd already made up a brother on this trip, why not a sister too? "She's waiting back in London for any word from me."

The jeweler shook his head. "When people go missing in Lisbon . . ."

I've observed over the years that some men are terrified of the sight of a woman crying and will do anything to prevent her from weeping. Standing in the jewelry shop, I mustered a few sniffles and let my voice waver a little bit as I said, "I—I understand."

"Maybe I do remember your father," the jeweler said quickly. "What is his name?"

I reached into my handbag and pulled out a handkerchief, dotting the corner of my left eye as I said, "Sir Reginald Redfern."

The man brightened. "Ah, Sir Reginald. A very distinguished gentleman."

"You remember him? Oh, that is good to hear," I said. "Do you recall what he was shopping for?"

The owner frowned. "He was not shopping, Menina. He was trying to sell. He described the pieces to me and wanted to know what sort of price I would give for them."

"Did he?" I mulled over that one. I wondered how the prices in this shop compared to what Morrison had promised him in London.

"It is not uncommon for foreigners to come into the shop and inquire about selling gold and gemstones," the jeweler continued.

"What did my father say when you told him what you would pay for those things?" I asked.

The man hesitated. "He was disappointed. It was clear he thought they were more valuable. However, I told him that the price of diamonds?" He made a downward-sloping gesture with his hand. "It is a very good time to buy, but not to sell.

"Your father insisted that he had paid top prices for the jewels when he purchased them twenty or thirty years ago, and that they would stand up to authentication," the jeweler continued. "I did not doubt that, but prices are what they are right now. If he comes back in a few months, maybe it will be different."

I suspected that if Sir Reginald wanted to dispose of *Maman*'s jewels, it meant that he needed funds now and couldn't wait. Besides, delaying gratification had never been one of my father's strong suits.

"Thank you, Senhor. You have been very helpful. I just had one more question. You said that my father described the pieces to you. He didn't show you anything?" I asked.

"No. He had nothing with him," said the jeweler, confirming that the jewels my father was inquiring about must have been the ones in the safe deposit box.

I thanked the man and let myself out of the shop door. Although I had two more jewelry stores in my notebook, I'd seen enough. Besides, it was time for me to make my way back to my hotel and hope David had forgiven me at least a little.

Back on the pavement, I turned left to round the left side of the square to pick up the road that would lead me back to Avenida da Liberdade. I passed the Hotel Metrópol, rounding a stack of luggage sitting on a cart outside the hotel's front door. In fact, I was just beginning to enjoy the warmth of the sun breaking through the clouds when, in the tables in front of a café just a few doors down from the hotel, I spotted the unmistakable beauty of Luiza, the switchboard operator, sitting at a table in the window. With her mustard dress and lack of coat, she stood out from the rest of the café patrons.

What was she doing at the café when she'd just taken a break to speak to me not long ago?

I slowed a little, using a taller man with a large suitcase as a shield to obscure me a little from the view of the café, although I needn't have bothered. Luiza was clearly deep in conversation with a man.

I paused on the pavement facing the road and opened my handbag, extracting my compact from inside. I opened it and touched my hair, making as though I was fussing with the way it fell from under my hat. As I raised the mirror, however, I angled myself to catch a glimpse of Luiza's companion. My stomach turned when I saw that the man on the other side of the table wore the unmistakable, easy smile of Berndt Köhler.

TWENTY-SIX

I snapped my compact shut and hurried off in the direction of the Hotel Tivoli, my sighting of Luiza and the Abwehr agent churning in my mind.

Phillips had warned David and me that there were German spies everywhere, but I hadn't considered that the Hotel Metrópol's switchboard operator might be one of their informants. It was entirely possible that Luiza and Köhler had been speaking about something unrelated to my case, but the timing was suspicious at best. It was far more likely that she had contacted Köhler just after I left, wanting to report my questions related to Jessup, which begged the question: where did Jessup's—and therefore Winn's—loyalties lie in this war?

As soon as I stepped through the lobby doors of my hotel, I hurried up to the front desk to inquire as to whether Mr. Slater had returned. Finding David was still out, I retreated to my room. I had only just pulled off my coat when there was a knock. My stomach flipped at the sight of him leaning against the doorframe.

"I thought you were still at Phillips's office," I said, letting him in.

"I saw you just as the lift doors were closing, but I didn't want to make a scene hailing you."

"Well," I said, pushing my dark fringe back from my forehead as I did whenever I began to feel a bit overwhelmed, "I'm very glad you're here because such a great deal has happened that I hardly know where to begin."

"Even more than at the Hotel Metrópol?" he asked with a raised brow.

I nodded. "Even more."

"Why don't you start with how you got on at Café Real?" he asked.

"It's definitely the right place." I found the matchbook the waiter had given me and held it up to show him. "Winn and Phillips's hiding spot was right there in the lip of Phillips's usual table, as he said it would be. It was empty, which was not a surprise. However, what was a surprise was the visit our friend Capitão Camargo paid me."

"Camargo?" asked David sharply. "What did he want?"

"He followed me from the Hotel Metrópol. I had to tell him a story about you having an appointment with a vintner who never arrived. You kindly allowed me to take the afternoon because of the canceled meeting."

"How generous of me," he said. "I can verify all of that, if Camargo asks me."

"Thank you. He still doesn't trust me—rightly so, although not for the reasons he thinks—and I don't want to give him any more reason to detain me. I feel as though I'm doing quite a bit of tap dancing to try to convince him that I had nothing to do with Jessup's murder," I said.

"Did he accuse you of anything?"

"No, but he did want to know whether I'd touched Jessup's attaché case. Apparently, when they examined it, the PVDE found it has a false bottom."

"Was there anything hidden inside?" he asked.

"Camargo said it was empty." I held up a finger. "I will come back to that in a moment. First, you should know Camargo knew that Jessup stayed at the Hotel Metrópol when he was in Lisbon. Now, we learned about that through the diary . . ." I trailed off.

"I suppose he could have found out because of a previous file on Jessup," said David, picking up the thought for me.

"Or old-fashioned police work. He could have had one of his junior officers ring around to all of the hotels in the city on the theory that a foreigner would likely have stayed in a hotel."

"Did he mention anything about the trunk calls?" asked David.

"No, but I don't think Camargo was inclined to share many more details of his investigation with me," I said.

"Well, I managed to track down who is on the other end of that London telephone exchange Jessup called," he said, pulling a folded sheet of paper out of his jacket pocket and holding it up between two fingers.

"That was quick," I said, impressed.

"Miss Larkin, Phillips's secretary, sent the telegram for me. I waited on the chance that Miss Summers might receive and fill the request swiftly, and I was right." He unfolded the paper. "Apparently the exchange is for a business called H. M. Barlow."

I sank down to the edge of the bed as the breath left my body. The exchange Jessup had run at the end of each trip was to the same jeweler who had ended up dead in an air raid shelter just days after Sir Reginald had sent me with instructions to deliver my mother's jewels to him.

"H. M. Barlow belonged to Christian Morrison."

"Your dead jeweler?"

"The one and only," I murmured. "I've been so stupid."

"What do you mean?"

"Remember how there was a pattern to Jessup's trips to Lisbon? They started off sporadically, and then during the summer they became more regular. Recently, he was coming to Lisbon every fortnight, staying for a week, and then flying back home."

"Yes?"

"But we don't know *why* Jessup was making these trips. Or at least we didn't until now." I swallowed and reached under my mattress, where I'd stowed Jessup's diary for safekeeping. "I think Jessup was smuggling jewels out of Lisbon, working with Morrison to sell them on, and bringing the money from London back into the country."

"Why?" asked David. "There are plenty of jewelers in Lisbon. If people want to sell their jewelry, they can do it here."

"Do you remember what Senhora Ferreira in the dress shop said about the price of jewels here? The market is overrun with people trying to fund their onward journeys. The jeweler I spoke to this afternoon said my father didn't seem interested in selling after the jeweler gave him an honest assessment of the pieces he described.

"What if Jessup realized he could act as a sort of middleman for people like Fortescue and my father who were short of money? The prices he could secure in Britain would be better than anywhere in Continental Europe given that all of those cities are flooded with desperate refugees. Even with a smuggler's commission, it might be worth it to some people to dispose of their jewelry in London," I said, things becoming clearer as I spoke.

"When I spoke to the switchboard at the Hotel Metrópol, one of the operators confirmed that Jessup broke his usual pattern of placing a trunk call at the end of his trip on the thirty-first of October," I continued. "We also know that's the date Fortescue said he spoke to Jessup because his hotel bill was due, and that was also around the time Sir Reginald went back on his request for Princess Petrova to get the word out to Winn that he needed help."

"You think Jessup saw an opportunity with Fortescue and Sir Reginald and made a trunk call to Morrison outside of his usual pattern to let Morrison know he would have an additional shipment of Fortescue's antiques coming in his false-bottom case," said David.

"And to tell Morrison to expect me to show up at his jewelry shop with a tea chest full of my mother's jewels. Only I didn't get the letter until much later because I was on the Blackthorn Park case with you."

"Jessup was a middleman who could move goods between London and Lisbon, all for a fee," said David.

"It wouldn't have taken much effort to put currency in his case rather than jewels for his return trips."

I could see it so clearly. Sir Reginald being approached by Jessup, listening to the man's pitch and promise, being tempted by the possibility of more money than he could get in Lisbon. For a man who, according to Aunt Amelia, was always short on funds, it would have been too tantalizing an offer to ignore.

"How does Winn connect into all of this?" asked David.

"I don't know," I admitted. "I thought at first that Jessup was poaching Winn's territory—and maybe he was—but a smuggling ring? That's an entirely different kettle of fish. It requires a network of people like Morrison."

"And we haven't found any evidence that Winn was in contact with Morrison," said David.

"Nothing."

The telephone in my room rang. David moved aside to allow me to pick up the receiver.

"Hello?" I answered.

"Menina Moore, there is a telephone call for you from a Senhor Phillips," said a switchboard operator.

"Please put him through," I said before covering the receiver with my hand and whispering to David, "It's Phillips."

"Miss Moore," said Phillips in my ear. "I hope I'm not disturbing you."

"Not at all," I said. "I was just finishing some work for Mr. Slater."

"Perhaps that is why the switchboard had some difficulty reaching him in his room," said Phillips. "Never mind. I wanted to inquire whether you and Mr. Slater intended to attend the casino this evening. I thought that perhaps we could continue our conversation about flying. You were keen to speak about a particular aviator, I believe."

I finally have the name of the man seated next to Jessup on your flight.

"I can imagine that would be a longer conversation than one might like to have over the telephone," I said.

Are you worried the telephone might be bugged or someone might be listening in?

"I could not agree more, Miss Moore," Phillips replied. "If you'd mind passing the invitation along to Mr. Slater, I should be delighted to meet you at Estoril Casino at half past nine."

"Thank you. I'm certain that time will suit Mr. Slater," I said before saying my goodbyes and turning to an expectant David.

"Well?"

"Phillips seems to have some information about the flight manifest and the man who was seated next to Jessup on the flight from Whitchurch," I said.

"Excellent. Where does he want to meet us?" he asked.

"Dust off your dinner jacket, David," I said. "It looks as though we have another date with Phillips at the casino."

TWENTY-SEVEN

After a quick dinner at our hotel, David and I met in the lobby at nine o'clock, refreshed and dressed in our evening best. In my case, that meant donning the same gown, shoes, wrap, gloves, and evening bag I'd worn the day before. I doubted that anyone save the princess would even notice.

Given that we were on our own and without Carter to act as chauffeur, we took a ludicrously expensive taxi from Lisbon to Estoril and, once we climbed out, made straight for the casino's bar.

After a moment's searching, David said, "There he is," and pointed to a table by one of the bar's huge windows where Phillips sat.

The intelligence agent was alone and, as we approached, I could see that there was what looked like a half-drunk martini next to his left hand. In his right, he was flipping a gold cigarette lighter end to end as he stared into the distance. When he saw us, he straightened and tucked his lighter into his jacket pocket. He rose and greeted us, taking my hand first and then David's.

"Please join me," he said, lifting a finger to signal to one of the waiters circling the room.

I ordered a sidecar while David took a whiskey and soda. As soon as the waiter was gone, Phillips asked in a low voice, "How has your search for Winn progressed?"

"We are making progress," said David.

"Would you care to share any details about that progress?" asked Phillips, annoyance edging into his tone.

In the taxi over, David and I had discussed how we would answer just such a question, knowing that saying anything about Winn's connection to Jessup would require revealing my father's connection to the case and, thus, jeopardize my continued stay in Lisbon. As such, we decided it would be best to hold our proverbial cards close to our chests.

"Winn left very little behind in the way of leads, and few people will admit to knowing him," I started.

Phillips shrugged. "That is the way of informants, I'm afraid."

"Are they all so . . . secretive?" I asked.

"Winn was a special breed, and perhaps a bit too well suited to the work. I found him rather paranoid sometimes. He rarely would agree to meet me indoors, it was always outside where there were more escape routes. About two months into his working for me, he became convinced that the telephone he had been using to speak with me was being monitored, hence the notes in the café and the drop point in the gardens here."

"Do you think that paranoia was justified?" asked David.

"It's hard to say," said Phillips. "Everyone is keeping an eye on everyone else in this city, and it would not be surprising to me if the Abwehr was bugging Winn's telephone if they had a suspicion about the work he was doing for our side. That's why I was so obscure on the telephone to you this afternoon, Miss Moore."

"I guessed as much," I said.

"I am very concerned that Köhler spoke to you yesterday evening," he said. "Approaching a British woman in Lisbon like that shows a boldness I hadn't yet attributed to the Germans."

"I think it's safe to say that in this war, the Germans will stop at very little to meet their ends," I said.

"Speaking of ends," said Phillips, reaching into his jacket pocket and extracting a folded sheet of paper. "Here is the flight manifest you were looking for. The man who sat next to Jessup is Emile Curzon."

"Emile Curzon," I read off before sliding the paper over so David could see it. "Do you know him?"

David shook his head.

"I took the liberty of doing a little digging for you," said Phillips. "Emile Curzon is the pseudonym for Adriene Baudin, a French refugee who arrived in Lisbon in July. It appears that, in his guise as Curzon, he was doing what most refugees try to do—secure the appropriate papers and passage to leave the country. That plan fell apart, however, when he ran into some difficulties when the PVDE connected him to a moniker used in a robbery in one of the border towns before the war. In Portugal alone, it appears he has had several brushes with the law, mostly for low-level crimes."

"If Curzon was a known criminal who was prevented from leaving the country, what was he doing on a flight from Bristol to Lisbon?" I asked.

"That is an excellent question and one that I am certain is sending both the PVDE and our own people into something of a frenzy trying to figure out. But what is even more interesting is that, after leaving Lisbon on an undetermined date, Curzon boarded a flight to return to the city," said Phillips.

"And he was seated next to Jessup," I said.

"That's right," said Phillips.

"Were you able to find any other connections between the two?" I asked.

"None," said Phillips. "As far as I can tell, Jessup appears to have been a law-abiding, hardworking man who had never had any brush with criminality in his life. Quite the foil to Curzon."

"What are the chances that a criminal with a known past would be able to secure himself transport to London and back without help?" I asked, gliding over the fact that David and I knew full well that Jessup wasn't the clean-cut character Phillips believed he was.

"Slim, I would imagine. He would need forged papers and a passport at the very least, not to mention his ticket," said David.

"Places on flights leaving Lisbon are at a premium," agreed Phillips.

"I think Curzon had help, and I think that person hired him to kill Jessup," I said.

"Murder for hire?" asked David.

I nodded. "An assassination."

Phillips scrunched up his face in doubt. "Who would want to assassinate a banker—and a rather junior one at that? Besides, this case didn't fall within our sphere of interest. This is a matter for the PVDE, not your lot. I would appreciate it, Miss Moore, if you would focus your attention on the matter at hand: finding Winn."

"Look, here's Carter," said David, lifting his chin as he looked past my shoulder and saving us all from the tension that was threatening to bubble up.

I twisted in my seat and found the junior agent striding toward us, the light of the casino chandeliers on his light blond hair lending him an angelic quality.

"Carter," said Phillips when the younger man stopped at our table. "I didn't realize you were coming this evening."

"I'm afraid I have the rather poor luck of being here for work rather than leisure," said Carter. "Good evening, Miss Moore. Mr. Slater."

"Is that right?" asked Phillips. "I can't imagine what that would be."

"I'm glad to find you both here," said Carter, ignoring his superior's rather pointed remark to address David and me. "I have some good news about your friend Bauer."

"You were able to secure him a visa?" I asked.

Carter nodded. "When Bauer finally decided that I was not there to drag him back to Austria, he realized that he could help his cause of securing a British visa by disclosing certain details about a project he had been working on before he fled. Something to do with refinement practices for wolfram. Apparently the Germans have been circling because they want him back."

"Why not snatch him off of the street?" asked David.

"Rather cleverly, Bauer has taken steps to let the Portuguese authorities know that if he disappears, he believes it will be because of a German plot to kidnap and return him to Austria," said Carter.

"If he disappears, the PVDE will suspect the Germans and that could trigger a diplomatic incident," I said.

"Precisely," said Carter. "I have made arrangements for Bauer to leave on a ship bound for Southampton tomorrow morning. One of our men will escort him so we can be certain he makes it onboard without any interference."

I breathed out a sigh of relief. "Hopefully he can help our side."

"He was—well, 'grateful' would not even begin to describe it," said Carter.

"Do you think Bauer and his knowledge of refinement practices could be the vital information that Winn was trying to convey to Mr. Phillips before he disappeared?" asked David. I could hear the doubt in my partner's voice, and I understood why. Bauer and his information *were* important, but it wasn't exactly a great secret. Bauer himself had told us he'd been approached by a number of different representatives from different countries.

Carter glanced at Phillips. "Not knowing Winn myself, I can't be certain," he said slowly. "However, I have my doubts."

"Why is that?" I asked.

"I don't believe Bauer is holding any great secrets about the Nazi strategy for this war," said Carter. "He doesn't appear to have been high up enough to be privy to specific plans around how his improvements would be used."

"He didn't reveal any German plots to take over Portugal's wolfram mines then?" I asked.

Carter smiled. "I'm afraid not at this time, no."

"Then why are we sponsoring the man's bid to relocate to Britain?" asked Phillips rather peevishly.

"To ensure that he does not fall into the hands of the Germans," David muttered.

If Phillips heard my partner, he ignored him, instead refocusing his attention on Carter. "Surely your news about Bauer didn't necessitate you coming to the casino tonight."

"No. I've been asking around about Sir Reginald Redfern again," said Carter, his gaze sliding to mine.

"That old chestnut?" asked Phillips. "I thought he left Lisbon weeks ago."

"We don't know that he has left. It's been ten days since a cigarette girl says she saw him here. I thought it might be prudent to reinterview her and some of the other staff I originally spoke to see if they recall him mentioning anything about going away," said Carter.

"Well, good luck with your search, although I can't imagine you'll find much. I had the impression while speaking to him at Princess Petrova's party a few weeks ago that he rarely stays in one place long," said Phillips.

"Thank you, sir," said Carter before giving a short bow and retreating.

I wanted to tell Carter what we'd found out about Sir Reginald having met with Jessup at the Hotel Metrópol's bar, but I risked raising Phillips's suspicions if I followed the younger man too quickly, so instead I said, "We spoke to Fortescue at his hotel today."

"That windbag?" Phillips scoffed. "I'm surprised you wasted your time."

"We were curious about his connection to Winn," I said.

"Winn? Why would Fortescue have any connection to Winn?" asked Phillips.

"It appears that he considered asking Winn for help with a spot of financial difficulty he's in," said David.

"Fortescue has some Egyptian antiquities—or at least the gold that could be melted down from them—that he thought he could sell off. It didn't sound as though Fortescue was terribly bothered with questions of legality," I said. "Were you aware that Winn might have had some connections to the criminal class?"

Phillips pursed his lips as though deciding how much to tell us. It wasn't unheard of for an intelligence agent to recruit someone from the criminal world—or at least connections to it—but it would have cast a certain shadow on Winn's information and therefore Phillips, who had clearly leaned quite heavily on his informant.

Finally, Phillips said, "I suspected he might, but I didn't make anything of it. It's not my job to police Lisbon, and Winn's information was good. Did Fortescue tell you what Winn proposed to do for him?"

"That's just the thing. Fortescue doesn't seem to have ever actually made contact with Winn," I said.

"Well, there you are. There's no need to question Winn's activities after all."

"Except there is," I said. "Princess Petrova herself told me that Winn had a reputation for being able to solve problems."

"The princess?" asked Phillips with obvious surprise.

I nodded.

Phillips let out a long breath. "I've known the princess as long as I've been in Portugal, and I've never once heard her mention Winn."

"She implied that he worked through a sort of whisper network. Rumors that someone needed his help had a way of making it back to him," I said. "Apparently Winn first established contact with her because there was an incident with a jeweler who claimed the items she'd sent for repair had gone missing. Winn was able to facilitate the return of her jewels."

"The princess told you that?" asked Phillips. "She's never mentioned anything of the sort to me. Clearly you are on your way to becoming one of her favorites. Perhaps she'll invite you to tomorrow's soiree."

"I'm here to investigate Winn's disappearance, Mr. Phillips, and that is precisely what I am doing," I said, taking exception to his tone.

He looked amused. "Of course you are."

"The princess is hosting a party tomorrow?" asked David.

"Once a month, on a Sunday. I think she enjoys the slight scandal it causes to hold it on the Lord's Day." Phillips turned to me. "Miss Moore, I would caution you to tread carefully around the princess. She might seem like a frivolous creature, but she has powerful friends."

"I will be careful," I said.

Phillips reached for his glass and drained the last of his drink. "Winn gone. A dead body on a plane, murdered by a French refugee and criminal. The princess bartering in favors. I thought the arrival of you two would help, but it's only made things murkier."

"I understand it seems like that now, but we can promise that we'll figure out who exactly is behind all of this and why and bring them to justice," said David.

"You seem very confident that you'll solve the case," said Phillips with more than a little hint of doubt in his voice.

I smiled. "That's because we always do."

TWENTY-EIGHT

A few minutes later, I extracted myself from the table with the excuse of powdering my nose. However, I was really on the lookout for Carter.

He had mentioned reinterviewing a cigarette girl, and I had assumed that was not random. Sure enough, as I passed into the gaming room, I spotted him, cigarette in hand, hovering against a wall a few tables over from the counter. I wound my way through the tables of spinning roulette wheels and smiled as I caught his eye.

"Contemplating whether you might have a little flutter?" I asked as I approached.

He laughed. "I'm not wealthy enough to even think about a little flutter."

"That's what my friend Moira always says." Of course, Moira could be that wealthy if she wanted to, but that would mean turning her back on her dreams of acting and returning to the cosseted life her parents wanted her to live.

"So, the cigarette girl?" I prompted.

"Yes," he said, straightening and putting out his cigarette in a tall brass ashtray next to him. "I was thinking about something you said yesterday. You told me that Sir Reginald has always been able to charm his way into people's good favor."

"Particularly women," I said.

"When I interviewed the staff at the casino everyone said the same thing: no one had seen Sir Reginald for days. But there was one woman—the cigarette girl—who seemed remarkably disappointed about that fact. I thought perhaps she might have harbored a little . . ."

"*Tendre* for him?" I suggested.

"Quite. When I hinted at it, she clammed right up, but I thought that if a woman were to ask her—"

"She might spill everything to a sympathetic ear. I suppose it's worth a try." I nodded past his shoulder. "Is that her?"

"One and the same," said Carter.

"Right. There's an alcove near the cloakroom. Why don't you wander over there and wait for me?" I suggested.

Carter ambled off, and I set my sights on the cigarette counter.

I waited at the counter, tapping my foot while the man just before me labored over his decision about whether to purchase American or French cigarettes.

"I do apologize, Miss," he said sheepishly. "It's just that I don't know how much longer I'll be able to find French cigarettes, even if these aren't my brand."

I smiled in understanding but, when he finally made his purchase, sent up a little silent cheer.

"I'm very sorry, Menina," said the cigarette girl in near-flawless English as I finally came up to the gold and glass counter. "The gentleman had some difficulty selecting."

"Never mind," I said, waving my hand as though it didn't matter at all.

"What would you like?" she asked.

Given that I didn't smoke, I really didn't care one way or another, but I bit my lip as though laboring over my choice as well.

"Well, let me think. A friend of mine mentioned that you had his brand in stock here. Now what was it . . ." I pretended to try to remember.

"Were they English?" she asked with a patient smile.

I pressed a hand to my temple, knowing that Moira would probably tell me I was doing rather too much acting, but I thought it added to the effect. "Oh, what was it that Sir Reginald said?"

The young woman brightened. "Sir Reginald?"

"Yes, do you know him?"

She dipped her head, her dark brown curls falling over her face, but not before I saw the deep blush in her cheeks. "He came to the casino for a time. He was very kind to me."

A pretty young woman like her? I'm certain he was.

"Oh goodness, that is good luck," I said.

"Sir Reginald always asked for Player's Navy Cut," she said.

"That's it," I said, pretending to remember. "A half dozen of those, please."

I would have to make an excuse about why I didn't have my cigarette case with me, but in that moment I was far more interested in what this young woman remembered of my father.

After she'd counted out the cigarettes and named the price, I said, "It's a good thing you have a better memory than I do. What is your name?"

"Iolanda."

"How do you do, Iolanda? I'm Evelyne," I said as I reached into my handbag for the coins to pay her. "It's a shame really, if only Sir Reginald were here I could have asked him his brand myself."

"He hasn't been to the casino in some time," she said.

"That doesn't seem like him at all. When was the last time you saw Sir Reginald?"

"A week ago Wednesday," she said.

Just before Carter filed his report.

"You seem very certain," I commented.

Her cheeks flushed once again. "Yes. My mother fell ill the next day, and I was home with her. I was worried I might lose my job."

"I'm very sorry to hear that. Has your mother recovered?"

She gave a little nod.

"I'm very glad to hear it. Did Sir Reginald seem in good spirits the last time you saw him?"

"No." She frowned. "Well . . . he seemed worried about something."

"Worried? I wonder why."

She shook her head. "He didn't say."

"Then how do you know he was worried?" I asked.

"Normally when he would buy cigarettes, he would have something nice to say to me. This time, he hardly seemed to recognize me. He seemed . . . I don't know the word for it."

"Preoccupied?" I supplied.

"Yes," she said.

"Was there anyone with him?"

"No. I don't think so," she said. "But he bought more cigarettes than usual."

"That's curious. I wonder why he did that?"

"He said that he might need them," she said.

Might need them? Unlike at home, where, despite not being on the ration, cigarettes could sometimes be difficult to come by if supplies ran short, it didn't seem particularly difficult to procure tobacco in Lisbon. So why would my father need extra cigarettes purchased from a casino counter where they were certain to be more expensive than at a tobacconist's shop?

Unless he knew that he was going away and wouldn't have the time to pick them up in town.

I took the cigarettes from Iolanda, made my excuses about not having a case, and thanked her. Then I navigated back out of the gaming room to the casino's main corridor, avoiding the bar and Phillips's scrutiny entirely.

I found Carter in the alcove, just as I'd proposed.

"You don't happen to smoke Player's Navy Cut, do you?" I asked as I sank down into the chair across from him.

He shook his head. "Craven A."

"Shame." I'd have to find someone else to foist the cigarettes onto.

"Any joy?" he asked.

"I think you were right about Iolanda having some affection for Sir Reginald. She couldn't stop blushing when I spoke about him."

"Did she notice anything unusual about his behavior the last time she saw him?" asked Carter.

"Actually, yes. She said that he bought rather a lot of cigarettes. Many more than usual. Do you think there is the possibility that he knew that he was going out of town and was stocking up?"

Carter frowned. "That would be an expensive way to buy a large number of cigarettes."

"My father has never been known for his prudence, but I am inclined to agree with you. I think he was in a hurry. There's something else you should know. David and I believe that, when he was last in town, Jessup spoke to my father."

"What business did Sir Reginald have with a murdered man?"

As quickly as I could, I explained about Jessup, the false-bottom attaché case, and the trunk calls.

"I believe that my father intended to have me remove the jewels from the safe deposit box in London, deliver them to Morrison, who would sell them on, and then have Jessup bring the money back to Lisbon in his secret compartment," I finished.

Carter crossed his arms and looked up at the ceiling for a moment, presumably thinking over everything I had just told him.

"I'm tempted to say that Sir Reginald might have fled because of Morrison and Jessup's deaths, but the timeline doesn't line up. Sir Reginald disappeared days before Morrison died," he said.

"I don't think my father fled. I think he left Lisbon to wait out Jessup's return from London."

"Why?" he asked.

I shrugged. "Everywhere I go, everyone tells me how expensive the hotels are and how difficult it is to live in this city without money. I suspect Sir Reginald was feeling the pinch and decided to hide out somewhere less expensive. The question is, where did he go?"

Carter seemed to mull this over before saying, “Give me a few hours to make some telephone calls, and I might be able to find out. Down the road from my office, there is a place called Café Pereira. Meet me there at eleven o’clock tomorrow morning and I’ll let you know what I find.”

TWENTY-NINE

I left Carter with the promise that I would see him at Café Pereira in the morning and then went to find the facilities closest to the gaming room to reapply my lipstick and lend credence to my excuse for leaving David and Phillips in the bar.

I pushed open the door and found myself in a sitting room awash in pale pink velvet and gold-framed mirrors. Two large vases of hothouse lilies framed either side of the vanity where three ladies sat, laughing and chattering away in French as they dabbed powder on their noses.

I sat down on one of the tufted velvet stools on the opposite end of the long vanity mirror as I could and snapped open my handbag. I was just touching up my carmine-red lipstick when I heard a woman say, "Miss *Moore*, what a delightful surprise to see you here."

I looked up in the mirror and found Princess Petrova standing at my shoulder, a smirk playing over her lips, no doubt at her own cleverness for using my cover name.

"Princess," I said, making to rise.

"Oh, do keep sitting," she said, perching on the stool to my right. "I came here for a bit of respite from all of those vultures out there."

"Vultures?" I asked.

"When you have been in Lisbon as long as I have and you have a certain reputation for entertaining, you acquire unwanted hangers-on," she said, extracting a gold compact from her bag and beginning to powder her nose. "I see that you're with Mr. Phillips again tonight."

"He has been very kind during my stay in Lisbon."

"I'm certain he has," she said, a rather sly tone to her words.

"I didn't mean to imply . . ." I started to protest, fearing she'd mistaken my comment as having some sort of hidden meaning, but I stopped when she began to laugh.

"Oh, don't worry yourself. I've seen what Mr. Phillips's taste runs to, and it isn't you. Let's just say you lack a certain amount of softness about . . . well, everywhere."

"Does he have something of a reputation?" I asked, remembering the waiter in Café Real that afternoon remarking that a woman sometimes joined Phillips for his morning coffee.

"Oh, he does. But many of these men dispatched from London with conveniently nondescript jobs do." She caught my eye in the mirror. "He also has a wife."

"Oh? He's never mentioned her."

She dabbed at her forehead. "She's back in England. She's exactly what you might expect, of course. All finishing school manners and perfect dinner parties, although I hear she does rather enjoy a gimlet or two more than she should most evenings. You might know her. Nancy Phillips?"

"I don't." But I wondered whether that was one of the reasons Phillips was so reluctant to see David's and my arrival in Lisbon. So much of the intelligence services and the rest of the government were full of grown-up public-school boys who all knew one another either personally or by reputation. If word about Phillips's romantic adventures in Lisbon got back to his wife . . .

"Does he ever bring these women out to your parties?" I asked.

The princess laughed. "You are attributing far too much courage to the man. He would never be so bold as that because too many people might recognize him. He did have a very attractive blond French girl at the casino a few months ago, but he told everyone who would listen that she was a friend of the family and he was looking after her while she was waiting for a visa to Britain. Not that any of us believed it for one moment.

"No, recently Phillips has been running around with a little brunette. Pretty in a common sort of way—aren't they all?—although she wears far too much makeup. She works in a restaurant or boutique or something like that."

"You've seen her?" I asked.

"From a distance. I was driving by a grubby little café, and there they were making love for all the world to see. Right out on the road at one of the tables when it was still warm enough to sit outside like a third-rate Casanova!" the princess cackled.

"If you disapprove of Mr. Phillips's . . . dalliances, I'm surprised that you invite him into your home," I said.

"Oh, if I struck everyone from my guest list who had a 'dalliance,' as you call them, my soirees would be a veritable ghost town. No, I am happy to overlook a few things here and there. Goodness, last time I threw a soiree someone walked off with the keys to my country house in Valverde."

"Did you report them missing to the police?" I asked.

She gave me a look out of the corner of her eye. "The last thing anyone wants in Lisbon is to bring the police to their door. No, I have no doubt the keys will turn up when someone realizes their mistake." The princess snapped her compact closed. "After all, who is perfect?"

"That is a very trusting philosophy."

"Yes, well, I will also be restricting guests to the ground floor in the future. And staff will be stationed at the staircases to make sure that everyone observes that rule. You should come. Bring that Mr. Slater with you tomorrow evening. He looks as though he could use a stiff drink and a little fun. The house is the Villa de Pietro in Estoril. A mad Italian built it for his mistress who ran off and married the son of a car manufacturer and died in a smashup on her honeymoon. It was all terribly romantic and tragic. Any taxi driver will know the way."

"That is very generous of you," I said, not entirely certain that, if we hadn't been mid-investigation, I would want to spend any more time with Princess Petrova.

"Princess," I said, stopping her as she began to put her evening bag together again, "there is something I wanted to ask you."

"For the daughter of an old friend, I am an open book," she said.

I very much doubted that was the case.

"When I asked whether you knew a man named Michael Jessup, you told me no. However, when I spoke to Mr. Fortescue, he said he believed you knew Jessup."

"Did he?" she asked, her voice positively chilly.

"In fact, he was rather insistent about the fact," I said, recalling that Fortescue had told me Jessup knew the princess well enough to believe her to be—what had he called her?—*a trumped-up wealthy woman trying to stave off boredom by pretending to have a connection to Winn.*

The princess's eyes hardened. "A word of advice, Miss Moore. I would not go through life trusting the word of liars who inflate their own sense of importance by concocting stories about their betters."

"Do you mean Fortescue or Jessup?" I asked.

"I don't know any man named Jessup, but given what you have told me I would say my advice pertains to both."

The princess was lying—I had no doubt about that—but what I didn't know was why.

Rising, she leaned a hand on the vanity to bend down, dropping her voice as she said, "There's very little that escapes my notice in Lisbon, Miss Redfern, and I can be a very good friend to those who need one. Your father knew that. I could be your friend too, but I trust my friends not to interfere in matters they don't understand."

Then she sauntered off, the pearl-gray silk of her evening gown shimmering in the sitting room lights.

When I returned to the casino bar, I found my partner sitting alone at the table.

"What happened to Phillips?" I asked.

"A waiter came up with a note. Apparently there's a telephone call for him. He sends his apologies," said David.

"Well, while you have been thinking about your second whiskey, I've been doing a little work," I said before relaying my conversation with both the cigarette girl and Carter. Then I told him about my conversation with Princess Petrova and her second denial of having any association with Jessup.

"Do you believe her?" asked David.

"Not even the littlest bit," I said. "I wonder if that nullifies our invitation to her soiree tomorrow."

"Invitation?"

"Yes, she told me to bring you along."

His brows jumped. "Your employer?"

I laughed. "I don't think the princess ever believed that I was your secretary. Not since she recognized me as Sir Reginald's daughter."

"We should go to her party," he said.

"At this rate, I'm going to have to purchase another dress," I said with a sigh. "I doubt the SIU's budget will stretch to that."

"It didn't stretch the first time," said David, taking a last drink of his whiskey.

I shot him a look. "What do you mean?"

"I bought you the dress," he said.

"David, you can't buy me a dress!" I protested.

"I thought you knew," he said as though it hardly mattered.

"Of course I didn't know. I wouldn't have said yes if I had."

I couldn't accept such a generous gift from my partner—especially when I considered that it wasn't just a gown but shoes, a wrap, a handbag, and evening gloves as well.

"Consider it a thank-you for being the one who was shot last month," he said with a smirk.

"Well, when you say it like that . . ."

He set his glass down and looked around. "Do you have a taste for gambling?"

"Not particularly," I admitted. "A junior copywriter's salary at an advertising agency never stretched too much."

"That's what you did before the war, isn't it?" he asked.

"Yes," I said, although we both knew that he would have learned that from my file when he'd interrogated me the first time we met.

"Do you think you'll go back when this is all done?" he asked.

I blew out a long breath. "I really haven't given it much thought since my change in employer."

Mr. Fletcher had come into my life and plucked me off the line at a munitions factory where I was doing my war work, having quit my copywriting job not long after the declaration of war. I had no idea I was auditioning for a place in the Special Investigations Unit, but when I learned that I could train and become a field agent, I'd jumped at the opportunity. Now, after everything I'd been through and everything I'd seen, I couldn't imagine myself going back to my old life.

"I don't know if it would be a fit any longer," I said.

The right side of David's mouth quirked up. "No, too much has changed, hasn't it?"

He held my gaze for a moment, and I had the sense that he wanted to say something, but then he gave a tiny shake of his head as though deciding against it. "Shall we go?"

"I think we should," I said.

The day and all the revelations had left me suddenly tired, and I wanted nothing more than to crawl into bed.

We made our way out to the entryway, where more people were coming in rather than leaving at this hour.

"I hope I don't fall asleep in the taxi," I said as we gathered my wrap and his coat.

"I'll find us one," said David. "You can stay here and keep warm while you wait."

I shook my head. "It shouldn't take long. One of the ones dropping passengers off will be glad of the business back to Lisbon, I'm certain. I'll come with you."

A doorman held the door open for us, and we stepped out into the cold night air. I pulled my wrap a little closer around my body, but I couldn't help my shiver. Without asking, David took off the coat he'd just donned and deposited it gently on my shoulders.

"Thank you," I said.

He smiled. "My pleasure."

I snuggled into the warmth of the coat while breathing in the scent of neroli and bergamot before catching myself. This was David. Not a handsome man in a dinner jacket taking me home at the end of an evening. *My partner.*

"Evelyne," he called, his hand on the open door of a taxi.

I took a step forward, but something in the casino's drive caught my eye. A man was poking his head around a hedge as though waiting to see whether he would be noticed. But it wasn't just any man. It was the man from the plane.

Emile Curzon.

Jessup's murderer.

THIRTY

Curzon turned, as though sensing that someone was watching him, and locked eyes with me, and I knew in an instant that he recognized me from the aeroplane.

"Curzon?" I called out.

The man darted out of the hedge and began to sprint down the drive.

"Wait!" I cried, throwing off my layers and dropping my handbag as I raced after him.

"Evelyne!" I heard David shout behind me.

"Stop!" I shouted after Curzon.

Before the gap began to open between us, I knew that I would never catch him. He was dressed in a dark suit and—most importantly—proper shoes, while I was trotting along on what amounted to three-inch nails.

"Bloody heels," I cursed under my breath as I picked my skirts up a little higher.

At the bottom of the casino's drive, Curzon darted around the corner, and moments later, a huge car swung around and nearly drove straight into me. I dove out of the way and into the flower bed, crushing several plants underfoot, before the coast was clear and I could hit the drive once again.

"Evelyne!" David shouted as I reached the bottom of the drive and a lorry trundled by. "What are you doing?"

I screamed in frustration because, in the road ahead of me, I saw Curzon swing himself up onto the lorry's running board and wave a cheeky hand in my direction.

"Evelyne," David prompted again as he came to a stop beside me.

"That was Curzon," I gasped out. "I saw him while you were securing a taxi, but he got away."

"Curzon was here?" asked David, incredulous.

"Yes, and if I wasn't dressed like a bloody wedding cake, I might have caught him."

"It's a wonder you didn't turn an ankle," said David, peering down at my feet. I dropped my skirt to hide my shoes, and my partner straightened. "What was he doing here?"

"I don't know, but he certainly didn't want to be caught," I grumbled as the rapid scrape of shoes on concrete filled my ears. I turned and saw Phillips jogging up to us, his brow etched with concern.

"What happened?" he demanded as he slid to a stop. "A waiter just ran up to me and said that the couple I had been sharing drinks with ran off down the drive in a tear, shouting all the way."

"Curzon was here," I said.

"Evelyne spotted him when I was negotiating with a cab driver. She gave chase, but he had a good start on her," said David.

"He jumped on the back of a lorry and spirited himself away," I finished.

Phillips gaped at me. "You chased the suspect in a murder investigation? Miss Moore, surely for your own safety—"

"I think, Mr. Phillips, that you'll find that Evelyne is more than capable of taking care of herself," David interjected.

"This *is* my job," I pointed out.

"Quite." Phillips cleared his throat. "Nevertheless . . ."

"What was Curzon doing here?" I asked, breezing past his awkwardness.

"What do you mean?" asked Phillips.

"Presumably Curzon is intelligent enough to know that the police would be looking for him. Why risk showing his face in a place like Estoril Casino where there are so many people about?" I asked.

"Evelyne has a point. It would make more sense for him to go to ground," said David.

"He's a criminal and a murderer. Surely you don't expect him to behave in a rational manner," said Phillips.

That was just the thing. From what little I'd seen of Curzon's behavior, he had been extremely logical. Even if he had the help of someone else, as seemed likely, he had managed to slip into Britain without detection, seated himself next to Jessup on a BOAC flight, chosen a method of murder that was silent, and kept himself calm and collected as he deplaned with the rest of us. Who knew how long the body might have remained undetected if I hadn't forgotten my book and been, admittedly, more than a little nosy?

"I want to check the hedge I first saw him look out of," I said.

"At this time of night? You won't be able to see a thing," said Phillips.

I reached up and undid one of *Maman*'s pearl earrings from my lobe before dropping it into my evening bag. "I'm certain there is a casino employee who would be happy to lend a torch to a lady who has lost her earring."

Phillips stared at me long and hard and then shook his head as though admitting defeat. "Fine."

While Phillips returned to his table, muttering about the bill, David and I scoured the bushes and the surrounding area for anything Curzon might have dropped that would give us an idea of where he had been or where he might be staying. When all we found were broken branches and a few footprints that abruptly stopped at a paved path in the garden, we were forced to admit defeat.

David negotiated a taxi to take us back to the Hotel Tivoli and, after handing the torch back to a slightly confused doorman, slid into the back seat of the cab next to me with a weary sigh.

"I could not agree more," I said, as I reached down to rub at the back of my aching ankle where I was certain a blister was forming thanks to my impromptu display of athletic prowess.

"This case . . ."

"Feels as though every which way we look we have nothing," I finished his thought.

"What *do* we know?" asked David.

I glanced at the back of the taxi driver's head and decided that caution was probably the best course of action as I began to wearily count off our leads on my fingers. "Mr. W. disappeared eleven days ago after not attending a meeting he arranged with our mutual friend, Mr. P.," I said, reviewing what we knew about Winn from Phillips. "No one will admit to having seen him or knowing where he is since, but I overheard Mr. F. badgering a prominent lady about the fact the late Mr. J. stole from him," I continued, recalling my overheard conversation between Fortescue and the princess. "Subsequently, we found out that Mr. F. wanted Mr. J. to help relieve himself of some of the trinkets he brought with him from abroad."

David snorted, no doubt amused by the idea of Fortescue politely asking Jessup to help rid himself of his stolen antiquities.

"We know that Mr. J. telephoned a London jeweler, Mr. M., on the last day of every trip he made to Lisbon, and that he did this after meeting with my father," I said. "Add to it that my father also hasn't been seen since the same week Mr. W. disappeared and we have a very concerning situation indeed."

"Meanwhile Mr. J. and Mr. M. have been . . . removed from the game by the man you pursued tonight," said David about the murders, "but we suspect that our runner had help in the form of documents, planning, and possibly payment."

"Which makes it sound as though our runner was a paid employee of sorts," I said.

"And yet the more we learn, the further it feels we are from finding Mr. W. or locating the runner and his employer," he said.

"I forgot to mention in the middle of everything, I'm meeting with Carter tomorrow down the road from his office. He believes he might have an idea of where my father has been these past weeks," I said.

"Really?" David asked. "What is his theory?"

I shook my head. "He said he needed to make several telephone calls before he would share that with me, and given our surroundings, I didn't think it wise to press."

"Then let's hope he has more to say tomorrow," he said.

THIRTY-ONE

David and I fell into a silence that lasted until the taxi pulled up to the Hotel Tivoli and a doorman ran out to open my door for me. However, David waved the man off and helped me out of the car himself.

When I winced with my first step, David grabbed my elbow. "Are you hurt?"

"Just my pride, but I do seem to have acquired a rather pesky blister chasing Curzon," I said.

"Here." He tucked my arm into the crook of his elbow. "Lean on me."

At one point, I might have pulled away just to prove that I would not be felled by something as insignificant as a blister, but my ankle hurt and my freshly healed gunshot wound was sore enough that I could feel it tug with every movement. I let my partner take some of my weight as we passed into the hotel lobby. The late hour meant it was emptier than I'd seen it, although a party dressed in evening clothes laughed as they spilled out of the doors leading to the hotel bar.

"I suppose there's very little we can do the rest of the evening except try to get a good night's sleep," I said with a sigh.

David nodded and leaned in to say, "I'll speak to Phillips about working some of his contacts to find out more about Emile Curzon's known associates in the morning. Someone must have helped him with his documents."

"Hopefully tomorrow will find Phillips in a better mood."

"I suspect in the bright light of day, he'll realize that anything that can help us find Winn and rid him of us will be worth it," he said. "Even more so if Winn's disappearance proves to be connected to Jessup's murder."

We stopped in front of the lift doors and waited for them to slide open. I glanced at David, catching his eye. For a moment, I saw how it might have been if he had just been a man I'd met at a casino escorting me home, rather than my partner. If things had been simpler.

"Would you like me to see you to your door?" he asked.

"Thank you," I said, my voice hardly a whisper above the sound of the lift doors sliding open.

The attendant stepped aside to let us in, and after David gave him my floor, we rode up in silence, my hand still on his elbow. I stared at the numbers ticking by as we climbed, knowing I should step away, severing the connection between the two of us, but the thought of that left me bereft.

There was a soft ding when we reached my floor, and the doors slid open. I thanked the attendant and stepped out. It was just a short walk to my hotel door, but when David and I stopped, neither of us spoke. I risked a glance at him and found him looking at me with such focus that I had to drop my gaze. Instead, I opened my evening bag to search for my key.

"Here it is," I said, pulling the key free and glancing up, a part of me hoping that his expression would have returned to the normal calm neutrality I was used to and finding myself profoundly disappointed when it had.

He took a step back. "I should go check my messages with the front desk."

"Of course."

When he gave me a little half bow, something cracked in me. It was the sort of gesture a man might make to a woman he had only just met. Distant. Formal.

I wished him good night. Then I jammed my key into the lock, twisting before I could call out to him or do something equally foolish. I half stumbled into my room, shutting the door swiftly behind me. I leaned against it, catching my breath. I wished Moira were there to listen to every foolish thought racing through my mind. She would have been sympathetic to a point before holding up a hand and telling me to stop being ridiculous. David Poole was just a man, after all, and it was never wise to make oneself ridiculous over a man.

I was tired and frustrated, and both of those things were compromising my judgment.

Pushing off the door, I unbuckled the straps on my heeled sandals and eased off my shoes. Then I sat down on the bed and let myself fall back onto the covers, exhausted.

This case . . .

As I lay there, I turned over all the things David and I had spoken about in the cab, holding each up and examining it from every angle I could think of. It felt as though all the jigsaw pieces were laid out in front of me plain as day but, no matter what I did, I couldn't make any of them fit.

A knock on the door pulled me out of my contemplation. I glanced at the time. It was nearing half past midnight. The witching hour.

With a groan, I hauled myself to my feet and went to open the door only to find David standing before me.

"You're back," I said.

"I think the events of tonight merit a drink." He held up a bottle of whiskey in one hand and two glasses in his other. "Do you mind?"

I pointed to the bottle. "Did you liberate that from the hotel bar?"

"If by 'liberate' you mean 'bought,' then yes," he said.

"Well, it's a good thing then that I never turn down good whiskey when it's on offer."

I stepped aside to let him in and watched as he strode over to the desk, set the glasses down, and poured out a measure of whiskey for each of us.

"Did you have any messages?" I asked, taking a glass from him and cradling it in my hand.

"Nothing, although I'm not entirely surprised. Mrs. White usually trusts me to report when there is news."

"That must be nice."

He huffed a laugh. "A few more missions, and she won't be able to deny how good you are."

It was a simple statement of faith in my abilities, but it tugged at my heartstrings nonetheless.

"Thank you," I said quietly.

He stared at his glass and then took a drink, as though summoning courage. "If we hadn't met in this . . . line of work, do you think we would have been friends?"

"Is that what we are? Friends?"

My question was genuine. David was my partner, yes, but there was more to it than that. There must be.

"I'd like to think we're friends. Perhaps . . . My apologies," he said, rubbing his eyes with his free hand. "I think the lack of sleep is beginning to weigh on me."

I peered at him, noting the bruises under his eyes were deeper than usual. "When did you last sleep?"

"On our flight."

"When did you last sleep *properly*?"

He leaned back, looking up at the ceiling as though counting the days. "Tuesday?"

"David Poole, go to bed," I said firmly.

"Spies—and investigations—wait for no one, Evelyne. You know that."

"They do if the spies are practically dead on their feet. I'll see you for breakfast at a reasonable hour." I reached out, intending to take his arm and guide him to the door, but he turned toward me and my hand connected with his chest. Before I could move, his hand was on mine, pressing it in place.

"What do you consider reasonable?" he asked.

For a moment, my mind went blank. All I could think about was his warmth and how good it felt to touch him properly. My fingers tightened a little in the wool of his dinner jacket, almost as though I wanted more.

"Evelyne . . ."

I looked up, lips parted—

All at once, the realization of what I—we?—were about to do slammed into me, and I jumped back.

"I am so sorry. I should have thought about your shoulder—"

David's brow furrowed, and he took a half step toward me. "You haven't done anything to my shoulder."

I fumbled with my glass, splashing a drop of whiskey onto my hand. "But you were hurt and—"

Another step, slow as though he was certain I would bolt. "Strangely enough, my first thought is not for my shoulder at the moment."

He stopped in front of me, a little too close for me to relax. Even with my height, I was forced to tip my head back to look at him, fully aware of how close this once again brought my lips to his. At this late hour, his hair had become a little loosened from whatever held it so perfectly in place and a lock hung down over his eye.

"David . . ."

He lifted his hand and used the very tip of his finger to pick up one of the ties of my dress where it fell from the knot at my neck. I sucked in a breath as he brushed my skin. His fingers followed the length of silk upward until they rested on the knot.

"Are you afraid?" he asked.

"I-I would never want to hurt you," I whispered.

"You couldn't." Then he gave one of those little half laughs I'd come to expect when he was amused and bemused in equal measure. "Actually I suspect you could. Quite badly."

"David." If he wouldn't, I was going to have to stop whatever this was before it became something we couldn't step back from. Before it could change everything.

He ran his fingers back down my dress's tie, the tug of slight pressure on the silk turning the bare skin of my back electric. I closed my eyes and clenched my fists as his hand traveled lower and lower.

He let the tie drop.

"You're about to be very practical, aren't you, Evelyne?"

"Reasonable," I countered softly. "There is a difference. We're on assignment."

When I opened my eyes, I read the hesitation in his expression. I thought for a moment that he might damn reason and sensibility and *do* something, but instead he gave a little nod and stepped back.

"I think, if you don't mind," he said, reaching around me to take up the bottle of whiskey from the desk, "I'll take this with me."

I watched him open my hotel room's door and let himself out, leaving me standing barefoot in my evening gown, wishing very much that there was a bottle still for me.

THIRTY-TWO

For all my insistence that he rest, I slept poorly after David left my room. At first, I'd been too hot. Then I'd been too restless. When finally, at four o'clock in the morning, I decided that the entire exercise was futile, I turned on the light to read.

I'm certain I could have come up with any number of reasons for my poor night's sleep, but I knew that the real culprit was David—or rather my reaction to him. Since we'd become partners in September, I'd seen our relationship as one bounded by a thick line of sand. For the last two months, I had been happy to stay on the professional side of that line despite all the teasing I'd received from Moira, who had witnessed a grand total of one interaction between David and me and declared that he would be the perfect distraction for me. However, in the early hours of that morning in my hotel room when he'd looked at me with those weary eyes as though all he wanted was to drink me in, I'd almost sprinted right past that line and straight into his arms.

Enough.

I was at risk of making myself look ridiculous, and I wanted no part of it.

At half past six, I put my book aside, stood, stretched, and immediately regretted it. I felt as though I'd been run over by the lorry

Curzon had absconded on. Despite my training with the SOE, which involved quite a bit of running, climbing walls, and leaping over obstacles, my little adventure in heeled evening sandals the night before had left my calves burning and my gunshot wound aching. After checking to make sure I had only aggravated the wound and not reopened it, I eased myself stiffly into as hot a bath as I could stand and let the water soothe my tired muscles.

After soaking for so long the water went tepid, I set about washing my face, brushing my hair into place, and generally making myself presentable to the world. A peek out from behind the hotel room's curtains told me that yesterday's sun had transformed into a fine mist, so I swept my hair up into an approximation of a twist and pinned it savagely in place. Then I pulled on my secretary's uniform of blouse, skirt, jacket, and stockings, wincing a little as I eased my sensible leather shoes over my blistered heel.

Deciding that eight o'clock was a reasonable enough hour for breakfast, I let myself out of the hotel room and went to the lift.

As with the day before, I found David already seated in the dining room, just starting his meal. I dropped down into the seat across from him and almost immediately a waiter was by my side with an offer of coffee. I accepted gratefully and, as he hurried away, said to David, "I don't know how I'm going to go back to rationed tea and coffee when we go home."

As opening bids go after nearly kissing a man, I thought it wasn't half bad. It showed I was willing to see past our near-indiscretion and pretend as though nothing at all had happened except a drink between colleagues. David seemed to agree because he didn't drop onto one knee and declare his undying love for me but instead said, "Twice-boiled tea leaves do lose their punch by comparison."

"Did you sleep?" I asked.

"Well enough," he said. "You?"

"Oh, very well," I lied through my teeth.

The waiter brought my coffee, and I ordered ham, eggs, and toast.

I was just about to take my first sip when an increasingly familiar voice called out, "Menina Moore."

I let my head fall back a fraction and set down my coffee with a heaving sigh.

"Who is that?" asked David, twisting to look over his shoulder.

"Camargo," I muttered before pasting a smile on my face and turning to find the officer closing the gap to our table. "Good morning, Capitão. I don't believe you've had the pleasure of meeting my employer, Mr. Slater."

"Ah yes. I believe one of your juniors interrogated me," said David.

"Interrogated? We merely asked questions, Senhor. A very reasonable thing to do given the circumstances."

"You detained my secretary for an unnecessary length of time," said David, stepping neatly into the role of annoyed employer.

"Sometimes justice is inconvenient." Camargo nodded to our table. "May I join you?"

When neither of us moved to stop him, he snapped his fingers and a waiter hurried over with a spare chair.

"I'm surprised that they allow you to sit on the job," I observed as Camargo lowered himself to seating while another waiter rushed to place a cup of coffee in front of the PVDE officer.

Camargo made a noise in the back of his throat that, if I wasn't mistaken, was slightly amused. "Do you have a very busy day ahead of you both visiting winemakers?"

"I would have to defer to my secretary," said David, continuing to play into his cover rather neatly.

"And I would have to consult Mr. Slater's diary," I said with a tight smile. I was doing a poor job of playing the breathless, innocent secretary, but I was still furious at myself for losing Curzon and I hadn't had any coffee or tea yet, so I hardly qualified as awake.

"Your secretary does not appear to be doing a very good job of keeping your appointments, Senhor Slater," said Camargo. "She said she missed a message about a meeting being rearranged at the Hotel Metrópol yesterday afternoon."

"She does her best," said David, which made me want to elbow him in the ribs very much.

"Were you looking for me, Capitão, or were you just stopping by to sample the Hotel Tivoli's excellent coffee?" I asked. It was plain that Camargo didn't believe for one moment that David and I were representing Berry Bros. & Rudd on a wine-buying trip.

This time the captain did chuckle. "There are not many women who would be so unwise as to question a PVDE officer's motives, Menina. I came as a courtesy."

"Did you?" I asked, hardly believing him.

"I understand that you were at the casino yesterday evening," he said.

"As I expect half of the guests at this hotel were," I said.

He smiled a little in acknowledgment. "I have had an interesting morning speaking to members of the casino staff. Several of them recall you chasing after a man like—what do you English say?—a madwoman."

I straightened my shoulders. "That is the expression, yes. Earlier in the evening, someone tried to grab my bag. I thought that he was the man."

"Is that right?" Camargo asked, glancing at David. "Was this in the casino?"

"It was on the grounds. Miss Moore went for a stroll," said David, playing along with my lie.

"I sometimes become lightheaded because of the smoke," I said.

"And did anyone see you walking in the garden?" Camargo asked.

"I don't recall seeing anyone. I was only out for a few minutes. My headache dissipated as soon as I was in the fresh air," I said.

"It must have if you ran after the man who you believe tried to steal your handbag," said Camargo.

"Yes," I said slowly. "It was foolish of me, really, but my instinct was to try to catch him."

"Not many women would do that in full evening dress, if you don't mind me saying so," he replied.

The aching blister on my heel would agree.

"If that is all, Capitão . . ."

Camargo held up a finger to stop me. "Just one more thing, Menina. Have you ever heard the name Emile Curzon?"

I was fortunate that my training had schooled me in how to control my expressions, otherwise I might have given everything away right then and there. "Should I have?"

"Perhaps," said the officer. "He was seated next to the man who was killed on your aeroplane."

I gasped, back to the Miss Moore act once again. "And you think that is the same man I chased after?"

"I can't be certain, but I must entertain all possibilities," said Camargo.

"Well, I hope you catch him," I said.

"Oh, of that you can be certain," he said. "He was found dead on the beach in Caxias just before dawn this morning. He was shot in the head."

It took everything in me not to turn to David, jaw open. First Jessup's neck was broken on a plane, then Morrison was killed in an air raid shelter in London, and now Curzon was shot on a beach in Caxias. A banker turned smuggler, a jeweler turned fence, and a criminal turned assassin, all dead.

"The discovery was made just in time for the newspapers," continued Camargo. "Perhaps you saw the article?"

"I haven't looked at a newspaper this morning," I said. "I'm afraid my Portuguese is very poor."

When Camargo glanced at David, my partner shook his head. "I haven't seen this morning's paper either."

"Does this make your investigation more difficult?" I asked, trying very much to sound like a young woman ignorant of these matters.

"I think, given the circumstances, it closes the case of Senhor Jessup but leaves me with the question of who killed Senhor Curzon," said Camargo.

A waiter chose that very opportune moment to appear with David's and my breakfasts.

"I think that is enough talk about shooting and killing people, Capitão. Miss Moore and I do need to eat before we start our day," said David.

Camargo looked rather unconvinced by the idea that either of us would be unable to handle conversation about death over the breakfast table, but nonetheless he said, "I shall leave you both to your meal."

David and I both waited until Camargo was out of earshot before looking at one another.

"Curzon dead too? Three bodies?" I asked. "This feels like someone tying up loose ends."

"And they're moving faster. Something's frightened them," said David.

I glanced at my watch. "I am meeting with Carter in about two hours. What will you do this morning?"

"Perhaps my secretary should tell me what is on the agenda," he said. "Or is Camargo right that you aren't a very good secretary after all?"

When I looked up, I found him wearing a cheeky smile, the awkwardness of that early morning's near-kiss gone.

"You are fortunate that your secretary hasn't seen fit to take her fork and jab you in the hand with it," I muttered, perhaps being a little more surly than necessary because how on earth could he simply move on as though nothing had happened between us? That is to say, in a way, nothing had, but it hadn't *felt* like that.

David laughed. "That would not be very in keeping with your cover."

"Oh, I wouldn't say that. I'm certain there are secretaries who want nothing more than to inflict cutlery-related injuries on their employers."

"That might be so, but I'd still advise resisting," he said. "To answer your question, I might go for a walk to clear my head. I need to think."

"Let's hope that walk of yours clears some cobwebs, because the death toll has gone from two to three, and David? I don't think we're any closer to finding the murderer."

THIRTY-THREE

It was half past eleven, I was almost done with my third cup of coffee for the day, and my nerves were positively jangling from its effects when I looked about Café Pereira with a sigh. It seemed as though Carter wouldn't be joining me after all.

I pushed up the sleeve of my cardigan and glanced at my watch for what felt like the tenth time in the past five minutes. Good manners said that Carter was well past the bounds of polite but explainable lateness.

I had yet to visit Phillips's and Carter's offices, but David had told me where it was just in case I had need of it. If I found Carter sitting at his desk, finishing one of those telephone calls he had been so intent on making the evening before, all the better. I would be annoyed but at least I would no longer be worried.

I was just fishing out a few escudos from my handbag when a shadow passed over my table.

"We meet again, Miss Moore."

What was it about that day that was bringing all the men I didn't want to see out of the woodwork?

Slowly and deliberately, I snapped my coin purse closed and relatched my handbag before fixing my smile and lifting my chin. "Herr Köhler, a pleasure, I'm certain."

The Abwehr agent lifted his black Homburg and smirked. "I am glad to hear it."

"I would invite you to sit down, but—" I stopped myself as the man unbuttoned his long black overcoat, pulled out the chair across from me, and sat. "Apparently it doesn't matter whether I invite you or not."

"Miss Moore, I have heard some very distressing reports that, despite our little conversation at the casino two nights ago, you persist in asking a number of delicate questions of people who find them upsetting," he said.

"Is that right? And I suppose these people have spoken to you about this directly?"

"Not in so many words." He pulled out a cigarette case and extracted a cigarette before offering me one.

"No, thank you."

"This is the second time you have refused a cigarette from me, Miss Moore. Do you not smoke?" he asked, putting the case away.

"I don't."

A flame jumped to life from the silver lighter he'd extracted from his pocket. "Herr Hitler would approve."

"I assure you, Herr Hitler's opinion on the matter of women smoking never entered my mind."

That earned me a tight smile.

"Back to the issue at hand, Miss Moore. I realize you have not been in Lisbon long, so allow me to educate you. A young lady such as yourself would do well not to ask too many questions of anyone, particularly when she is a member of British intelligence," he said.

I sat back in my chair and crossed my hands over my knee, prepared to do battle. "I'm not with British intelligence."

"No?" He cocked his head to one side. "If that is the case, you are in the very unfortunate situation of having attracted the attention of people who believe you are."

"Tell me, Herr Köhler, who are these people and why are they so distressed about a few simple questions?"

He wagged a finger at me. "Ah, Miss Moore, that is not playing fair, and I understand the English pride themselves on their fairness. 'Not very cricket'—isn't that what you say?"

"Not quite cricket," I corrected him.

He flicked a hand through the air, dismissing me and my knowledge of my own country's idioms.

"Herr Köhler, why exactly have you taken such an interest in me since I arrived in Lisbon? There must be other young British women you could follow around and corner in cafés if you wanted to."

"But none so pretty as you," he said.

My hands tightened on my knee as I resisted the urge to flip over the table.

"I also believe we have some mutual interests, Miss Moore. Even mutual friends," he continued.

"Would one of those friends happen to be a rather lovely if haughty switchboard operator from the Hotel Metrópol named Luiza Barbosa?" I asked.

For the first time since he'd accosted me in the casino, Köhler looked a little taken aback. However, that was swiftly replaced by a sly smile. "I cannot imagine what you mean."

"I saw the two of you in a café on Rossio yesterday," I said. "I thought you looked rather cozy—or you would have if she hadn't clearly been so distressed."

"The cafés of Lisbon are the most interesting places. One meets so many people over coffee these days, don't you agree?"

"Does one also order those people to seduce Austrian engineers who have managed to flee the Nazis?" I asked sweetly, remembering Bauer's story about being approached by a Portuguese woman not long after arriving in Lisbon. The engineer had been certain she had been part of a honey trap, and by the way Köhler's eyes hardened, I knew Bauer had been right.

"I don't know what you mean," said Köhler.

"Did you put Luiza up to trying to bring Bauer back over to your side? I can't imagine that the Nazis like their scientists and engineers fleeing. It's bound to earn the Fatherland a poor reputation." I leaned in, my elbows on the table. "Tell me, Herr Köhler, what other mutual friends do we have?"

"Ah, but if I were to tell you that, the game would no longer be fun," he said.

I contemplated reaching over the table and popping the odious man in his smug nose, but before I could say or do anything else, the café's door opened, and Phillips walked in, shaking out his umbrella. He lifted a hand to hail me. "Miss Moore, I saw you from the pavement and—"

He broke off mid-sentence when Köhler turned around.

"Mr. Phillips," said the German. "What a coincidence to find you here."

I thought I saw Phillips swallow. "Herr Köhler."

"I was just enjoying the pleasure of your countrywoman's company. Miss Moore is a fascinating woman," said Köhler. "Very . . . opinionated."

"Is that right?" asked Phillips. "Well, I'm afraid I shall have to cut this social call short. I have urgent need of Miss Moore's help."

Köhler raised a brow. "You need the help of a wine buyer's secretary? How resourceful you British are."

"It's one of our better qualities," I said.

"Miss Moore," said Köhler, clicking his heels together and executing a bow before striding out of the café.

"Miss Moore," Phillips began as he sank down into the chair his rival had just occupied, "I should not need to remind you again how dangerous it can be consorting with a member of the Abwehr."

"I was hardly consorting. And for your information, he again approached me—not the other way around."

"Still, I would urge you to exercise due caution when dealing with the likes of Berndt Köhler. He is a ruthless man. I should hate to be the one to have to write a report for London about your disappearance under less-than-desirable circumstances."

A little unwelcome shiver danced down my spine.

"No, I shouldn't like that any more than you would," I said.

"What did he want?" asked Phillips.

"Word made its way back to him that I've been asking questions of various people in our search for Winn."

"I thought that your lot were meant to be discreet," said Phillips.

"We are, and we have been. However, if someone has been talking to Köhler about Mr. Slater and me, no amount of discretion can help that. He already admitted that we have 'mutual friends.'"

Phillips frowned. "Mutual friends?"

"I suspect that one of them is a young woman who works at the Hotel Metrópol's switchboard."

"What were you doing at the Hotel Metrópol?" he asked.

"That is where Mr. Fortescue is staying. We also believe Winn may have met contacts there. Did he ever arrange to speak with you at the bar?"

Phillips's frown deepened. "No, he was always insistent that we use the casino or leave messages at the table at Café Real. I had the impression he was concerned with discretion, but if he was holding meetings in the middle of a hotel bar, perhaps I was wrong."

"After I left Luiza at the Hotel Metrópol yesterday, I saw her sitting with Köhler in a café nearby. They were deep in conversation," I said.

"And you think that means she could be working for the Germans?"

"Didn't you yourself warn me that they have informants all around, just like we do?"

"Yes. Yes, of course." He kneaded his forehead. "Forgive me. All of this worry about Winn is beginning to affect me."

"Mr. Slater and I are trying our very best."

He sighed. "I know. I can't fault you for that."

I supposed that in a way I should be grateful because it was the first time the man had conceded that David and I might actually be helpful.

"Do you mind if I use the telephone in the office?" I asked. "I should probably ring my hotel and check my messages."

"I am heading there myself. Please allow me to accompany you," said Phillips, standing and then presenting me with the crook of his arm.

I let him lead me out of the café and onto the pavement outside. The rain had grown heavier, so Phillips put up his umbrella to cover us both.

"Are you limping?" he asked.

"A blister after yesterday's footrace," I said.

"Miss Larkin, my secretary, keeps some moleskin in her desk drawer. She would be happy to assist you."

"That would be very kind of her. Do you ever miss England, Mr. Phillips?" I asked as we walked.

"In some ways," he said. "I miss a good cup of tea and the way that the countryside smells when there's been a heavy rain overnight. It's a different scent in Portugal."

"Do you spend much time out of the city?" I asked.

"As much as the job allows me to. I have a little place I go in Azenhas do Mar. It's about an hour from here," he said. "I find it is a good escape from Lisbon. Things have become very crowded recently."

"I can imagine," I said.

"Where do you live when you're in London?" he asked.

"Chelsea."

"And this is your first time in Lisbon?" he asked.

"It is."

"How do you find it?"

"It's beautiful. I should like to see it in the summer, but I can see what you mean about it being crowded. It feels sometimes as though it's bursting at the seams with so many people," I said. "I was amusing myself this morning, sitting in the café and trying to pick out all of the different languages being spoken."

"I meant to ask," he said as he opened the door of his office's building for me, "how did you choose that particular café? There are many closer to your hotel."

"Carter suggested it," I said as we began to climb the stairs to the second floor.

"Carter?" he asked with surprise.

"Yes. We were meant to meet there at eleven o'clock, but he never showed up. He must have been detained."

"I'm very sorry, Miss Moore, but Carter left Lisbon early this morning to chase a lead on an investigation he's been undertaking for the fellows in London."

I frowned. "This morning?"

"Yes. We've been keeping tabs on an old explorer named Redfern. It appears he resurfaced in a place called Valverde in the Alentejo region. Carter hopped straight in the car to try to intercept him."

"When was this?" I asked.

"Just after half past eight this morning. I had only just reached the office. We crossed paths as he was leaving and I was walking in," he said. "He really should have left word for you at your hotel if he'd arranged to meet. That's very poor form."

It was possible that, in the time between breakfast and leaving for the day, I'd missed a message or telephone call, but it seemed odd Carter hadn't also left word for me at Café Pereira.

Just ahead of me, Phillips opened a door with ALBION IMPORTS CORP. painted on it, and I stepped into the entryway of one of the British intelligence operations in Lisbon. It was a modest space with a brunette woman dressed in a russet cardigan typing at a desk in the middle of the room. Flanking her were two doors leading to what I could only assume were offices.

"Good morning, Miss Larkin," said Phillips with a nod to the secretary. "This is Miss Moore. She is assisting Mr. Slater on his visit to Lisbon."

That wasn't quite right, but I was growing tired of correcting men who seemed unable to remember that I wasn't merely David's helper.

"I'm very glad to make your acquaintance, Miss Moore," said Miss Larkin, her typewriter falling silent.

"Miss Moore is in need of some first aid after sustaining a nasty blister," said Phillips.

"I have just the thing," said Miss Larkin.

"Thank you," I said.

"I will leave you in Miss Larkin's safe hands," said Phillips.

He made to turn for one of the closed doors when Miss Larkin called out, "Mr. Phillips, you're meant to be meeting Senhor Guerra at Martinho da Arcada at a quarter past noon."

"So I am. Thank you, Miss Larkin. Miss Moore." With a nod to both of us, he made his way out of the office.

"Time to set you right, Miss Moore," said Miss Larkin, opening her desk drawer and drawing out an envelope and a pair of nail scissors.

"Thank you," I said, easing my shoe off.

"Do you need a plaster as well?" she asked, pulling a bit of moleskin out of the envelope.

"I think so," I said, glancing at the back of my heel. I would have to peel my stocking off to apply the bandage.

"Here." She handed me a plaster. "If you'd like to put that on, you can use Mr. Phillips's office."

"You're certain he won't mind?" I asked.

"He won't be back from Martinho da Arcada until at least three o'clock. You go right ahead," she said.

If Phillips was playing the role of the quintessential English public-school boy grown up as a convenient cover here in Lisbon, his office certainly reflected it. While his desk was virtually empty except for a box of cigars, a cutter, and a lighter placed on one side of the blotter, there was a well-stocked bar close at hand and a stack of newspapers neatly laid out on a low coffee table next to a pair of club chairs. Hanging on one wall was an old map of London, and the framed photographs on his desk revealed not the wife Princess Petrova had mentioned but a portrait of eleven men all dressed in their cricketing whites. I peered down at the photograph, taking a moment to pick a slightly more youthful Phillips out of a crowd of men who, quite frankly, all bore a rather strong resemblance to one another, with their clean-cut hair and scrubbed-fresh faces.

Setting the photograph down again, I rolled down my stocking on my blistered foot, applied the plaster, and replaced my nylon. After making sure my undergarments and skirt were securely in place again, I let myself out of the office and found Miss Larkin just finishing cushioning my shoe.

"Thank you," I said, taking it from her to slip back on.

"You're welcome," she said.

"Miss Larkin, you didn't happen to see Mr. Carter today, did you?" I asked.

"Yes, he must have come in very early because I arrived at eight o'clock and he was already inside his office with his door closed. I think he was on the telephone."

"Did he say anything about going to the countryside today?" I asked.

"I really couldn't say. I directed a call to him about quarter past eight, and a few minutes later, he was straight out the door without a word. He had his coat and hat with him, so it's entirely possible that he left for an unexpected trip."

"And he didn't stop to leave a message or say where he was going?" I asked.

"No, he didn't. Were you expecting him?"

"I was at eleven, in the café down the road. Only he never appeared."

She smiled. "That does sound rather like Mr. Carter. He can become rather single-minded when he has the bit between his teeth. Shall I tell him you asked after him if he rings?"

"I would appreciate that, thank you," I said. "Do you mind if I use your telephone to ring my hotel?"

"Please," she said, gesturing to the telephone on her desk.

I picked up the receiver and asked the operator to connect me to the Hotel Tivoli.

"Hello," I said as soon as the front desk picked up. "I'm Evelyne Moore, staying in room forty-two. Do I have any messages?"

"No, I'm very sorry, Menina Moore," said the front desk clerk on the other end.

Nothing from Carter, and nothing from David either.

"Thank you," I said. "Would you be able to tell me whether Mr. Slater in room thirty-six has returned?"

"Just one moment, Menina Moore," said the clerk. There was a pause on the line and then the clerk returned. "I believe he is in his room. Would you like to be connected?"

"Please," I said.

There was a pause for the switchboard to make the connection, and then there was a ring.

David picked up immediately. "David Slater."

"It's Evelyne."

"Where have you been?" he demanded.

My brows jumped. "I'm at Phillips's office. Is something the matter?"

"How soon can you come back here?" he asked, ignoring my question.

"Maybe ten minutes? I can take a taxi, but it will probably be a moment before I can hail one in this rain."

"That doesn't matter. Just get back here as quick as you can," he said before hanging up and leaving me staring at the receiver in my hand.

THIRTY-FOUR

Precisely twelve minutes later, my taxi pulled up to the Hotel Tivoli. I paid the driver and then hurried into the lobby. I bypassed the front desk and made straight for the lift, taking it up to David's floor. At his door, I lifted my hand, but before I could even knock, he yanked it open, his eyes bright and a little wild.

"I've found something," he announced.

"What is it?" I asked.

"Come in, come in," he said, ushering me into the room. The curtains were still drawn, and the light was dim.

"How long have you been back?" I asked.

"Half an hour. You caught me not long after I returned. How was your meeting with Carter?"

"He never showed up."

That pulled David up short. "Didn't he?"

"Phillips said that Carter received a lead in an investigation into a man named Redfern and that Carter raced off straight away this morning."

"Then Phillips still doesn't know Sir Reginald is your father?" asked David.

I shook my head. "It would appear not. It's strange Carter didn't tell me he was going to chase after my father. I checked with the front desk, and there were no messages for me telling me that Carter had gone."

"Then you sat in a café and waited for no reason?" asked David.

"It was a waste of time unless you consider an encounter with Berndt Köhler to be worthwhile," I said.

"Köhler approached you again?"

"Yes."

"Did he threaten you?" he asked.

"Only in that charming-with-a-touch-of-menace way of his." When I saw David's frown deepen, I added, "Don't worry, Phillips came into the café shortly afterward and broke everything up. I think he was quite rattled by seeing Köhler and me together. Hopefully he hasn't decided that I'm a German spy."

David huffed out a laugh and said, "Well, while you were entertaining the enemy over coffee—"

"Unfair and untrue," I interjected.

"I went on a walk and had an idea. I went over to the Hotel Metrópol and paid the switchboard a visit."

"The switchboard? But I've already spoken to the ladies there."

He held up his hand to stop me. "Just wait. I wasn't getting anywhere at first—I gather that the supervisor does things rather by the book—but one of the girls managed to slip me a note telling me to meet her around the back of the hotel while she was on her break."

"Her name wasn't Luiza, was it?" I asked.

His brows lifted.

"She's the rather surly switchboard operator who placed Jessup's regular trunk call, and also the woman who I saw speaking in a café with Köhler yesterday," I explained. "This morning, when I mentioned her name to Köhler, I thought he seemed surprised at first. Then, on a guess, I suggested that she was the woman who tried to seduce Bauer on behalf of the Germans. He did not like that one bit, so I suspect my guess was correct."

"Luiza was the one having coffee with Köhler yesterday?" David asked.

"One and the same. I didn't expect him to confirm the identity of one of his agents, but I wanted him to know that he's not the only one who has been keeping an eye out recently."

"Well, that is interesting . . ." David trailed off. "I'll come back around to that. Leona—she is the operator who met me this morning—said that normally the switchboard doesn't make note of domestic calls because there are so many of them coming in and out of the hotel. However, she and the other girls on the switchboard were interested in Jessup because of who called *him* while he was staying at the hotel."

"Who was that?" I asked.

"Apparently every time he stayed, a woman would ring up and ask to be put through to Jessup's room. And every time, she would announce that she was calling on behalf of Princess Petrova," said David with a satisfied grin. "It seems it became something of a game between the switchboard girls, seeing who would be the one to put through the princess's call that visit."

"Then not only did Princess Petrova know Jessup, she knew him well enough to ring him regularly," I said.

"Multiple times a visit, apparently. Which makes me wonder if the princess had a role to play in Jessup's smuggling scheme."

"Introductions to Winn. Telephone calls to Jessup. We need to speak to the princess," I said, turning for the door.

"Wait!" David stopped me before I could cross the room. "There's more. There was one other peculiarity of Jessup's that Leona also told me about. He had a habit of ringing down from his room and hanging up on whichever operator answered his call."

"Perhaps he was indecisive," I said.

"I thought so too, except he would ring again and again until finally one operator picked up."

"One operator?" My eyes widened. "Luiza."

David nodded. "Given her connection to Köhler, I think we should be very concerned that Jessup insisted on her taking his calls."

Suspicion—a vast, nebulous thing—was beginning to grow in the back of my mind. It was too much of a coincidence that Luiza had been the one Jessup had insisted on speaking to when placing calls to the princess, and I suspected that there was only one person still living who could tell us why.

"Come on," I said. "We need to catch a cab to Estoril."

"Where are we going?" asked David.

"To pay a little visit to Princess Petrova."

We reached the sweeping drive of Villa de Pietro in the early afternoon. After the rainy morning, the sun had decided to make an appearance, and its soft late-autumn light made the bright white walls and warm terra-cotta roof of the house on top of the cliff glow.

"That's quite a house," I said.

"One of the largest in the neighborhood by the looks of it," said David as the taxi rolled to a stop at the base of the steps leading up to the front door.

"Somehow I doubt that Princess Petrova would settle for anything less."

David paid the driver, and then we climbed the steps up to the black painted door with a large iron knocker hung in the middle of it. I lifted it and let it fall a few times before stepping back to wait for the door to open. Sure enough, a young woman dressed in the white and black uniform of a maid appeared a few moments later.

"*Bonjour*," she said, her eyes sweeping over first me and then David.

"We would like to see Princess Petrova," I said in French. "Is she at home?"

The maid sniffed. "Madame is not at home to social calls, Mademoiselle. She is preparing for tonight's soiree."

"That's fortunate then that we are not here for a social call. Where is the princess?" I asked.

"I am not at liberty to say," she replied tartly.

"Who is it, Marie?" The princess's voice drifted down to us, but not from inside the house as I might have expected. Instead, it came from above.

I craned my neck and spotted the top of the princess's head wrapped in a mottled blue and green silk turban poking over the edge of the roof above us. A pair of large tortoiseshell sunglasses obscured her eyes.

"Good afternoon," I said, switching to English as I shielded my own eyes from the glare of the sun.

"Miss Moore, you are hours too early. Your invitation is for tonight," the princess called down.

"There's a matter I must discuss with you," I said.

"It could not wait until tonight?" she asked.

"It's urgent," I said.

"Urgent and you have brought your employer along with you. How intriguing. I hope neither of you have a fear of heights. Show them up, Marie," the princess instructed her maid.

Marie sniffed again but said, "If you will follow me."

Up the stairs we went before Marie showed us into a light-filled drawing room, the French doors of which stood wide open to air the house out.

"You may join Madame on the roof," said Marie in a tone that betrayed how much she disapproved of the fact that she was seeing *anyone* to a rooftop.

When I stepped out of the drawing room's French doors and onto the roof of the porch, I found Princess Petrova wrapped in an enormous mink ornamented by a diamond fur clip in the shape of a panther. With her hair bound up, the enormous pair of citrine teardrop earrings she wore were free to flash in the sunlight. In front of her was a table set for one, a plate of baked chicken and some picked-over vegetables sitting next to a glass of white wine filled nearly to the brim.

"Good afternoon, Miss Moore," said the princess before sliding her gaze to David. "Or do you go by Miss Redfern in front of Mr. Slater?"

David took a half step closer to me, but I touched his arm to reassure him that I was not concerned with the use of my real name. The princess might seem high-handed now, but I suspected she would be far less superior after our conversation.

"Princess Petrova, I hope you don't mind us interrupting your lunch," I said.

"Hardly, my dear. Marie hates it when I call for lunch on the roof in the autumn, but I find myself desperate to soak up what little sun and warmth I can, otherwise I should have to fly even farther south for the winter like those migratory birds. What are they called?"

"Swallows?" asked David.

The princess dipped her chin to look at him over her sunglasses. "Clever man. Am I still to call you Mr. Slater?"

"I think that would be best given that it's my name," said David.

"If you say so. About what did you wish to speak?" asked Princess Petrova, reaching for her glass. "I am a very busy woman, especially today."

"We wanted to ask you a few questions—"

"Not more questions, Miss Redfern," groaned the princess. "I've had enough of those for a lifetime."

"We wanted to ask you a few questions about a man named Michael Jessup," I said.

"Who?" asked the princess.

"You might recall me having some questions about him the first night we met. I said he was a friend of my brother's," I said.

"And I suspect I told you then what I will tell you now. I have never met such a man in my life," said the princess. "Now if that is all . . ."

"Are you certain you never met him?" asked David. "He was a banker, working between London and Lisbon. It's possible that you invited him to one of your famous parties."

She waved a hand vaguely. "Perhaps someone brought him along. That does happen sometimes, you know. I would consider it rude to arrive with an uninvited guest if it wasn't how I've met so many very interesting people. Just the other day—"

"We know you telephoned Jessup at his hotel whenever he stayed in Lisbon," I said.

"My dear Miss Redfern, if I didn't know the man, how could I possibly telephone him?" she asked with an air of entitled annoyance.

"Jessup was a guest at the Hotel Metrópol. According to the switchboard operators there, someone in this house called there regularly saying they were ringing on your behalf. This happened multiple times a visit," said David.

"I'm not sure I appreciate what you're implying—"

"Jessup was found dead two days ago," I said, growing tired of the woman's evasion.

She touched a manicured hand to her chest. "Dead?"

"He was murdered on a BOAC flight from Britain to Portugal," I said.

I noticed the princess's fingers tighten in her mink. "Was he? How ghastly."

"It was, actually," I said. "His neck was broken. Did you not know?"

"Clearly not," she murmured.

"The PVDE is very interested in learning the identify of Jessup's killer," said David.

"We gather that the punishment for anyone withholding information about his death would be both swift and brutal. It would be a pity if you were mistakenly caught up in their investigation given that you are not a Portuguese national," I said.

"I'm certain I can't imagine what you mean, Miss Redfern," said the princess, but some of her earlier haughtiness was gone, replaced by a distinctive shake in her voice.

"The PVDE are also upset to have discovered that Jessup was not just in Lisbon on business for his British bank. It also transpired that he was a smuggler." I paused and then smiled. "Those are beautiful citrines you're wearing, if you don't mind me saying."

She touched her right earring as though reassuring herself that the jewels were still there. "They're topaz, actually."

"Back home in London, matters look even more dicey because Jessup has also been linked to a murdered jeweler who traded in Hatton Garden," I continued. "If the situation in Portugal were to change and the country decided to ally itself to the Axis powers, it would be very difficult for any Briton who had been connected to the murders of two British men to make her way back into the country. Don't you think, David?"

"Without a doubt," said my partner firmly.

"*Two* murders?" the princess asked in a shaky voice.

"Did I say two? I should have been clearer. There are three. The man who we believe killed both Jessup and the London jeweler was shot and killed in Caxias early this morning."

"And James Winn is missing," said David.

"James Winn missing . . . ?" she murmured.

"We think that the smuggling ring worked like this," I said. "Jessup carried jewels from Lisbon to London secreted away in his luggage. Then the jeweler found buyers for the goods and Jessup returned to Lisbon with the money from those transactions in a compartment in his attaché case.

"Now, I have a theory that someone has decided that the smuggling ring poses a danger to themselves and is trying to shut it down and tie up loose ends. I imagine this would be a very dangerous time for anyone who was involved *unless* the person behind all the killings is caught." I leaned in. "And I think that you were the one who used your extensive knowledge of wealthy but desperate people who routinely wash up in Lisbon to identify those who might want to sell their jewelry in a market that is not quite as flooded as the one here."

The princess swallowed and peeled off her sunglasses with a shaking hand. She looked tired and even a little old.

"That is what you did for Jessup's smuggling ring, isn't it?" I asked. "You would handpick targets and introduce them to Winn. Then he would hand the jewels off to Jessup, who would ferry them to London."

The princess swallowed.

"With your superior knowledge due to your own jewelry collection, you must have been quite the asset," I said.

"You must understand . . ." she trailed off.

"Princess Petrova, did you help identify well-heeled refugees who needed to sell their jewels for more money than they could raise with Lisbon's jewelry dealers?" I pressed.

"Yes," she croaked out. "But that is all I did. I didn't kill anyone or order anyone's murder. I swear it."

THIRTY-FIVE

I leaned back on my heels, satisfied as one of this case's puzzle pieces finally clicked into place.

I'd never for a moment thought that Princess Petrova had killed Morrison or Jessup—it seemed clear that the person at the top of the smuggling ring had directed Curzon and I didn't think she had the ruthlessness in her to run the operation—but her confession to being involved in the smuggling scheme felt like a triumph.

"What exactly did you do?" I asked.

"We want to know everything," said David. "If you leave anything out, it could delay us in finding the killer."

"A killer who seems intent on doing away with the rest of your associates," I added. "We can help you, Princess, but only if you help us."

Princess Petrova grabbed her wineglass and took a large gulp before asking, "How can you help me?"

"We know people who can help you leave the country." Phillips wouldn't thank us for the extra burden but that would be his responsibility.

"I don't want to leave Lisbon. I've made my home here now," she said.

"I doubt the PVDE would look kindly on your participation in a smuggling ring, but if you help us, I'm certain arrangements can be made to help keep them from your door," said David.

"But only if you tell us what you know," I reminded her.

The princess took another large swallow of wine and nodded. "I know people. I hear things. It means that I have information about who has just arrived in Lisbon, who might be desperate to lay their hands on ready money. I am known for my jewels so naturally men and women began to ask discreetly for my advice on how to dispose of theirs for a fair price. There are some shops in the city, but in the past few months it has become nearly impossible to sell anything for what it's worth, especially diamonds."

"Were any of these shops you were directing people to dealing on the black market?" asked David.

"I-I didn't like to ask," she admitted.

"How did you become involved in Jessup's scheme?" I asked.

"A letter appeared on my desk," she said.

"A letter?" I asked skeptically.

"I found it the morning after one of my soirees. To this day my staff swear they don't know how someone managed to slip past them into the private areas of the house to leave it, nor how they managed to unlock my study door without a key."

"First the keys to your country house, then a letter," I said, remembering the story of why her guests were now confined to the ground floor of her home during parties. "You really should think about the company you keep."

She pulled a sour face.

"What did the letter say?" asked David.

"I can show you," said the princess, rising. She tossed her mink on the sofa in the first-floor drawing room with little regard as to the value of the beautiful jacket, almost as I might throw aside a pair of gloves at the end of a long day's work. Then she led us up a flight of stairs before stopping in front of a white painted door. She pulled a key out of her white silk trousers and unlocked it.

"This is my study," she said. "Only I hold the key."

Having picked more than my share of locks over the last few months, I knew that for someone with even a modicum of skill, a standard study door would present virtually no obstacle. Sure enough, I peered down at the lock and found the telltale scratches I'd suspected would be there.

"Someone picked the lock," I announced. "Likely someone who doesn't regularly make a practice of it if the scratches left behind are anything to believe."

The princess paled. "But my safe was undisturbed."

"That wouldn't matter if they were not concerned about the contents of the safe," I said.

"Oh," said the princess, as though the thought hadn't occurred to her.

With a slightly trembling hand, the princess unlocked the study door and, after letting us in, went to the wall opposite a bank of windows. She pulled back a gold velvet curtain, exposing a hefty safe with a heavy combination lock.

"I keep the most valuable of my jewels in a bank vault, but my everyday pieces and the things I have on hand stay in here," she said, stepping in front of the safe's dial to obscure our view as she began to twist it. Then she lifted a bejeweled hand to depress the handle. With a solid *thunk*, she opened the door.

"The letter is in here. I thought about destroying it, but I thought it would be a good idea to keep it if something happened," she said.

Turning around, she held an envelope out between her two fingers. I took it and drew out a single sheet of paper covered in typewritten text.

Dear Princess Petrova,

Please excuse me for not being able to deliver this note myself, but circumstances required a more discreet approach.

I believe we can be of mutual service to one another. I have a little scheme that requires someone with both an eye for fine jewelry and those who might need to part with it. Please do me the courtesy of telephoning the Hotel Metrópol and asking for the guest in room 527 tomorrow at three o'clock. He will give you further instructions.

I urge you to take this task seriously, and I must warn you, if you believe that you have a choice in the matter you are sorely mistaken. I am privy to certain information about your late husband's estate and the conditions under which his will was executed. Given that your living is dependent upon such conditions being met, it would be in your best interest to follow my instructions to a T.

You will find that I am not an unfair man, so you may expect to be generously compensated for your participation.

Sincerely,

J. Winn

I immediately passed the letter to David as the significance of it sank in. Winn wasn't involved in Jessup's smuggling scheme. He was running it.

As soon as he finished reading the letter, David exhaled heavily. "Winn was pulling the strings?"

"So it would seem," I said.

He shook his head. "London isn't going to like this."

"No." Given the war, British intelligence could happily overlook an informant who operated on the shadowy side of a city full of spies so long as that informant proved to be as useful as Winn had been. However, finding out that an asset was running a full-fledged smuggling ring across two countries that could now be connected to three murders? That was entirely different.

I held up the letter. "When did you find this?"

"June," she said. "I thought of ignoring it at first—I had never heard of a J. Winn in my life—but then another note followed the next morning. This one was sent with the regular post and included a copy of a page of my husband's will and a photograph." She touched her earring again. "There is a condition in it that states that if I develop a . . . close friendship with another man, I forfeit the living granted to me. The money would instead revert to my son. If that happened . . . well, I shouldn't have a thing to live on."

Having seen only a portion of the princess's collection of jewels and knowing her propensity for parties, I suspected that maintaining her lifestyle required a very substantial income. If her son decided he didn't approve—well, the princess didn't strike me as the sort of woman who would willingly economize.

Princess Petrova cleared her throat. "After receiving the second letter, I placed the call at the allotted time. A man named Mr. Jessup answered. He told me that he would be my point of contact in all matters. Then he gave me my instructions. I was meant to identify people who may wish to relieve themselves of their valuables and then contact him to pass along their names."

"And then what?" asked David.

The princess looked away. "I took the jewels from their owners and arranged for Mr. Jessup to collect them. Don't ask me what happened to the pieces after that. I don't know."

"You must have had your suspicions," I said.

She turned back to me, her pale blue eyes hard. "Given the nature of the letters I received, I did not think it wise to have suspicions."

"Then the story you told me at the casino about Winn helping you retrieve your jewels from an unscrupulous jeweler was a lie?" I asked.

The princess had the good grace to look away. "When you asked if I knew Winn, I thought it was a greater risk to tell you about the letter and Winn's blackmail than to tell you a story about some missing jewelry."

"Why not lie to me about knowing Winn in the first place like you did about Jessup?" I asked.

"Because, if you had asked enough people, someone would have told you I had a reputation for being able to discreetly contact Winn. That much of my story was always true," she said. "However, no one was supposed to know that Jessup and I knew each other except for my staff."

"Where did you make these exchanges with Jessup?" asked David. "His hotel?"

She scoffed, a touch of the aristocrat returning. "I'm not an errand boy. He came here. After the first exchange, he would bring an envelope with bank notes as a thank-you for my work. Pounds sterling."

"How much?" I asked.

"Enough," she said firmly. "It went along like this for months until the start of this month."

"What happened then?" I asked.

She shrugged. "I made my telephone call to Mr. Jessup, saying that I had identified a client, but when I named the man, Mr. Jessup said that he would handle the exchange himself. I was a little surprised as that had never happened before, but it wasn't as though Winn disclosed his business dealings with me. If he had decided to change the manner in which we were meant to do things, who was I to criticize?"

A sinking feeling washed over me, but before I could say anything, David asked, "Who was the client you had identified?"

Princess Petrova lifted her chin. "Sir Reginald Redfern."

Click. Another puzzle piece.

"It sounds as though, after Jessup approached him in the hotel bar, my father decided that it would be best to deal with Jessup directly," I said to David.

"Because the jewels were already in London?" asked David.

"Maybe."

I had a sneaking suspicion Jessup had far more lucrative reasons for the change, but I didn't want to discuss it in front of a suspect.

"Did you hear from Jessup again after that telephone call?" I asked.

"No," said the princess.

"Are you certain of that?" asked David.

"I would hardly forget something like that, Mr. Slater," she replied tartly. "Besides, I wouldn't have been able to because of Mr. Fortescue."

"He wanted your help," I said.

"First he wanted *Mr. Winn's* help, and then he wanted Mr. Jessup's," said the princess. "I was shocked when he asked me to track down Mr. Jessup because Mr. Jessup had taken one of these gold artifacts from Mr. Fortescue with the promise that Mr. Jessup would have it valued. When Mr. Jessup didn't reappear, Mr. Fortescue began to insist I knew where he was.

"Mr. Winn made it very clear that we were to speak to no one about our connections to him or each other. I will never understand why Mr. Jessup told Mr. Fortescue that he knew Winn or me."

"I suspect that Jessup thought it lent credence to his offer to act as a middleman for Fortescue in the sale of his antiques. He was setting himself up to do what Winn did, only for less money," I said.

By revealing his connection with the princess and Winn, Jessup also would have sown discontent among the smuggling ring and given himself more opportunity to take over Winn's territory. After all, avarice was at the heart of one of my favorite detective novels, Dorothy L. Sayers's *Unnatural Death*. Why could it not be a factor in this case?

"Did you make an attempt to inform Winn of Jessup's decision to handle Sir Reginald's exchange yourself?" I asked.

"No," said the princess. "Correspondence between us only went in one direction when I received those letters, which suited me just fine. The last thing I wanted was to come face-to-face with the man who was blackmailing me."

“Do you mean to tell me that this entire time you’ve been following the instructions of a man you’ve never met?” I asked.

“One doesn’t need to lay eyes on a man to be afraid of him,” she said.

All at once, the haze in my mind lifted and I could see the case clearly for the first time. All of this racing around Lisbon, trying to find someone—anyone—who had seen Winn since Phillips’s last message from him, and David and I had neglected to answer the one fundamental question we should have asked from the very moment we stepped off the aeroplane at Sintra.

How could we have been so blind?

“Thank you, Princess Petrova,” I said quickly. “If Mr. Slater and I have any further questions, we will be in touch.”

David gave me a quizzical look, but when I jerked my head toward the door, he followed.

“But what about me? What will you do?” the princess called after us.

“Don’t join any more smuggling rings if you can help it,” I shouted over my shoulder, trotting down the stairs as quickly as I could.

“How will you protect me? You promised!” shouted the princess.

“We’ll make arrangements!” I shouted back up at her.

“Evelyne, where are we going?” asked David in a low voice.

“Outside,” I replied.

“This better be good,” he muttered.

“Oh, don’t fret. It is.”

THIRTY-SIX

For the first time since arriving in Lisbon, I wished that David and I had been given use of a car. However, since we'd arrived at Princess Petrova's villa in a taxi, I set off at a march down the long drive to find another. To David's credit, he waited until we were out of earshot of the house to ask, "What is going on, Evelyne?"

"We've been looking at this case all wrong."

"Yes. It seems hard to deny now that Winn was at the top of the smuggling ring, which means he must be behind the murders—whether ordering them or committing them himself."

I shook my head. "No. I mean, yes, I think we were right in part. When Jessup encroached on Winn's territory and decided to set up his own smuggling operation starting with my father's request, Winn must have realized that he was vulnerable. It was time to wind down his own operation, so he paid Curzon to kill Morrison and then Jessup."

"And then he killed Curzon himself because Curzon was the last link back to him, save the princess," David finished for me as we reached the end of the drive. "It's possible that the princess's notoriety around Lisbon is what has saved her so far."

"So it would seem, but David, I think we've failed to answer one very simple question."

"What do you mean?"

I stuck my arm out to hail a passing cab. "Come along."

"Where are we going?" he asked as the taxi came to a stop next to us.

"Alfama," I said as I opened the car's door. "There's someone we need to speak to."

All through the ride back to Lisbon, my leg bounced with anticipation, and when the driver finally dropped David and me off at the bottom of the steep steps that led to Calçadinha da Figueira, it was everything I could do not to leap out and sprint up the hill.

"This is the way to Winn's flat," said David as we began to climb.

"It is," I said.

"What are we doing here?"

"Think back to Winn's flat. Was there anything strange about it?" I asked as Winn's door came into sight.

"His flat? I don't know. It was spartan, but he could be one of those types who prefer to live simply."

"I thought so too at first, but something about it bothered me. It's almost *too* spartan. As though it's hardly been lived in."

"Winn had been missing for nearly a week and a half when we went to search it," David pointed out.

"Yes, and there was a newspaper conveniently placed there for us to find to provide us with a date from which to mark his disappearance," I said, bypassing Winn's door and stopping in front of that of his landlady, Senhora Vidal.

"What are you saying?" asked David.

I lifted my hand and knocked. "What if the newspaper wasn't just a discarded newspaper but a prop? Something that we were supposed to find?"

Before David could answer, the door swung open to reveal Senhora Vidal wearing an apron and a frown.

"Good afternoon, Senhora," I started.

"The flat is gone. No one paid," she said, looking us up and down.

Knowing what I knew now, that was not a surprise.

"We were actually hoping to speak to your daughter," I said. "Just for a moment."

She studied us and then said, "Wait," before closing the door on us.

"Evelyne, are you certain about this?" David whispered. "Shouldn't we be reporting what we learned about Winn's role in the smuggling ring to Phillips? He's going to have to figure out what to tell London about—"

The squeaking door cut him off and Senhora Vidal once again filled the doorway, except this time there was a young woman around my age hovering just behind her.

The landlady said something in rapid Portuguese, and her daughter asked us in English, "You wish to speak to me?"

"Your mother told us that you were the one who let the flat next door to an Englishman named James Winn," I said.

"Yes," she said cautiously.

"If we could show you a photograph, do you think you would recognize Mr. Winn?" I asked.

"Yes," she said slowly.

If my theory was right, I would know soon enough.

"Senhora Vidal, would you please allow your daughter to come with us to identify your tenant?" I asked.

"No."

"*Mamã*," the girl said in a low tone.

Senhora Vidal pulled her shoulders back. "Why should she go with you?"

I could not blame the woman for her suspicions of David and me. We were two overly excited foreigners standing on her front doorstep, asking questions about a former tenant she clearly disliked and requesting that her daughter travel with them.

"Senhora, I can understand your hesitation," I began, "but your daughter could be the key person in identifying a man who is wanted by the PVDE. I hope that by going with us, it will be possible to keep your family from becoming involved."

Senhora Vidal's eyes narrowed. "The PVDE?"

I nodded.

The landlady looked back at her daughter and then reached behind her for a coat and a hat that hung on a peg in the entryway to her home. "I will go with you too."

We all trekked down the hill to the road where David hailed a cab, then climbed into the front seat while I crammed in the back with the Vidals. My partner raised a brow when I gave the driver the address, but he didn't say anything. In fact, no one spoke for the entire trip until finally we pulled up in front of our destination.

David climbed out and held the back door open for us, handing first Senhora Vidal and then her daughter out before reaching for me. When I stepped out onto the pavement, he stopped me and asked, "Are you certain it's a good idea to bring them here?"

"Trust me," I said before leading the Vidal women to the building that housed Phillips's and Carter's offices.

I knocked on the door for the Albion Imports Corp., and moments later, Miss Larkin answered.

"Mr. Slater, Miss Moore," she said, clearly surprised to see us. "I hadn't expected to see you again today. And you've brought us guests."

I gestured to the two women who were glancing around them. "Miss Larkin, this is Senhora Vidal and her daughter . . ."

"Mariana," said Senhora Vidal.

"Shall I make tea?" asked Miss Larkin, as though the idea of two women she'd never met before appearing at the offices of a branch of British intelligence was perfectly normal.

"That would be lovely," I said before casually asking, "Is Mr. Phillips in?"

"I'm afraid he's still at that lunch," she said.

I glanced at my watch, which told me it was half past three. "My, that is a long lunch. He asked us to bring the Vidals here to meet him. Something about an interview."

Miss Larkin gave me a small smile. "You know these business lunches. They can get away from one."

"I certainly do," I said, although I'd never had a business lunch in my life.

"I'll just make that tea. If you wouldn't mind staying in the reception while I'm gone," said Miss Larkin.

"Of course," I said, having no intention whatsoever of following that request.

As soon as she was gone, I turned to David. "Is Phillips's office locked?"

He strode over and tried the knob. "Yes."

"Right," I said, opening my handbag and pulling out my lock-picking tools. However, before I could cross the room, the door to Carter's office opened.

"Mr. Slater, Miss Moore, how good to see you," said Carter glancing around at the rather full reception area. "I was hoping I might run into you at Princess Petrova's party, Miss Moore. I'm sorry we missed one another this morning."

"I'm very sorry, Carter, but something rather urgent has come up," I said, hook and tension wrench on full display.

He held up his hands. "Not a worry. I just wanted to let you know that I'd received your note."

I stopped. "What note?"

"The note that you left me saying that you wouldn't be able to meet this morning? It turned out to be fortuitous. Phillips decided at the last minute yesterday evening that I should be the one to escort our Austrian friend to his ship," said Carter, referring to Bauer.

"I didn't leave you a note," I said.

Carter frowned. "Miss Larkin said you'd taken a message. Did you not speak to her?"

"No, I didn't," I said. "Carter, I don't suppose you have a key to Phillips's office, do you?"

He shook his head.

"Right," I muttered to myself, hoping my theory was correct. Otherwise I was going to embarrass myself in front of David, Carter, and the Vidals and probably find myself censured as a result.

I crossed to Phillips's door and crouched on one knee before sliding my tension wrench and hook into the lock.

"What is she doing?" I heard Carter ask David behind me.

"It would appear she's breaking into Phillips's office," said my partner.

"Why?" asked Carter.

"I don't have the foggiest," said David.

The lock clicked open, and I turned the handle. Phillips's office was quiet, the blinds drawn against the afternoon light. I flicked on the overhead switch and then made a beeline for Phillips's desk.

"Menina Vidal," I said, sweeping up the photograph I'd seen when I had stood in this office just hours before. "Could you please look at this photograph and tell me if you recognize any of these men?"

Mariana inched into the office, followed closely by her mother. I held up the photograph, and she peered at it, carefully studying the faces.

"Him," she finally said, pointing directly at a younger Peter Phillips dressed in his cricket whites.

Click. The last puzzle piece fell firmly into place.

THIRTY-SEVEN

I stared down at the photograph of Phillips in my hand. "This is the man you let your family's flat to? You're certain of it?"

"Yes," said Mariana.

Behind me, I heard David mutter, "Bloody Hell," but I ignored him and smiled at Mariana.

"Thank you. *Obrigada.* We're very sorry to have disturbed you, but you have been most helpful," I said.

"That is all?" asked Senhora Vidal.

"Yes, you are free to go," I said.

"And the PVDE will not bother us?" she asked.

"They will not bother you," I said.

The landlady said something to her daughter, and the young woman edged away from me. Then Senhora Vidal leaned in and asked, "She is not in trouble?"

"No, far from it. Your daughter has been a great help," I said.

That earned me a quick nod.

"Perhaps I should find a cab for these ladies," said Carter.

"Thank you," I said.

The moment he led the women from the room, David asked, "Did she just identify Phillips as the man who let Winn's flat?"

"Yes. Yes she did," I breathed.

"But why would Phillips tell her that his name was Winn? And why wouldn't Phillips tell us that he was the one who acted as Winn's agent to secure him the flat?" he asked.

"Yes, and why would Winn go through such pains to never meet Senhora Vidal that he sent a woman to pay his rent for him so that that same flat might still be available and undisturbed when we arrived to investigate Winn's disappearance?" I asked, starting to become more excited as I went. "Isn't it strange that out of all the people we've spoken to about Winn, each one knows bits and pieces about him but no one seems to actually have met the man? Princess Petrova was threatened by Winn via letter. Fortescue had heard of him, but he couldn't tell us who Winn was. Carter's never met him because Winn is Phillips's asset. I think Winn isn't a person but a threat and a distraction rolled into one convenient fiction." I paused. "David, what if James Winn doesn't exist?"

He stared at me. "What do you mean, doesn't exist?"

"It was Princess Petrova who made me realize it when she said, 'One doesn't need to lay eyes on a man to be afraid of him.' What if Winn isn't a real person?"

"You think that James Winn is a figment of all of our imaginations?" asked David, sounding very much the skeptic.

Once I might have taken offense at his doubt, but I'd become used to my partner's rather straightforward nature. It pushed me to examine things from all angles. To anticipate where I might be overlooking some key detail in my excitement to connect the dots.

"You're forgetting something. Someone *has* seen Winn," said David. "Phillips."

A grin broke out over my face. "That's right. Peter Phillips. The one man who not only claims to be able to identify Winn but also actually regularly met with him. The man who Mariana just identified in that photograph," I said, waving at the frame I held with my free hand.

David looked shocked. "Evelyne, you're not saying—"

"That Winn and Phillips are the same person?" I asked. "I don't think there's any other explanation that makes sense. After all, what better way to run a smuggling ring than to be the puppet master pulling the strings of a phantom? If Winn was a cipher, it would make it all the harder for the PVDE or our own authorities to connect Phillips back to the smuggling ring if the authorities did get wind of it."

"But Phillips is a member of British intelligence," said David, clearly shaken by the very idea of such a deception.

"I suspect Phillips would not be the first person to use that fact to his advantage," I said.

"He filed reports based on what Winn told him," David sputtered. "Remember the report about the brothel that was stealing secrets from British soldiers?"

"Isn't it convenient that the very first tip Winn gave Phillips was the one that would solidify Winn's value as an asset? I think Phillips realized that if he had a valuable contact in Winn, no one would question his loyalty to British intelligence or the efficacy of his work. His position in Lisbon was safe," I said.

"If that's true, that means that Phillips and not Winn is responsible for ordering the murders of Morrison and Jessup."

"And after Emile Curzon was foolish enough to appear at the casino yesterday night, no doubt trying to make contact, Phillips killed him too," I said. "If you think about it, Phillips reporting Winn missing was a stroke of genius. Who is going to find a man who never existed at all and who is going to suspect the very person who raised a flag about his disappearance?"

"All Phillips had to do was tie off the loose ends of his smuggling ring by killing the main players, and then weather our investigation into Winn's disappearance until we came to the only conclusion we could make: Winn vanished without explanation," said David.

"After which Mrs. White would have called us back, and Winn would have become yet another unexplained disappearance in a war full of them," I said.

David looked about to reply when there was a cry from behind us.

"Oh! What are you doing in Mr. Phillips's office?"

I whipped around and saw Phillips's secretary standing in the doorway with a tea tray.

"Miss Larkin," I started, but she put the tray down and rushed forward to snatch the photograph from my hand. Carefully, she placed it back on the desk.

"The door was locked. You cannot be in here," she said, pushing David and me out of the office and closing the door behind us.

"Miss Larkin," I tried again as Carter came back through the reception door.

"What's going on here?" Carter asked.

"They were in Mr. Phillips's office," said Miss Larkin.

"You did let me adjust my stockings in here mere hours ago," I pointed out.

She drew her shoulders back. "Under my supervision and only for a few moments. This is an entirely different matter. Mr. Carter, there is sensitive material in his office. It cannot be compromised."

"I admit I would also like to understand why Miss Moore decided she needed to pick the lock of Phillips's office," said Carter slowly. "But first, Miss Larkin, perhaps you had better tell me why you lied and said you'd taken a message from Miss Moore for me this morning."

All the secretary's defiance seemed to drain from her, and she looked as though she wished in that moment that the floor would open up and swallow her whole.

"I'm very sorry, Mr. Carter," said Miss Larkin. "Mr. Phillips dictated the message. I thought that perhaps Miss Moore had telephoned him before I arrived . . ."

"When was this?" I asked.

"First thing," she said. "I'm usually the first to arrive, so I was surprised to find Mr. Phillips already in his office. I didn't think there was any harm in taking his dictation."

"Phillips told me you were the first to arrive this morning," I said to Carter.

"I haven't been in the office at all until about a half hour ago," said Carter.

We all turned to Miss Larkin, who looked terrified.

"Phillips told me that he had run into Carter on his way in, and then *you* told me that Carter had been in his office early this morning before taking a telephone call and leaving," I said.

Miss Larkin's lips began to tremble, and then all at once she cried, "Mr. Phillips made me lie! I didn't want to, but he made me! He always makes me!"

"What do you mean 'always'?" asked David.

"He keeps his own diary, and sometimes he makes me write down appointments in the diary I keep for him to make it look as though he was in a place when he wasn't," she said.

"Does he keep that second diary in his office?" asked David.

"I don't know," she said.

I glanced at my partner and he nodded. "I'll go look."

"What other things did Phillips make you do for him, Miss Larkin?" I asked.

She swallowed. "Just little things. At first it was things like booking his tables for dinner, but then he asked me to start buying gifts for him," she said.

"What kind of gifts?" I asked.

"Perfume. Jewelry."

"Were they meant for his wife?" asked Carter.

Miss Larkin looked miserable. "I thought they might be, but then he asked me to send them to an address here in Lisbon."

"Who was the recipient?" I asked.

"I never met the woman," she said.

"Evelyne!" David shouted from the other room. "You're going to want to see this!"

"You go," said Carter.

"You're certain?" I asked.

Carter shook his head slowly. "Let's just say there's little love lost between Phillips and myself. I work for the man, but that doesn't mean I particularly like him, his manner of conducting business, or his personal life. I'll keep an eye on Miss Larkin."

There was a whimper from the secretary, but I was already halfway to Phillips's office.

THIRTY-EIGHT

I found David standing behind Phillips's desk, the wood and leather chair pulled away from where it must usually sit. David had his hands planted on his hips, and he was staring hard at the floor.

"What is it?" I asked.

"Look at that," he said, waving me over.

As I rounded the desk, he pointed at something near his feet, and when I crouched down, I spotted a brown leather suitcase tucked under Phillips's desk.

"That is not good," I said.

"No, it is not," David agreed. "No one keeps a fully packed suitcase under their desk unless they believe that they might one day need to make a quick getaway."

"Is there any clue as to where Phillips is going or when?" I asked.

"Let's see," he said, pulling the case out to set it on Phillips's blotter. Then he unsnapped the clasps and opened it up.

My stomach sank as I began to lift out shirts, trousers, a spare jacket, socks, and a pair of shoes. I set them all on the desk along with a leather wash bag. Everything that a man might need if he were absconding from his double life.

With the case empty, I slid my hand into the elasticated pocket on the inside of the lid. My fingers brushed paper, and I pulled out a passport and an envelope. I handed the passport to David and opened the envelope myself, pulling out a single ticket for a Mr. Richard Masters on an American Export Lines ship, set to sail tomorrow.

"He has a ticket to New York under the name Richard Masters," I said.

"That explains this then." David held the passport up so I could see Phillips's photograph.

"Richard Masters," I read the name out.

"He had false documents made."

"No doubt by the same person who forged Emile Curzon's papers so Curzon could enter Britain in order to kill Morrison and Jessup. Carter!" I called. "Come here, and bring Miss Larkin, would you?"

Carter stuck his head in, eyes going wide at the sight of Phillips's suitcase. "What's that?"

"An escape plan," I said as Miss Larkin cautiously edged out from behind Carter. "Miss Larkin, you said Phillips made you do things. Did that extend to booking him a place on a New York–bound ship under a false name?"

"No," she breathed. "No!"

"You're certain? Now is not the time to lie to us," David warned.

"I swear I'm telling the truth," she insisted. "Most of the things I did for him were small. That is all."

"About those gifts you mentioned, what was the name and address of the woman he was sending them to?" I asked.

"I have it in my desk," she said quietly.

"Write it down for me," said David, before taking her gently by the elbow and leading her away.

Carter crossed his arms and leaned against the doorframe. "Normally I have an abundance of patience, but before things go any further, I'd better ask what all of this is about."

I weighed the possibility that Carter was a part of Phillips's schemes but quickly dismissed the thought. Phillips had fooled him too, sending Carter off to escort Bauer to keep him out of the way this morning.

"We have reason to believe that Phillips has constructed an elaborate smoke screen in the form of his informant James Winn. First, he concocted an entire fabricated identity for Winn, and then he fooled London into thinking that Winn was a valuable informant. In reality, Phillips was using Winn as a front man for a smuggling ring ferrying jewelry and money between Lisbon and London."

"Smuggling?" asked Carter. I was pleased to find that he didn't sound outraged or incredulous but instead curious.

"I think Phillips set things up in such a way that no one could trace things back to him, even if someone were to figure out Winn's involvement," I said. "But that was before Jessup betrayed him by striking out on his own, and Phillips began to see the vulnerabilities in his scheme and decided to shut the entire operation down."

"And killed Jessup for good measure," Carter finished, letting out a long breath. "Bloody Hell."

"And Morrison in London and Curzon yesterday evening after we all left Phillips at the casino."

"Phillips has been a busy boy."

"Busy and ruthless," I agreed.

"How could he manage all of that without raising my suspicions? Or London's, for that matter?" asked Carter.

I shrugged. "How many leads are you working on at any given time?"

"Too many," he said.

"And how many reports does London expect you to file?"

"More than I can possibly manage in a week," he said. "Phillips was always putting work off onto me."

"Everything except his reports based on information gathered from his supposed meetings with Winn," I said.

"Bloody cheek," muttered Carter before peeling off the doorframe to let David and Miss Larkin through.

"I've got it," David announced as he strode in holding up a piece of paper, Miss Larkin on his heels.

"Who was the woman?" I asked.

"Luiza Barbosa."

"The switchboard operator at the Hotel Metrópol?" I asked.

"The very one," said David, grinning.

"Princess Petrova did say that she'd spotted Phillips sharing an intimate moment with a Portuguese woman at a café," I said. "Had he been sending gifts to her for long?"

"Since late spring," said Miss Larkin.

"It all makes perfect sense," said David.

"Does it?" I asked.

"I asked around the operators at the Hotel Metrópol's switchboard. They said that Jessup would typically make and receive three types of calls on every visit: a trunk call to London; telephone calls from Princess Petrova, presumably to arrange for the collection of the jewels; and another call."

"Calls down to the switchboard from his room until one particular operator answered," I said, recalling what David had told me earlier that day.

"One thing has been bothering me when it comes to your theory, Evelyne, and that is the money. If Phillips was so intent on making sure that no one connected him back to Winn, how did he collect the money that Jessup brought back into Lisbon with him after his trips to London? There must have been someone who acted as a middleman between Jessup and Phillips."

"Luiza," I breathed. "I would wager anything you like that she's the woman who paid the weekly rent for his flat after Winn had gone missing. When I met Luiza, I didn't think anything of it because—to me—she didn't match Senhora Vidal's description of plump or the princess's recollection that she wore too much makeup. But her job at the switchboard of the hotel Jessup stayed at would make her uniquely positioned to act as a go-between for Jessup and Phillips. She could have collected the money from Jessup at the hotel and passed it along to Phillips at the flat in Alfama."

"We need to find her," said David.

I glanced at my watch. "She's likely on her shift. We'll start at the hotel, and if she isn't there, we can go to that address."

"What if Phillips comes back before then?" Carter asked.

"His ship sails tomorrow and his suitcase with his papers is packed and stored here. It seems unlikely that he's already on the run," I said. "Which means that, presumably, he will want to pretend that everything is business as usual so no one suspects him of planning to leave the city."

"Excuse me," came Miss Larkin's meek voice. "I think you'll find that Mr. Phillips RSVPed to Princess Petrova's party this evening. He asked me to send the reply last week, and yesterday I picked up his dinner jacket from the tailor. He was having it repaired."

"It would be just Phillips's brand of arrogance to go to a party with the knowledge that in twenty-four hours he will be fleeing on a ship to America," said Carter.

"It would be the ideal place to take care of his last loose thread," said David. "The princess."

"You think she's in danger?" asked Carter.

"I think she will be tonight, after the guests go. If Phillips wants to make sure no attention is on him, he'll need to wait until then to kill her," I said.

"She needs police protection," said Carter, rubbing his forehead. "I can sort that out too."

I glanced at David. "I think it's time we bring Camargo in."

"Are you certain?" he asked.

"We need to if the princess is in danger," I said.

"Right," said David. "Carter, you contact Camargo and explain what we've told you. See if you can also make arrangements for the princess's protection without tipping Phillips off that we're on to him. We'll go to the Hotel Metrópol and find Luiza. Then we'll meet back here in an hour and make a plan to grab Phillips at the party."

"Consider it done," said Carter.

"Oh, and keep Miss Larkin with you, would you, Carter?" I added.

"Me?" Miss Larkin squeaked.

"I'm afraid we can't risk word getting back to Phillips that we're looking for him," I said.

Miss Larkin began to stammer her objections, but when Carter raised a brow in her direction, she stopped. "Yes, Miss."

"We should repack the suitcase just in case we're wrong and Phillips returns for it earlier than we expect," said Carter.

"I'll do that," said David.

"Take Miss Larkin back to her desk with you, would you?" asked Carter. "I just need another moment with Miss Moore."

"Come along, Miss Larkin," said David, ushering the disheartened secretary in front of him.

As soon as David shut Phillips's office door, Carter said, "I should have known that you wouldn't have canceled our meeting today without good reason. It was stupid of me not to have asked more questions."

"Phillips has had so many people on a string for so long, I don't think any of us really stood a chance of seeing what was really going on," I said.

"You did."

I smiled. "I had help. What did you want to speak to me about?"

"I think I've found your father."

"Really?" With the excitement about Phillips, I had almost forgotten about Sir Reginald.

"Yesterday evening after the casino, I placed some calls as I promised. This morning, one of my contacts rang me at my flat before I left. He said that a man matching Sir Reginald's description had been staying at a house in the countryside."

"Where?" I asked, my heart beating a little faster now.

"A village called Valverde in the Alentejo region. The locals say that a wealthy family owns the house, but they hardly ever visit. That's why people noticed the Englishman who started coming and going out of the garden's side gate. The Englishman matched Sir Reginald's description.

"However, when my contact's source went around this morning to check if Sir Reginald was still there, the house was shut up," said Carter, pulling a slip of paper out of his pocket with an address written on it. "I was going to drive up there this afternoon, but then all of this happened."

"Did you say the village is called Valverde?" I asked.

"Yes, it's near the city of Évora. Do you know it?"

I nodded. "Princess Petrova told me that she has a house there."

"Then your father was staying at the princess's second home this entire time?" asked Carter.

"I doubt it was with her knowledge," I said. "She told me that, at her last party, someone walked off with a set of keys to her country home. She was convinced it was an accident, but I suspect Sir Reginald may have seized on an opportunity to help himself to them. And now he's disappeared again."

"We will find him," Carter said.

I nodded in agreement. "Just as soon as we catch Phillips."

THIRTY-NINE

To his credit, David showed great restraint in not asking me about my conversation with Carter until we were on our way to the Hotel Metrópol in what felt like our twentieth taxi of the day.

"What did Carter want to speak to you about?" he asked.

"He thinks he found my father's trail. One of his contacts got word that someone matching Sir Reginald's description was seen at a house in the countryside about an hour and a half's drive out of Lisbon, but by the time the contact went to see for themselves, Sir Reginald was gone."

"Do you think he fled Portugal?" David asked.

"Not unless he suddenly came into money. I think my mother's jewels were something of an emergency fund to him. He wouldn't have tapped them unless he was truly desperate. Given that it took some time for me to read the letter he sent me, I suspect that Sir Reginald has been hard up for money for weeks.

"I wonder too if that means Jessup found himself stuck in London, checking in on Morrison every day as they waited for me to arrive with the tea chest. Jessup probably went to the shop the day I did—before or after I don't know—saw the state of the place, realized that something had happened to Morrison, and ran. I remember how nervous he seemed at the hotel in Bristol and as we boarded in Whitchurch."

"If Sir Reginald does prove to be connected to Winn and Jessup as more than just a client, what will you do?" asked David.

"What do you mean?"

"Will you be able to bring your father in?" he asked.

It was the question I had refused to ask myself ever since I'd first made the connection between Winn, Jessup, and Sir Reginald at the bar of the Hotel Metrópol. Finally, I said, "Yes. He is a virtual stranger. That will make it easier."

"Are you certain?" asked David.

I pursed my lips. "Yes."

"Even so, let's hope you won't need to make that decision," he said as our taxi pulled up in front of the hotel.

Inside the Hotel Metrópol, the manager spotted us from across the lobby and hurried over.

"Mr. Slater, you've returned again," he said with a slight edge to his voice. "So soon."

"Yes," said David. "I need to speak with one of your switchboard operators again. Luiza Barbosa."

The manager's eyes darted between us. "I'm afraid that will not be possible."

"Why not?" I asked.

"Menina Barbosa is no longer in the employ of the Hotel Metrópol," he said.

"Since when? She was here this morning," said David.

"It is a very recent development," said the manager.

"What happened?" I asked.

"I am not at liberty to share that information—"

A furious scream from the other side of the hotel lobby had every head turning toward the commotion, including mine. Luiza Barbosa was being half led, half dragged out in handcuffs by four uniformed officers, yelling what I could only assume was her innocence in Portuguese as she went. Behind them I could see Camargo wearing a satisfied expression.

"*Meu Deus*," muttered the hotel manager.

I could tell the moment the PVDE man spotted David and me as soon as the furrow on his forehead appeared. He clasped his hands behind his back and strode over.

"Menina Moore, why am I not surprised to see you here?" asked Camargo.

"Good afternoon to you too, Capitão," I said. "I see you've taken Luiza Barbosa into custody."

"Yes. We received an unusual telephone call from an Archibald Carter. I believe he is a friend of yours?"

"He is indeed," I said.

"He told me that I should arrange for police protection for Princess Petrova. He also mentioned that Menina Barbosa should be questioned in connection to the deaths of Senhor Jessup and Senhor Curzon. He finished this extraordinary call by saying I should speak to you about it, although he did not mention why. The strangest thing about all of this is, we were just on our way to the Hotel Metrópol to arrest Menina Barbosa on a different charge."

"What is that?" asked David.

"Suspicion of being a German spy. She was found carrying messages to a man named Berndt Köhler. He will be taken into custody and deported as soon as he is found."

The captain's lip twitched, and I could be forgiven for thinking that the man almost smiled.

"You will understand why I might have some questions about why a wine buyer and his secretary would have suspicions about Menina Barbosa's ties to two murders. Not to mention"—Camargo glanced at something over my right shoulder—"an importer. Senhor Carter?"

"Yes," said Carter, racing up to us out of breath.

"What are you doing here?" I asked.

"I telephoned Camargo's office and found that he was already on his way. I didn't want to miss out on the fun," said Carter.

"Where is Miss Larkin?" asked David.

"I grabbed one of the policemen milling around outside and told him to guard her," he said.

"I will have to speak to him about taking orders from an Englishman," said Camargo. "Now will someone explain what this is all about?"

"We believe that the murders of Michael Jessup, Emile Curzon, and a third man in London are all connected to a smuggling ring operating out of this hotel and other locations across Lisbon," I said, quickly laying out the case for him as it stood.

When I finished, Camargo stared at me for a moment and then said, "You seem to be remarkably well-versed in a case you have claimed to know nothing about until this point."

"I'm a quick study," I said.

"And you think Peter Phillips is the man behind all of this?" asked Camargo.

"We do," I said. "We also believe we can lead you to him so that you and your men may arrest him, but only if we have your agreement that we will work together."

For a moment, I thought Camargo would shake his head and decide to arrest *me*, but instead he sighed and rubbed his brow. "This Peter Phillips, he is your supervisor at Albion Imports Corp., Senhor Carter?"

"Yes, sir," said Carter.

Slowly, Camargo began to nod his head. "Then you should know that we believe Menina Barbosa was recruited by the Abwehr because of her relationship with Peter Phillips."

"Did she have orders from Köhler to try to turn Phillips?" asked Carter.

"It would seem so," said Camargo.

"Did she manage it?" I asked.

"We don't know. Yet," said Camargo.

"It goes from worse to worse," muttered Carter, and I could understand why. Everything Phillips had reported wouldn't just have to be reexamined for accuracy given that his informant was a fabrication.

He would now have to be treated as a possible double agent. It would set back our intelligence efforts in Portugal months, and an entirely new structure would have to be put in place to scrub our network clean of his damage.

But that was a concern for later.

"We have reason to believe that Phillips will be at Princess Petrova's party tonight," I said.

"I will go," said Camargo.

"*We* will go." When Camargo began to object, I added, "Phillips isn't aware that Slater, Carter, and I know he and Winn are one and the same. We have a better chance of slipping into the party and finding him without causing a scene that would set off his suspicions. If you bring your officers in and raid the house, he might try to escape into the gardens and we'll never find him. We need a plan."

Camargo seemed to mull this over for a moment before finally nodding. "We will go to my office and take two cars. Menina Moore, you may come with me."

"I'll be joining you," said David, taking a step forward so that his left shoulder covered part of me from view.

"David—"

Camargo shrugged. "If you insist, Senhor."

David glanced over his shoulder at me and gave me a small nod. "I do."

FORTY

It was eight o'clock and dark by the time that we left Camargo's office. The PVDE officer drove David and me to Estoril, and Carter took his car with Miss Larkin in the back seat.

We'd spent the time since leaving the Hotel Metrópol recounting what we'd discovered in greater detail, and Camargo's normally stern expression went from unsmiling to openly furious several times over.

"And how long has this smuggling ring been operating?" he had asked.

"The princess told us she was first approached in June. That would fit with the timeline of Jessup's more frequent visits to Lisbon," I said.

"How do you know about Jessup's trips to Lisbon?" asked Camargo.

"I have friends," I lied, as I suspected that was not the moment to reveal that the captain had interviewed me on the morning of Jessup's murder with the man's diary secreted in the top of my stockings.

"As do I," said David.

"Do these friends of yours have names?" asked Camargo.

"They do not," I said gravely.

Then something extraordinary happened. The PVDE captain

laughed. It was just a short, sharp bark of a laugh, but there was no mistaking it.

"Now it's your turn," I said, taking advantage of the moment. "How did you figure out that Luiza was working for the Germans?"

"I came across her when interrogating the staff at the Hotel Metrópol about Jessup's murder. Her colleagues were all too happy to tell stories about how she'd been spotted meeting with Köhler or how she always seemed to have money for a new handbag or a lipstick. At first, we thought Köhler was the boyfriend, but after putting them both under surveillance we realized that she was meeting with Köhler and then going to a flat Phillips gave her money to rent in Alfama in the evenings," said Camargo, neatly tying together our suspicions that Luiza had been the go-between to collect Phillips's cash all along.

"Then there can be little doubt she was also paying James Winn's rent. Phillips must have cut her in," I said.

Camargo had nodded, and then we had gone on to planning our trap.

Now, with the princess's party well underway, Camargo swung the wheel and steered his car into the drive of the Villa de Pietro.

The approach to the house was full of parked cars, their drivers lingering a few feet away with cigarettes or sitting in the front seat reading their newspapers. Camargo parked at the end and killed the ignition while Carter pulled up behind him.

We all climbed out of our cars except for Miss Larkin, who remained trembling in the back.

"All right, Menina Moore, since you seem to have so many ideas, what is your plan?" Camargo asked, looking through the trees at the lights of the house.

"The house has multiple floors," I said, "but the princess has told me she intends to confine the party to the public rooms on the ground floor. Then there are the gardens. I think we should split up. Two take the ground floor in case Phillips spots us and slips out, one takes the front garden here, and the fourth takes the back garden."

"*Bom*," Camargo said. "You take the back gardens. Senhor Carter will enter the ground floor. I will go around the back so that I make less of a scene. Senhor Slater, that leaves you with the front of the house."

"Very good," said David.

"There are police officers in place on either side of the road, so if Phillips tries to escape on foot or by car, he will be caught," said Camargo.

"What do we do about Miss Larkin?" I asked. "We can't risk her leaving the car to alert Phillips."

Camargo retreated to his car and, a moment later, walked back with a pair of handcuffs dangling from his fingers.

"I'll do it," I said, grabbing them. "The poor thing is terrified enough as it is without one of you handcuffing her."

I opened Miss Larkin's door, and she shrunk away. It was clear she'd been crying.

"Miss Larkin," I said in as gentle a voice as I could muster, "I do apologize but I'm going to have to handcuff you to the door."

"I'm so very sorry! I won't tell him anything," she said quickly. "I promise!"

"I'm afraid I must insist. You were his secretary. We can't risk that you might still be loyal to him. I will give Carter the key, and he will make sure that you're released as soon as we have Phillips in custody. Would that be okay?"

Her lip trembled but, to her credit, she stuck out her wrist to be handcuffed.

"I promise we will be back to release you as soon as possible," I said.

With that done, I returned to the men who were waiting for me. I gave the key to Carter.

"Whoever spots Phillips will try to reason with him. Tell him that he is under arrest and the building is surrounded," said Camargo.

"And in the unlikely event that he tries to run, be prepared," I said.

"I should add, he may or may not be armed," warned Carter.

Camargo muttered something under his breath that I suspected might have made me blush if I understood Portuguese profanity.

"Once you see Phillips, make enough noise that the others will hear you," I said. "Whoever is closest will come running and help."

"Ready?" David asked.

"Ready," I said.

We walked up the drive together before Camargo and I broke off to round the side of the house via a small path that led along the top of the cliff. At some point, someone had installed an iron fence to keep residents and guests from straying too close to the dangerous drop.

At the far corner of the building, there were steps up to the veranda. I recalled spotting the gardens sprawling out from the other side, and so I too climbed the steps.

"What do the English say in these moments?" asked Camargo, as we reached the top.

"Good luck," I said.

He nodded. "Good luck."

I watched him slip into the party, conspicuous in his uniform. I suspected that even without it he would have stood out as a law enforcement officer for the straightness of his carriage and his rather severe expression. However, the other guests seemed to neither notice nor care as they continued to chat, laugh, and drink.

For my part, I began to weave my way across the wide veranda, checking the figures in the shadows to see if there was anyone familiar. I wondered what all these people would think if they knew that their host was part of a smuggling ring. That she had been blackmailed because of her affairs, and that she had risked her reputation for the sake of maintaining the lifestyle that allowed her to throw these parties. Perhaps they could have understood, knowing that if they had been faced with the same decision, they might have chosen reputation and money over doing the right thing.

This war, I realized, had pushed all of us to the brink of what we thought was good and fair. Men who never dreamed of hurting anyone were now on the battlefields, fighting for their lives. Back home, housewives were buying off the black market. People were cheating coupons and writing letters that would never make it past the censors—little things that on their own were nothing but when put all together made up the murky gray we'd all been living in.

And then there were the men like Sir Reginald. I might have disapproved of my father and his choices before the war, but I'd never heard of him doing anything illegal. Yet there remained the fact that he had friendships with Nazi sympathizers in South America and elsewhere that, while not strictly illegal, were certainly reprehensible at best and treasonous at worst. Had he simply been desperate when he'd written to me to try to retrieve *Maman*'s jewels, or were his intentions more nefarious?

I turned to glance back over my shoulder and there he was, walking through the French doors of Princess Petrova's house and onto the veranda, almost as though I'd conjured him up.

My father.

I shrank back into the shadow cast by a manicured potted bay and turned to hide my face. As his footsteps approached, I struggled to control my ragged breath, convinced that I would give up who I was before I was ready. However, his step never faltered. Instead, he walked right by me and down the garden steps.

From my spot, I could just make out a flash of his features as he descended—the fine point of his chin that I'd inherited from him, the hollow cheeks that I hadn't—but what struck me the most was how *old* he looked.

It had been four years since I'd seen him last, yet somehow he seemed to have aged decades. The newspaper photographs Mr. Fletcher had showed me in his office hadn't revealed the tiredness around his eyes or the way his skin seemed to sag from his jowls.

For years, I'd wondered about what I would do if I met my father again. What I would say? Would I take him to task for what he'd put *Maman* through? Would I ask him why he'd fought so hard for me only to move me away from the comforting familiarity of my childhood in

Paris and dump me in a boarding school as soon as he could? Did he feel any remorse? Any guilt?

And yet, before I could make the decision for myself, he disappeared into the shadows.

I hesitated, knowing that my mission was to find Phillips and bring him to bear for his crimes. However, something tugged at me, and I found myself sneaking down the garden steps in pursuit of Sir Reginald.

FORTY-ONE

Even amid the well-tended perfection of the Villa de Pietro, the scent of damp fallen leaves and earth wrapped around me as I hurried into the heart of the garden, keeping to the little grassy strip on either side of the path. Ahead of me, I could hear the scrape of Sir Reginald's heels against the stone pavers even though the English borders that must have been a nod to Princess Petrova's childhood in Britain obscured my view of him around the twists and bends down the gentle slopes leading away from the house.

The footsteps stopped, and I stopped too, my ears straining in the dark to find any sound. Slowly, I crept around the corner ahead of me.

In the middle of the path stood Sir Reginald, pointing a revolver right at me.

"Who are you?" he demanded.

I stepped clear of a broad-leafed shrub hiding the corner and into the dim light cast off by the grand house.

"I've been looking for you," I said, as calmly as I could.

"Who are you?" he repeated, not lowering his weapon an inch.

I scoffed. "I really shouldn't be surprised you don't recognize me. At least it points to consistency in your character."

I could see him squint, his eyes searching mine as he tried to figure out who I was. Then, the moment of recognition.

"Evelyne?" he asked, lowering his gun.

"Congratulations, you managed to get there in the end."

"What are you doing in Lisbon?" he asked.

"You wrote to me, or did you forget?"

"To clear out the contents of the safe deposit box and deliver it to my colleague. That was all."

"Your colleague? Do you mean the fence who would quietly sell off *Maman*'s jewelry for you?" I asked.

His mouth dropped open, and it took him a moment to reply.

"You weren't supposed to open the box. I expressly wrote—"

"Did you really think that the same woman who would figure out that you'd sent an address written in invisible ink would leave a mysterious box with instructions not to open it untouched?" I asked. "Why did you let Aunt Amelia and me believe that you'd sold *Maman*'s jewelry years ago?"

"It was my insurance policy," he said, rolling his shoulders back, his cool mask back in place. "It was there if I ever needed it."

"And it never occurred to you that your daughter might want her mother's things?"

"What did you need jewels for? You were a child."

"I'm not a child now," I argued.

"Amelia would have taken care of you if you'd needed anything."

"It sounds as though she already has been for some time. Aunt Amelia told me about the cheques for my school fees, just like she told me that you're short of funds these days."

"My sister always did have too much of a taste for gossip," he grumbled. "Whatever Morrison gave you, I need it, so you just tell me where it is."

I jerked back. "Then you don't know?"

"Know what?"

"Morrison is dead."

I watched him blanch.

"He can't be dead. He—"

"And so is Jessup," I cut him off. "He was your contact, wasn't he? Did he arrange to meet you in the garden at the next of Princess

Petrova's parties to give you your money? Is that why you came tonight, hoping that he would produce the bank notes you so desperately need?"

I could see the bob of his throat as he swallowed. "If they are dead, where are the jewels?"

"First, tell me what you want the money for."

"My assets in London have been frozen," he said.

I raised a brow. That was news to me.

"I've been staying at the house of a friend in the countryside, waiting," he added.

"The house in Valverde belongs to the princess, doesn't it?" I asked. "Did you two have an affair? Or have there been so many women you can't recall?"

"That's none of your business," he said. "Now, it's time for you to give me my jewels, Evelyne."

"I can't do that," I said.

"Why not?" he demanded.

"Because I didn't come to Lisbon to give you anything. I know about South America. I know about the company you keep."

"You don't know anything, Evelyne," he gritted out.

"I know that you have so-called friends, many of whom have not-so-secret Nazi sympathies," I said.

"Why do you think I left South America? I'm trying to get away from that lot," he sneered.

"Then why not go to London?" I challenged.

"Because he can't." Phillips stepped out from the shadows. "Sir Reginald, we meet at last."

"Who are you?" demanded my father.

"Peter Phillips. I apologize for not calling on you at the princess's country home. I only just found out you were there, which is a shame because you are not an easy man to find when you wish to disappear, Sir Reginald," said Phillips.

My eyes darted from man to man. This was not how this was supposed to happen. I needed to apprehend Phillips and speak to my father, but I could do neither effectively while they were both right there.

"I am with British intelligence. We have taken a keen interest in your activities, and we are eager to speak to you," said Phillips. "Miss Moore, will you please go telephone Carter and let him know that I have located Sir Reginald."

"Miss Moore?" asked my father.

"Phillips—"

"Her name is Redfern," Sir Reginald blurted out before I could finish.

Shock flashed across Phillips's face, but then his lips spread into a smile. "The daughter? That is an interesting development. What would you do to make sure that that little tidbit of knowledge doesn't make it back to London?"

"They already know," I said, half lying. "I was sent here in part to help find him."

"Sent to find me?" asked my father.

"And there I thought your time in Lisbon was an utter failure." Phillips gave me a condescending smile. "Not that I should be surprised. I don't know what the SIU was doing sending a woman to do a man's job."

"You're right," I said. "I haven't been able to produce James Winn. As you said, he seems to have vanished."

"I told them that," scoffed Phillips.

"It's strange, really." I pretended to muse it over. "Almost as though he never existed."

Phillips stilled.

"I know who you are, Phillips. I know about Morrison and Jessup and Curzon. I know about the smuggling too," I said.

His eyes narrowed slightly. "You think I had something to do with their deaths? You cannot be serious."

"I think you had *everything* to do with their deaths. You ordered Curzon to kill Morrison and Jessup, and then you killed Curzon because he was the last link between you and the murders. I suspect you believed no one would really care about the death of a refugee and a criminal. You almost managed it too. Just one more day, and you would have been on a ship to America, leaving all of this chaos behind you. By the time we figured out who Winn actually was—if we had managed it at all—you would have no doubt assumed a new identity and a new life," I said.

"Absolute rubbish," scoffed Phillips.

"We found the ticket for your crossing, along with your suitcase," I said.

"I am taking a trip," he pushed. "It is not illegal."

"Under another name?" I asked.

"We use covers all the time in our business," he argued.

"Which made it all the easier for you to not just commission the documents that Curzon used to enter and leave Britain, but to create an identity for James Winn," I said. "In fact, you were so good at it that you set up an entire life for him complete with a girlfriend and a flat and a collection of associates who spoke in hushed, reverent tones about him as though he was a real person, because to them he was, even if they'd never laid eyes on him.

"But it was you all along, pulling the strings, wasn't it?" I continued. "It must have been quite the feat, convincing everyone to work for you without actually meeting them. Making sure that your entire network was airtight so that none of the smuggling could ever be traced back to you. But then something went wrong."

I smiled. "Everything was working smoothly until Sir Reginald came to Princess Petrova for help selling jewels that were already in London. Jessup realized that if the princess wasn't necessary to collect the jewelry here in Lisbon, this job would be the ideal opportunity to strike out on his own. He met Sir Reginald at the Hotel Metrópol and instructed Sir Reginald to tell the princess he'd changed his mind about using Winn's services.

"Then Sir Reginald wrote to me with instructions to bring Morrison the jewels at his shop. Once they were sold, Jessup planned to use his usual trip to Lisbon to carry the money back. All Sir Reginald had to do was find a place to wait out Jessup's return." I turned to my father. "What was it that convinced you? Did Jessup offer to take a smaller cut than Winn?"

"That Jessup fellow said he could do it for ten percent," said my father. "The princess told me Winn would carry everything out for twenty and nothing less."

"Jessup didn't know what he was doing," Phillips hissed.

There it was. The crack. Time to take a sledgehammer and smash it wide open.

"You got wind of Jessup's double cross, and that upset you, didn't it, Phillips?" I asked.

"Jessup was nothing more than a scheming crook. Even before Sir Reginald came along, he tried to convince Winn to meet him to try to negotiate a better cut of the profits," Phillips spat.

"The bar of the Hotel Metrópol, Jessup's favorite spot," I said with a nod, remembering Jessup's notation in his diary. "Naturally, Winn never showed up for that meeting because he didn't exist.

"You must have realized then that you had made a mistake in trusting Jessup, and it left you rather exposed," I continued. "You couldn't negotiate with Jessup in person because Winn didn't exist. Besides, if you pushed too hard Jessup might decide it was time to learn more about the elusive James Winn. There was a risk that he could have discovered that Winn didn't exist and that would have prompted some very powerful people to ask a series of many uncomfortable questions about you."

Phillips made a low growling noise in his throat.

"You decided it was time to make Winn disappear. Informants must vanish all the time in this war. It wouldn't be out of the realm of possibility that Winn slinked away into the shadows—or even be done away with by the Germans because of his final tip, never to be heard from again. But that was when you realized your second mistake. You made Winn's first tip about the brothel too good. London wanted to hold on to him at any cost, so they sent David and me. That must have infuriated you," I said.

"You were a complication. Nothing more," Phillips snapped.

"And Luiza? Was she a complication too?" I asked.

That seemed to make Phillips falter for a moment.

"Who is Luiza?" asked Sir Reginald.

"Phillips's girlfriend and the woman he thought he had fooled into being the final link in the chain of his smuggling ring," I explained. "But he didn't realize until it was too late that she'd been recruited by the Germans to spy on him. Köhler knew perfectly well what he was up to because Luiza told him everything. I suspect she even might have tried to recruit him as a double agent, which Phillips knows would amount to treason. You know what happens to traitors, don't you, Phillips?"

In a flash, Phillips whipped a hand around his back and pulled out a gun. He trained it on me.

"They die. Isn't that right, Miss Redfern?" Phillips gritted out. "But I'm not going to die, am I?"

"You bastard. Stop pointing that bloody gun at my daughter," my father ordered. And then he leveled his own weapon right at Phillips.

FORTY-TWO

If I hadn't been staring down the barrel of a revolver, I might have rolled my eyes at the display of fatherly bravado coming from Sir Reginald. It was, after all, about two decades too late.

"You can shoot me, but the house is surrounded," I said. "Camargo and his men are here. One gunshot, and they all come running."

Phillips looked up the garden path, as though he expected the full force of the PVDE to storm down from the house at any moment.

"Give yourself up, Phillips. It will be cleaner and easier that way," I said.

"I'm the one with the gun!" Phillips shouted.

"So am I," said my father.

"For Christ's sake," Phillips muttered, and then in one swift move he shot my father cleanly through the hand.

Sir Reginald cried out, dropping his gun. I dove for it, but Phillips was closer. He scooped it up as I skidded on the ground, scraping my forearms raw against the paving stones.

"Get up!" Phillips ordered me while my father rolled on the ground clutching at his wounded hand.

Slowly, I hauled myself to my feet, my hands raised over my head. I was secretly pleased that he'd shot my father, not because it had resulted in my father whimpering like a child, but because it meant that David, Carter, and Camargo must have heard it.

"You have been in the way from the very moment you landed," hissed Phillips, training both guns on my father and me. "You couldn't leave well enough alone but had to find Jessup's body and lead London and the PVDE right to my door."

"Perhaps if you had refrained from killing people, you would have avoided that attention yourself. Or better yet, what if you had never set up your little scheme at all?" I asked.

"I had no choice," said Phillips.

It was my turn to scoff. "No choice? You absolutely had a choice when you decided to use Jessup as a mule for your smuggling ring and to blackmail Princess Petrova. Or what about when you executed three people? You certainly had a choice then, but you wanted the money."

"Not everything is *just* about money, Miss Redfern," said Phillips. "Foolish girl. You really have *no idea* what you have stumbled into, do you?"

There was something in his tone that caught my attention. "What do you mean?"

"You think you know the whole picture, coming to Lisbon in search of Winn and to look for your father, but it goes deeper than that. Sir Reginald isn't just a person of interest for British intelligence," said Phillips.

"No, he has contacts that could be useful for infiltrating groups of—"

Phillips's laugh cut me short. "You think *that* is why we've been trying to recruit him? To turn some men who want to cozy up to the Nazis to our side? You're just as blind as the rest of them."

I glanced down at my father, who had stilled even as he continued to press a blood-soaked handkerchief against his wounded hand.

"Evelyne, don't listen to him," ordered Sir Reginald.

"What is he talking about?" I asked.

"He's clearly mad," said Sir Reginald, panic creeping into his voice.

"That's not what you said when you told Jessup you needed something smuggled out of Lisbon, is it?" asked Phillips.

"I thought you were just trying to secure money," I said. "What did you want smuggled out of Lisbon?"

"Evelyne . . ."

"Let's just say we have a mutual friend and it is a very bad idea to say no to him," said Phillips with a wicked smile.

"Who is—?"

But before I could finish my question, Sir Reginald sprang up from his crouched position and knocked Phillips to the ground with a rugby tackle around the waist. One gun went off again, throwing up a shower of dirt, even as the other skidded a few feet away from the struggling men. I dove for the second and rolled onto my knees, aiming at Phillips.

"Sir Reginald! Move away!" I cried.

"You should listen to your daughter," ground out Phillips, training his gun on me.

My father released the man and stood back, his handkerchief gone and blood streaming down his hand once again. I could hear shouts from the house above us.

"What did you want taken out of Lisbon? And who is this mutual friend Phillips is talking about?" I asked my father.

"Why don't you tell her?" Phillips taunted, his eyes trained on Sir Reginald.

"Evelyne, this man isn't who he seems," said my father.

"Your father always would say anything to get out of a sticky situation, wouldn't he, Miss Redfern?" asked Phillips. "He *lies*."

"Who sent you?" asked Sir Reginald, staring at Phillips in horror.

"I think you already know," said Phillips. "Cerberus sends his regards and regrets that he is not able to attend to you himself."

"Cerberus?" I repeated. "Will someone *please* tell me what is going on?"

"Evelyne, leave. I'm begging you. There are things at play that you do not know or understand," said Sir Reginald.

"I am not leaving." I planted my free hand on my hip. "I'm the one who has the gun now, and I've had rather enough of this."

Phillips smiled slowly. "That makes two of us."

Phillips pulled the trigger, and my heart leapt into my throat.

Click.

Nothing happened.

He tried again.

Click.

Nothing.

With a roar of frustration, Phillips threw the gun away.

I heard the shout of "Down here!" in the distance, certain now that reinforcements were coming.

"It's not loaded," said Sir Reginald triumphantly. "I bought it off of a fellow, but he didn't have any bullets."

"You pulled an unloaded gun on me?" I asked in exasperation.

"You're my daughter!" said Sir Reginald, as though that made even the littlest difference.

"You didn't know that at the time!" I cried.

Phillips lunged at me, grabbing my scraped forearm. Off balance, my knees gave, and we crashed to the ground.

"Let go of the gun," he gritted out as he fought me hard for control, thrashing us about.

"Not on your life," I gasped.

As we grappled, Phillips rolled me onto my back, pinning my arms. Slowly he began to turn the gun on me, but before it could fully rotate, I brought my knee up into his groin. Phillips buckled with a guttural cry, his hand loosening its grip on the gun just enough for me to wrench it away.

"Stay where you are," I demanded, grasping the gun with two hands as Phillips rolled off me. I staggered to my feet, gasping for air, the weapon still trained on him.

"David! I'm here!" I yelled over my shoulder. Then I turned my attention to Phillips again. "Who is Cerberus?"

The corrupt intelligence agent looked up at me then, his eyes narrowed into a hard stare. "You are safer not knowing, Miss Redfern."

"Is it a man or a woman?" I pressed.

"Evelyne!" I heard David shout, his voice closer this time.

"Who is Cerberus?" I repeated.

"If I tell you, far worse things will happen to me than being hung for treason," said Phillips.

Then his cheek bulged as his tongue dislodged something and he bit down hard.

"Goodbye, Miss Redfern," Phillips said.

"No, no, no, no, no!" I shouted, as David skidded to a stop by my side.

"Evelyne, what happened? Are you all right?" demanded David.

I shoved the gun into his hands and dropped to my knees as Phillips lost consciousness.

"He's taken something—a cyanide pill, I think. Stand back," I warned.

I forced Phillips's mouth open and then grabbed a handkerchief out of my pocket to cover my own nose and mouth. Sure enough, I could see the chewed capsule resting against his tongue. "He'll be dead in minutes."

"Why would Phillips take cyanide?" he asked. "I thought he was trying to escape, not to kill himself."

"I don't know." I sat back on my heels, exhausted. "Have you ever heard of anyone who goes by the name Cerberus?"

David opened his mouth and then shut it with a frown. "I don't think so."

"Me neither," I said, glancing around me.

"What are you looking for?" he asked. "Were you hit?"

"Not this time, no." I squinted in the dim light. Sure enough, on the edge of the path there was a spattering of blood and a collection of broken stems in the border. When the moment had really mattered and my life had hung in the balance, Sir Reginald had decided to save himself.

"My father was here," I said.

As I proceeded to tell him everything that had happened, David stayed stony silent, his expression giving nothing away until he asked, "And you think he got away?"

"Through there," I gestured to the mangled plants.

"We should tell Camargo. He can put out an alert for hospitals and doctors to be on the lookout for a British man of his description seeking medical attention," he said.

I gave a shallow nod.

"Come on," said David. "Let's go home."

FORTY-THREE

I have learned over the years that the moments after capturing a criminal are not neat and clean like in the detective novels I love so much. Instead, the reality is that they are filled with a strange mixture of urgency and waiting.

As Carter and Camargo arrived at the scene of Phillips's death, followed by a trail of morbidly curious party guests following the sound of shooting, David put his arm around me and steered me through them, pulling me away from the scene.

I had enough experience by then to know that the adrenaline that had pumped through my veins and sustained me through my showdown with Phillips would soon be gone, replaced by bone-deep exhaustion. I needed food and a place to sit to wait for shock to cover me like a veil.

"We'll go to the house," said David, as Princess Petrova clattered past us on the garden path, the tails of her saffron dress flying out behind her as she no doubt saw her social standing as Lisbon's doyenne flash before her eyes, because who wanted to go to a party that ended in suicide by cyanide pill?

"I should debrief Camargo," I said.

"As soon as you take care of yourself," he said.

Up at the house, an ashen-faced butler and Marie, Princess Petrova's maid, hovered about.

"Food for Mademoiselle, please," David ordered.

Marie, clearly grateful for the task, jumped to it and returned a moment later with a plate nearly overflowing with food. The butler, for his part, set about mixing an excellent martini dry enough to make my mouth water.

I was just finishing my drink when Camargo walked through the sitting room door and dropped onto the sofa across from me.

"I would like the chance to speak to Menina Moore alone," said Camargo to David.

My partner planted his hands on his knees and rose. "I'll go tell Carter he can release Miss Larkin. He'll have to break the news to her."

"Good idea," I said.

Camargo waited until the sitting room door closed and then said, "Senhor Phillips is dead."

"I imagined as much," I replied.

"What did he tell you before he died?" asked Camargo.

"He confessed, if that's what you mean. He admitted that he was the head of the smuggling ring and responsible for Jessup, Morrison, and Curzon's deaths."

"Just as you said?" he asked.

"Just as I said."

"And then Phillips killed himself with a cyanide pill?" Camargo asked.

"After I tackled him to the ground, wrestling for the gun."

"Were you shot?"

"No."

The captain considered this for a moment. "Neither was he. But there was a trail of blood leading across the path and through the bushes."

The blood from my father's hand.

"Was there someone else there?" he asked.

It was on the tip of my tongue to tell him what had happened, but something held me back. It wasn't loyalty to my father or any sense of gratitude that he'd tried to stop Phillips but something else.

Curious.

"It is entirely possible Phillips was speaking to someone before I arrived on the scene," I lied. "In fact, it's likely. I heard a gunshot."

"And that is what made you run in that direction?" Camargo asked.

"Yes."

It was obvious from the way the captain looked at me that he didn't believe a word I said, but all he did was shake his head.

"I'm afraid, Menina Moore, that I must insist that you and your . . . employer leave the country on the next flight from Sintra. Senhor Carter must go as well," he said.

I had expected as much.

"Will we be able to retrieve our bags from our hotel?" I asked.

"I will escort you there myself," he said. "You will be permitted to sleep and then prepare for your flight."

"Thank you, Capitão. That is very kind of you."

He gave me a small smile. "Given that you helped me solve two murders, I can afford to be a little kind, but do not expect such treatment again."

I let my head drop against the back of the sofa. "I wouldn't dream of it."

Camargo was good to his word, and he dropped David and me back at the Hotel Tivoli. With the exception of the two armed guards who now stood in the corridor on either side of my door, I almost felt like a traveler who was wearily bathing, repacking, and resting before the long trip home.

The following morning, our guards became our driver and escort to Sintra. When we pulled up at the airfield, we discovered that Carter had arrived just before us.

"Only two bags, Carter?" I asked, wandering over as David took care of our luggage in deference to my scraped-up arms and hands. "You travel rather light."

"A consequence of my profession," said Carter with a smile.

"Importer?" I asked with a raised brow.

He shrugged. "What else?"

"Well," I said, looking out at the aeroplane where already the crew was weighing baggage and checking passengers' names, "I hope that the events of last night don't render your business here completely moot."

"Oh no. Phillips's office was just one of several. London has always found it useful to diversify its interests in places like Lisbon."

"I'm glad to hear it," I said.

"Are you ready to go home?" asked David, laden with our things.

I gave him a firm nod. "I certainly am."

FORTY-FOUR

Hours later, while we were on our descent into Whitchurch, David leaned over the armrest between our seats and said, "I was in Scotland."

I leaned in, wondering if I had misheard him over the sound of the plane's propellers.

"When I hurt my shoulder," he continued.

"What were you doing in Scotland?" I asked, keeping my tone low to match his.

"Training. They have special places for"—he glanced from side to side to make sure he couldn't be overheard and then whispered—"commandos."

I knew about the commando training grounds in Scotland thanks to our last case, but I didn't know that he'd been reassigned to one of them while I'd been on desk duty due to my own injury.

"I was on a jump, and I pulled my parachute. Everything seemed fine at first, but as I descended, one of the cords snapped. I deployed my backup, but I was too low and moving too fast. I braced myself, but my shoulder took the brunt of it and I managed to dislocate it. I was lucky that was the worst that happened, really. I was sent down south to convalesce until Mrs. White sent me a message that I was needed in Bristol," he said.

"Do you know what you were training for?" I asked.

"France."

I sucked in a breath as the wheels touched down and we bounced slightly with the impact of our landing. "France?"

David stared at the seat in front of us for a moment. "I have unfinished business there."

Something about the way his voice cracked made me move my hand to his where it rested on the arm between our chairs. Before the war, he had spent a great deal of time in the country of my birth, when he really and truly had been a wine buyer. However, that was the extent of what I knew about his history, because David was many things, but an open book was not one of them.

"When we returned from Blackthorn Park, Mrs. White told me there was an opportunity for an operation in the occupied zone," he explained as the aeroplane came to a stop. "She knew that I have been looking for a way back to France for a long time. I didn't ask any questions but simply said yes."

"I can understand why."

"No, Evelyne, you don't. Mrs. White doesn't do things without strings attached. I wanted something from her, and she wanted something from me. It was a trade," he said.

I frowned when David twisted in his seat. I mirrored his movement to look behind me and saw four men in uniform walking down the aisle toward us.

"Evelyne, I'm very sorry," said David, rising from his seat.

"What is—?"

"Miss Redfern?" the first man said as he stopped in front of us. "I'm afraid I'm going to need you to come with us."

"Why?" I demanded.

"I'm not authorized to answer that question," said the officer.

"Am I being arrested?" I asked, acutely aware of how the other passengers were staring at me.

"Miss," said the officer.

"Miss Moore?" Carter called out from a few rows away.

"Am I being arrested?" I repeated, louder this time.

"It will be better for everyone if you come with us and don't resist, Miss," said the officer.

"David—"

But when I looked to my partner, I found his shoulders slumped, head hung.

"David, where are they taking me?" I asked.

"I don't know. I'm sorry, Evelyne. I wish it could have been different," he said, standing and moving out into the aisle to make way for the first officer to reach over and lay a heavy hand on my arm.

"Don't touch me," I hissed, wrenching away.

"If you won't come willingly, Miss, I'm afraid we'll have to use force," said the officer.

"You appear to be afraid of a great number of things," I snapped, but still I made to stand, reaching for my handbag.

"Leave that," the officer ordered.

I shot a glare first at him and then at David.

"Slater, what is happening?" Carter called.

"What are they taking me away for?" I asked my partner.

David swallowed but then set his jaw. "I'm afraid that the decision has been made that you can no longer be trusted."

A chill went through me at that.

"What have you done?" I asked in a whisper.

"I'm sorry, Evelyne, but we all have our orders we must follow," said David.

"What is going to happen to me?"

"I expect you'll find out soon enough," he said.

I didn't see that I had any option other than to go with the uniformed men, my head held high. However, as I passed David in the aisle, I whispered, "I hope that, whatever you've done, it was worth it."

He didn't reply as I walked away as steadily as my quaking legs would carry me. I had been trained for what to do in the case of enemy capture. I knew how to weather a hostile interrogation. Yet I hadn't been prepared for what would happen if I was escorted off a BOAC aeroplane on British soil by my fellow countrymen like a traitor.

When I reached the top of the metal stairs leading to the airfield, I hesitated. Through the light rain, I could see a large black car with dark windows parked a little way away from the aeroplane. It was flanked by two more uniformed officers standing guard.

"Go on, Miss," said one of my unwanted escorts.

My heels clattered on the metal steps as I made my way down. As soon as my feet were on solid ground, one of the guards standing next to the car moved into position at the back door. As I approached, that guard asked, "Are you armed?"

"Of course not." Ragged though my cover had become in Lisbon, I couldn't imagine a wine buyer's secretary traveling with a gun strapped to her thigh.

The guard reached over and opened the door.

"Is that an invitation to climb in?" I asked petulantly.

When he didn't respond, I sighed, slid into the back seat, and found myself seated next to Mrs. White.

"Miss Redfern," said my handler, her voice grave but her eyes glinting in the fading light.

"If this is your idea of a warm welcome home, I'm afraid I remain unimpressed," I said.

"I see that Lisbon has not dulled your keen sense of humor," she said, sounding less than amused.

"I do apologize, but being marched off an aeroplane after a seven-hour flight without explanation does put one's nose rather out of joint."

"In that case, I'll cut to the chase. In Lisbon, you confronted a man who spoke about Cerberus. What did he tell you?" she asked.

I stared at her for a moment. "Not much."

"Tell me exactly what you remember," she ordered.

"I asked who Cerberus is, and Phillips wouldn't answer. All he said was, 'If I tell you, far worse things will happen to me than being hung for treason.'"

She sucked her teeth. “And your father. Did he seem to know about Cerberus?”

“Yes,” I said. “Phillips said something like, ‘Cerberus sends his regards and regrets that he is not able to attend to you himself.’”

“Blast,” she murmured.

“Mrs. White, who is Cerberus?” I asked.

The question seemed to snap my handler back to attention. “That is not something you need to know. All you need to concern yourself with, Miss Redfern, is the future.”

“The future?” I asked, fear choking me.

“Specifically *your* future.” She crossed her hands over her knee and pinned me with a stare. “For your utterly misguided decision in Lisbon to conduct an independent investigation into your father’s whereabouts, and—when it became clear that Sir Reginald was connected to not one, not two, but *three* murders and a smuggling ring—your failure to disclose this information to me, your handler, you are suspended from all Special Investigations Unit duties. Effective immediately.”

“You’re grounding me?” I asked in horror.

Mrs. White leaned forward. “Miss Redfern, you will be lucky if you ever see the inside of headquarters again.”

ACKNOWLEDGMENTS

Every installment of the Evelyne Redfern series has been an adventure, and I could not be more fortunate to have some of the best people along for the ride.

Mary, thank you for keeping me company as I scribbled away next to you at the London Library, plotting, scheming, and generally making up mayhem for my characters.

Thank you, Jordan and Jake. You have both been unfailing cheerleaders for Evelyne Redfern since your first read.

I am lucky enough to have been able to celebrate wins big and small over the years with Alexis Anne, Lindsay Emory, Mary Chris Escobar, Alexandra Haughton, and Laura Von Holt, some of the best writer friends a girl could ask for. Thank you also to Madeline Martin, who is always generous with her wisdom and experience.

As always, huge thank-yous must be reserved for my wonderful agent, Emily Sylvan Kim, and also for Ellen Brescia, who keeps us all on track.

I am fortunate to work with some incredibly talented, passionate people at Minotaur including my editor, Madeline Houpt, whose edits have made this book so much better. Thank you also to Kelley Ragland, Allison Ziegler, Kayla Janas, Gabriel Guma, Rowen Davis, Alisa

Trager, Laurie Henderson, Diane Dilluvio, Maria Snelling, Isabella Narvaez, and Esther de Araujo for everything you have done for this series.

Thank you also to Marisa Calin who has brought Evelyne's voice to life through her wonderful narration of the audiobooks.

As always, special thanks must be given to my wonderful family. Mum, Dad, Justine, Mark, and Diana, I appreciate all the ways you have supported me over the years, encouraging and lifting me up every time I needed it.

Arthur, my love, thank you for everything you do always. I have no doubt that I'm the lucky one.

And finally, to all my readers, thank you for making it possible for me to write stories like Evelyne Redfern's. I'm still amazed I write books for a living, and I will never stop being grateful for all you have given me.

ABOUT THE AUTHOR

Scott Bottles

Julia Kelly is the international bestselling author of emotional historical fiction about extraordinary women, and intriguing historical whodunit mystery novels. Her books have been translated into fourteen languages. In addition to writing, she's been an Emmy-nominated producer, journalist, marketing professional, and (for one summer) a tea waitress. Julia called Los Angeles, Iowa, and New York City home before settling in London with her husband.